pale grey

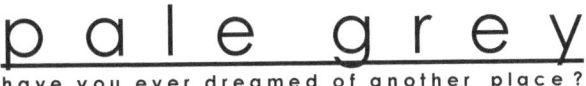

have you ever dreamed of another place?

by

BARRY P. CONNORS

New Adventure Publishing
P.O. Box 298
Rondebosch
7701
Cape Town
South Africa

First published in 2011 by New Adventure Publishing

Internet Electronic Mail Address: info@newadventurepublishing.com

ISBN 978-0-620-49373-4

Dedicated to my mother, Kathleen Megan Connors.
In loving memory of a soul who was too good for this world.

ACKNOWLEDGEMENTS

Firstly, thanks to my publisher, Llewellin of New Adventure Publishing for all the time and dedication put into the publication of this book. He went far beyond the call of duty on this, and for that, I am eternally grateful.

Moreover, for his belief in my work, there are no words.

Thanks also to my brother, Sean, who never doubted my ability to tell this story for one second, and never hesitated to criticize it at the first opportunity.

Difficult bastard.

A very big thank you, also, to my agent and friend, Nick Rosenthal, for his phenomenal patience in dealing with a sometimes very headstrong and eccentric writer. You never lost your cool. Not once.

I probably would have.

Thanks, also, to those who believed in this book long before it became what it is: Lara Dold, Gary and Cheryl Townsend, Dave Walsh and John Newman. You guys will never know the difference you made.

Keep the faith.

PART ONE
The Gathering Dark

Prologue

I entered Nu Caynan in the driving rain.

It was after dark, the glOlamps hovering at the edge of the flyover leading into the city casting orange reflections on the corners of my windscreen, zooming from the dashboard up to the roof in a constant stream of light as I approached the limits of a city I'd hoped never to see again.

The City Wall loomed ahead, and even in the downpour I could make out the storm lights, red and pulsing in perfect harmony, lining the walls from one edge of my vision to the other, and the search lights overhead, scanning the sky, cutting through the rain with blinding intensity, sweeping across the night in white arcs of light.

Arriving at City Gate 24, I slowed to a stop.

An armed guard in black fatigues approached my hovcar, took the proffered I.D card from my hand, and studied it carefully. The torch shone up to my face, back down to the card. He said nothing, his eyes scrolling slowly over the tiny holographic text.

There was definitely a bit of tension then, my breath coming to me with a lot more difficulty than it maybe should have.

Did he recognize me?

No, of course not.

That was ridiculous.

I'd never seen the guy before in my life.

But in a place like Nu Caynan, you never knew who knew whom. Money goes a long way in the social scene, and the bastard I was dealing with had way too much of it.

I entered Nu Caynan at Ground level. It's the only way in unless you want to get shot out of the sky. Hovcars shot by above me and all around, people on their way to some place or other, moving like ants through streets aglow with orange light. I found myself wondering if they knew what they were doing, where they were going, and what they would do when they got there. If any of it had a point, beyond money or sex or the Next Big Thing.

Probably not, but that was okay because I, on the other hand, knew exactly where I was going.

And what I would do when I got there.

I was here to kill someone.

Not for money.

Or for sex.

But because I wanted to.

The camera pans, taking in the City at ground level. Street lamps burning, hissing in the downpour. All is ensconced in a fine mist, and at this level, the city seems almost insubstantial, ethereal. Like a place you go to when you dream, or one seen through the dusty lens of ancient memory. Misty and pale, a haze of muted colour and faded contours.

Moving up now, out of the fog, the rain coming straight down. Neon signs and bright digital banners light up the night, from advertising slogans and corporate logos, giant and alive in crystal clear hi-res, to *Ahmed's Delic tes n*. Past offices and shops and businesses of every shape and size. Moving through one lane of hovcars after the next. Up a level, past apartments and mega gyms and franchised

8

pizzerias, the camera swerving around corners and zooming in on advertisements for companies with more money than small countries and nothing much to do with it except maybe make more.

Higher still, past casinos and deluxe spas and penthouse apartments, all the while winding through the maze of buildings and multicoloured neon light, blurring and slightly distorted in the downpour. Moving onwards and upwards.

And then, in the distance: one building towering above the rest. Giant in scale and beautiful in design, a massive rectangular megalith, soaring up into the night, pointing a finger at God. A huge neon sign perched on top. One word:

N e u_r o_L O G

Moving still, spiralling up and around this place, the rain beating down all the while. People in the windows. Some exec at work at his computer, another practising what seems to be some obscure form of yoga, a newly wed couple doing something experimental. Up and up, and finally to a cocktail bar, two thirds of the way to the top, windows surrounding almost the entire floor, except for a space where three elevator doors stand. Soft blue lights illuminate the interior at floor level. Suits standing around, talking shop, a wife on one arm and a whore on the other, and some guy standing alone at the window lost in thought, looking out at the night, a glass in one hand and a smoke in the other.

That's me.

I stared out at the city lights far below, wondering what the fuck to do next. I'd come this far; there was no point in backing out now.

That was a physical impossibility for me anyway; there was no way I could bring myself to walk away even if I'd wanted to.

Not this time.

In the reflection of the glass I saw him enter the room, accompanied by five bodyguards, all of them dressed in black and sporting headsets and matching shortRifles that could probably blow a hole through to China. I saw him motion to his guys to stay put and he crossed the room, coming to stand behind me. I gripped my glass tightly, fighting the urge to turn around and stab him in the head with it.

"Ash," he said, his voice daring me to remember something best forgotten.

"Hello, Cole," I said softly, turning to face him, "I see you've brought some friends."

"Wasn't gonna take any chances. You and I aren't on the best of terms."

I looked down, shaking but trying not to let it show.

"So what do you want?" he asked, "I'm a busy man."

"I've come to give you a message, from someone who couldn't be here tonight."

Cole raised an eyebrow, "Really? Now who could that be?"

"He would very much like to give you something."

"And what is that?"

Amused now, he smiled at me, a big, bright smile full of light and wholesome fucking goodness.

My arms came up, a gun in each hand, "A few of these! " and I started firing, both guns snapping back as bullets wove a path through the air straight at his face, throwing myself backwards even as I watched his head explode and his body reel back from the impact, smashing through the window behind me in a hail of glass and slugs. And then I was falling, flying through the air on a vertical course with only one destination.

I remember thinking that it was okay to die now, because I'd taken that bastard with me. I wondered if she'd be proud of me, if somehow this made things all right. Also, I found myself wondering how long it would take to sail past all two hundred and fifty floors, before finally exploding onto the sidewalk below in a fountain of colour. I didn't get a chance to find out because at that moment, life threw me a line.

Darkness. A void, black and lifeless. I can't tell how long I've been here, perhaps forever. Life fades back in. A cigarette, the tip burning orange, blurred, the same hand gripped a steering wheel. And a voice, heard as if from a great distance.

I knew that voice.

"You're gonna be alright, Ash. Just take it easy."

Something else, but I couldn't make it out.

Getting dark again, the bright orange lifeline fading back into endless night.

"Where are we?"

"We're leaving town."

Fade to black.

Time passes. Floating and insubstantial, I move through it. Occasionally I glimpse movement. Try to make it out. But it's fleeting, lost to me before I even notice it's there. And a voice, whispering softly. Telling me something. But I can't make it out. I strain to hear, but the more I focus on it, the more it shies away. And then I'm pulled from this place, the bright orange beacon once more pulling me back to the light. A face, illuminated in the soft blue dashboard lights: Dex. Staring straight ahead.

It was raining, and I realised we were speeding, the scenery beyond the passenger side-window streaking past me with a fluid intensity.

"Dex." My own voice sounded strange in my ears.

He turned his head, grinned.

11

I looked out at the rain-drenched night, trying to get my bearings. Downtown, business district.

We were speeding down the main thoroughfare, above us, high up above us, streams of cars could be seen through the rain, their landing lights blinking and their headlights cutting a swath of light into the gloom.

"Here we go," said Dex.

We were about to enter Gate 12, just one of forty-seven giant portals allowing access to the MegaCity of Nu Caynan.

"Dex..."

"Relax."

We drove up to the portal entrance, and a security guard came to the window.

"Pass and identification please." He sounded bored.

"You heard the man," Dex said to me.

I looked at him, then handed over the stuff.

The guard looked over the cards we'd handed him. His left eye twitched, ever so slightly, but just enough.

Shit.

Dex noticed as well.

"Time waits for no man," he said.

The guard stopped, hand almost at the collar-button that activated his headset, swallowed hard, and then nodded slowly. He leaned forward, face at the car window.

He nodded again. "When I open this portal, drive like hell."

We nodded.

He turned from us, walked into the guardhouse, and activated the gates. They started opening, sliding silently apart.

"Always have a back door," Dex said.

And then I heard a roar behind me, and I turned my head to see a black sedan hovcar come screaming around the corner, followed by another, heading straight for us. I had no idea whether our pursuers were cops or NeuroLOG security or some of Cole's thugs, but Dex decided not to stick around and find out.

The guard came out, drew his gun, "Go go go go!" he yelled at us.

Dex floored it, the hov roaring off into the night. And as I watched, the guard behind us started firing at the approaching hovcars. The first car took a bullet in the driver's side, swerved violently to the right, and rolled, spinning through the air, over and over, crashing into the guard and smashing against the half-closed gate. It exploded on impact, the night alive with orange fire, and we were away, speeding along the highway like fugitives from the devil.

One

If there's one thing I really hate, it's getting a call at the crack of dawn while you're trying with incredible difficulty to eat breakfast and stay awake at the same time.

Okay, it was closer to twelve, and breakfast was a very strong cup of coffee and a cigarette that I didn't feel like and wasn't enjoying, but the principle is still there. The wallscreen in my kitchen flashed turquoise and green (a migraine-inducing colour scheme if ever there was one, but hell, I lost the manual) and the words **Incoming Call** blinked on the screen.

I realised it was a miracle I could see that far through the haze of cigarette smoke hovering in the still air.

Who the hell wanted to speak to me at this time of the morning?

I checked the time.

Eleven forty-eight.

A.M.

"Answer," I muttered, increasing the dull aching in my head a hundredfold.

The screen came alive, and I found myself staring at a big, grinning, bearded man, blonde hair dishevelled and everywhere.

Dex.

"Morning Ash. Long night?" he said, one eyebrow raised.

"Long night," I muttered. " What's up?"

Dex leaned a bit closer into the screen, dropped his voice, "Got a guy here, says he's got a job for you. Something big. Something very big."

"For me? Last I heard, you and I were partners."

He nodded, "That's what I said, but he doesn't seem to give much of a shit."

I let out a deep sigh, "Alright, I'm on my way."

"And Ash," Dex said.

"Yeah?"

"Prepare yourself. This one's a bit weird."

I nodded, "On my way... Computer, end call."

I rubbed my eyes, got up off the sofa and walked out onto the balcony, thinking maybe the fresh morning air would somehow nullify the adverse effects of sucking smoke into my lungs.

Tanis. My home, and my second favourite place on the Planet.

It was a beautiful morning, which is extremely rare nowadays. Just the barest wisp of a breeze in the air and not a cloud in the sky, the sun's sparkling reflection glimmering on the surface of the sea like a million diamonds floating on the waves. I took in the scene, enjoying it while it lasted. God only knew when I'd see this again.

Tanis is definitely one of the nicer places on the Planet. It's an island city, all beaches and tall buildings and sunshine. And my apartment block is one of the nicest on Tanis. A glorious old-school stone building (complete with gargoyles) built around the highest strength titanium, soaring up one hundred and forty two floors, the third tallest building on the island.

I don't have much of a problem with money. Although I'm not as filthy rich as some of the bastards on Tanis, I am fortunate enough to own an apartment with a hell of a view, and I drive the kind of car teenage boys masturbate over and middle-aged men lose their wives over.

The social scene on the island is quite something. This place seems to be the destination of choice for a lot of NetStars at the moment. I get commissioned by the bastards on a regular basis. Once by a guy called Tommy Slid, you've probably heard of him. The director of *The Sands Of Tabania*, the multi-award-winning flick that came out a little while ago. He wanted me to check out his wife, thinking she was doing something dodgy, like fucking another guy. The truth was a bit worse, actually. It's never been my policy to discuss other people's affairs (pun not intended) in business or otherwise, but this woman was really out there. She thought she was the devil, and therefore being the highest ranking official Satanist on the planet, felt the need to sleep with as many fellow Satanists as possible, recording it all on disk. Anyway, after I'd shown Tommy the proof, gained after breaking into her place (black ski mask and all), beating my way past four of her henchman, and blowing open her safe, he promptly left the planet. Last I heard he was mining for minerals out towards Neptune.

So I stepped inside, changed into the usual black shirt and pants with matching jacket and twin glock nine-millimetre handguns tucked away in their shoulder holsters (well, you never knew), and walked out onto the deck area of my apartment, down a few steps to the berth where my hovcar floated peacefully in the morning breeze.

Sensing my approach, the driver's door slid back silently.

"Good morning, Ash," said the car.

I got in, slid the door shut, started her up.

"Computer, open top."

The roof retracted and I reversed out of the berth.

Below me one hundred and eleven lanes of space: not much in the way of traffic. That's what separates this place from Nu Caynan for me. If you're anywhere above the thirty floor mark, you're guaranteed to be surrounded on every side by hovcars, zooming around like a bunch of crazed, glowing, flying ants. But Tanis is different. No one ever seems to be in a hurry around here. I drove at a relaxed pace, enjoying the morning breeze, the sun on my face,

My thoughts drifted to the brief conversation with Dex.

This one's a bit weird.

17

I accelerated.

Ten minutes later I pulled in to my office berth, ground level, across the road from the beach. I got out, told the car not to go anywhere, and stepped inside.

Dex was seated behind his desk. Across from him, on a couch by the window, sat a total stranger, his face putting me in mind of a balding Doberman. His forehead shone like a bowling ball, glinting in the light, and his dark eyes stared at me intently. I suddenly had the unnerving feeling that he wanted to eat me, or at the very least chew on my earlobe.

Dex stood up, "Ash, this is Mr. Mathers. Mr. Mathers, Ash Corben."

The Doberman stood, and we shook hands.

"Tell me what I can do for you, Mister Mathers," I said, taking a seat across the way from him.

He looked at Dex.

I cleared my throat, then, "There is nothing you can say to me that you can't say to him, sir."

"That is the way you wish it?" he asked – accent strange, not something I'd heard before.

I nodded.

"Very well, then I wish you gentlemen a good day, " and he started to rise.

Dex got up, hands out in a placating gesture, "Sit. Please. I was just leaving anyway. Ash, catch you later."

Dex left, and I sat staring at the strange bastard.

"You haven't answered my question. What do you need from me?" I asked.

A laptop sat on the table, and he turned it to face me.

"Computer, call Mister Rainer," he said. The computer screen flashed **Calling...**, it connected and an old man, thinning white hair to his shoulders, sat facing me at the other end.

"Mister Corben?" he said.

"Yeah, and you are?"

"Howard Rainer."

"What can I do for you, Mister Rainer?"

"My employer is in need of your services, and he is prepared to pay you very well for them."

Ah, the usual story then.

I nodded, "Carry on."

He cleared his throat, "Mister Corben, are you at all familiar with something called Project Gateway?"

I thought for a while, then, "Yeah, I think so. Wasn't that a theory about dreams and how they played a role in the real world?"

The old man let out a dry cackle, possibly his idea of a laugh.

"You are right in one way, it did involve dreams, but not in the way you're thinking."

I gestured for him to continue.

He watched me intently for a second.

"Mister Corben, you dream."

I nodded, "Of course."

"It wasn't a question."

I said nothing.

"And some of those dreams," he continued, "they feel a bit...strange?"

I shrugged, "Sometimes, yeah."

The old man nodded.

"And have you ever woken up after a particularly lucid, atmospheric dream, and felt the rest of the world was almost...flat, lifeless...by comparison?"

"Maybe once or twice. Where's this leading?"

"Thirty years ago, someone had an idea. A man by the name of Terrence Manning. Mister Manning had an idea that he believed would change the world. He believed the dream world and the ordinary world were linked; linked in some strange and inexplicable way, and that if you could open your mind to the true existence of it; move past some hidden barrier in your head; that the two worlds would become one and the pieces of the puzzle of life would fall into place. That feeling of... missing something... in the waking world was due to the fact that we only saw half the picture. He believed there was another place... on the other side of this one."

I groaned inwardly. Another crackpot.

"His theory," continued Rainer, "was widely viewed by academics and scientists as that of an eccentric and possibly deranged individual. However he did gain a large following among certain fringe scientific sectors and so-called New Age factions. He built a large habitat, housing the latest technology, in a remote part of Antarctica called Ciegan's End, a place so cloaked in storms that visibility from space was an impossibility."

"No spies," I said.

Rainer nodded, "Privacy was key. The construction of this place took over two years. And then, one day, he gathered his followers together, put them on board a great big hovship called the *EAV Gatekeeper*, and set off to "unlock the secrets of this world".

"About two and a half years later, certain government officials became concerned as to what was happening out there, their fears no doubt sparked by the fact that their satellites could find no trace of the place, and attempted to make contact. They launched a search and rescue mission, comprised of scientists and marines, manning two EA Navy Tracker hovships, the *EAV Cirrus* and the *EAV Nimbus*. After the launch the expedition kept in permanent contact with base up until they reached the edge of Ciegan's End, about four weeks into the journey, when all communications ceased. This was expected, as the snowstorms in the area made any electronic communications all but impossible. The *Cirrus* was the first to reach Ciegan's End, about thirty-six hours later at their last recorded speed. It arrived alone, the other vessel having had engine trouble: trouble that would ultimately be their saving grace.

When contact was eventually re-established with the *Cirrus*, it was clear that all was not well. Of a full complement of thirty-two marines, four scientists and a ship's crew of ten, only a handful were now on board. Two marines, a crewman, and two evacuees: a man and a baby girl."

Mister Rainer stopped, took a sip of coffee.

"Base attempted to establish what had happened on the habitat in Ciegan's End, but the responses of the crew were unintelligible, and what little sense could be made was confused and horrifying. It became obvious that they were insane, having witnessed and somehow survived atrocities that defied nature."

"Atrocities?" I said, eyebrow raised.

"The *Nimbus* rendezvoused with them a few hours later. They found the *Cirrus* floating adrift on a snowfield about twenty clicks from the habitat, dead in the proverbial water. Nothing could have prepared them for what they would find. The remaining members of the crew of the *Cirrus* were, when they found them, shaking uncontrollably, suffering from extreme and intense hallucinations, and all but the child were burned, scarred badly, and bleeding from lacerations all over their faces and bodies. One marine was lying in a corner, body curled up, his hands to his face. When they attempted to move him, his hands fell away, and, " he swallowed. "His eyes... Mister Corben ... something very bad was happening on that habitat, something terrible. And it had been going on for some time before our boys arrived, possibly years. What little we were able to gain from them was frankly horrific.

Stories of torture, cannibalism, total insanity. A council was put together and a vote put forward. It was unanimous. A few days later the habitat and every soul in it was blown off the face of the earth with tactical land-to-land weapons. That was twenty-six years ago."

"I'm guessing what you're telling me didn't hit the papers," I said.

The old man looked at me.

"Oh, but it did," Rainer replied. "Mister Corben, open file Article 17b3."

"Computer, access Article 17b3."

A pause.

Rainer's face disappeared from view, replaced with an old news report:

Seventy Dead In Antarctic Disaster

A team of scientists and civilians were found dead earlier this week after a freak storm destroyed their habitat in Antarctica. Earlier this year the Earth Alliance Navy, after consistently failing to make contact with the outpost, launched a search and rescue mission in the form of two navy tracker hovships. Their four week journey ended in tragedy late last week when, arriving at last at their destination, the first of the two ships, a vessel called the *Cirrus*, discovered the habitat destroyed and the inhabitants dead and perfectly preserved in the freezing climate. While the bodies were being placed on board their transport, the area was hit by a ferocious storm. An SOS was sent out but when the sister vessel *Nimbus* arrived a few hours later, the ship and all souls on board were lost beneath the ice. The general consensus ...

I looked up, "A freak storm?"

Rainer grinned, "The military has never had much of an imagination when it comes to cover-ups."

"What happened to the survivors after all of this?" I asked.

"The two marines were committed to a naval asylum, on the grounds of total mental collapse; one of them killed himself. That was the one I had found curled in a ball. The other crewman seemed to be more together than the others, and was released after three months of physical and psychological treatment. A year later he was found in the woods outside his hometown, living in a shack of his own building, with a collection of dead children he called his babies. On his way to the death chamber he was asked a question by a member of the media and his reply was very strange. He said: 'They're safe now.'"

"And the other two?" I said, "The man and the baby girl?"

"The man collapsed into a state of catatonia shortly after boarding the *Cirrus*, and remained that way. He was placed in a military institution with the others, to be cared for until he 'came back' or passed away. The girl was placed in foster care. She was badly traumatised, but at her age the chances were good that therapy could undo most of the damage."

I was silent a while, then, "Mister Rainer, the story you've told me is intriguing, but where exactly do I come into it?" I asked.

"I represent a gentleman who has a somewhat personal interest in the events that took place at Antarctica twenty-six years ago. A close relation of his was one of the civilians on the outpost. He was recently made aware of the true nature of the events that took place on the habitat, and he wishes to discover the whole truth."

I looked Rainer in the eyes, "And what exactly am I required to do?"

"Simple," he replied. "You, Mister Corben, are a private investigator. My employer would like to commission you to find the only person on the planet who might possess the answers. The last living survivor of the atrocities that took place at Ciegan's End: that little girl."

On the way back to my apartment I thought through the conversation with that strange old bastard, Rainer. It had ended with a lead, the name of the orphanage

23

the girl had stayed at briefly before her placement with foster parents, and a bank account transfer on the laptop that had shown a very healthy addition to the company account.

I was in business. There was definitely something a bit weird about the whole thing, but in my line of work that isn't particularly unusual.

I had asked why, for instance, my services were required if he was already in possession of the only piece of information that would have presented a problem. Why, for example, could Mathers here not undertake to find her? To which he had replied, "Ah, my employer prefers to remain anonymous. Indeed, even after the initial investigation is successful and the young lady's whereabouts are discovered, he will then undertake to speak with her in a place that even I will have no knowledge of. In short, he doesn't trust anyone except a stranger who will do it for money. You."

For some reason, that last comment had pissed me off a bit. But I'd let it slide, and ended the meeting soon after that.

As I said, I was in business.

I slowed the hov, pulled into my apartment berth and came to a stop.

"Computer, any visitors today?" I said.

"Two entries. Anonymous at twelve thirteen. No messages. Ash Corben at twelve sixteen. Access granted," the computer replied.

I sat dead still.

"Computer, repeat second visitor entry."

"Ash Corben at twelve sixteen. Access granted."

Unless I was losing it, I didn't recall coming back here this afternoon. Not even to pick up my smokes.

"Computer, scan the apartment for foreign objects as of twelve p.m. today."

24

There was a brief silence.

If someone had somehow used my voice, my prints, and the DNA in the skin of my thumb to gain access, the computer would not have notified me automatically of any little changes. It would simply assume that I had made the changes. Mental note: Fire security people. And buy a new computer.

"One object detected. Size: four point three one cubic centimetres. Weight: unknown. Internal mechanisms: present. Extern/al sensors: present. Explosive content: none. Warning: twenty-eight percent of total mass unknown."

Unknown...

Oh shit...

Let me give you a brief history lesson. About twenty years ago there was a full-scale war on the Moon. Maybe you remember it. The Lunar Colonies, having started out as nothing more than a collection of industrial mining sites, warehouses and staff bunkers, had developed into a vast society encompassing civilian, industrial and corporate citizens. Everyone coexisted in a society with a near-perfect infrastructure and a hell of a view. But the corporate mineral mining was beginning to encroach on areas that had already been settled on and developed. Whenever a mining site needed to expand, the colonists occupying the targeted area simply had to pack their bags and move on, or face immediate deportation. In the early years the corporations owned the Moon. But after a few generations were born on lunar soil, the distinction between corporate property and civilian homeland began to blur. And it wasn't long before the lunar citizens began demanding rights, both in the form of official Lunar Citizenship and land deeds. They attempted to reach a compromise with the companies and failed on every level, the suits reminding them that it was corporate funding that had put them there in the first place.

The colonists said fuck you and everyone started fighting. The war was small in scale but it is a generally acknowledged fact that it was also one of the most vicious and brutal battles in history. There is a reason for this.

The vBomb.

One of the Corporations, a company called OreTech Industries, was also involved in weapons research and development, and they had been working on an explosive device using antimatter. They had tested it under secure conditions but had no idea what the impact would be in the open, and being the sick bastards they were, they saw this as the ideal time to find out. So they leaked one of these things to a suit who had his living quarters in one of the nicer parts of the civilian colony. He was able to get it into the central promenade. When they activated it, they unleashed hell.

The bomb created a mini blackhole, first exploding, then sucking the entire colony and a few mining structures into it before winking out of existence, leaving a giant, gaping hole in the surface of the Moon that you can see from earth. Needless to say, OreTech was brought down with a bang. When the media got hold of this they had a field day. Families sued. And the Earth Alliance government promptly shut them down and took their research. Including the bomb. What actually happened to the company was slightly different, but I'll tell you about that later.

All was quiet for a while until, one lovely spring morning several years later, during a weapons' conference in Nu Caynan, the latest in smart weapons was unveiled: The vBomb. The Earth Alliance Army claimed it to be the perfect bomb, an antimatter containment bomb that would destroy only within the specified parameters, then suck all the debris into oblivion.

26

They staged a test explosion that totally obliterated a small dining chair in the conference room, leaving not a speck of dirt on the EA suit standing right next to it. Everyone loved it, no one realising for one second that if, when programming the parameters, you accidentally put an extra zero in ....well, there goes the neighbourhood.

They discovered this the hard way, and after one too many accidents in battle, the vBomb was outlawed.

There was one in my apartment right now.

I took a deep breath.

Let it out.

So it was going to be one of those days. I found it pretty interesting that this should happen directly after my new commission. But hey, this was the job, like it or not. Besides, I'd had worse.

Hell, I'd been married.

I gunned the hov's engine, shifted into reverse and roared backwards out of the berth, pulling sharply into the skylane.

"Computer, close top!" I said, and floored it.

Two

Life, for me, began simply enough.

I was born.

Came kicking and screaming into the world, underweight and overwhelmed, wondering what the hell I was doing here and looking immediately for the first exit, or maybe the next train back. I found neither and realised with a sinking feeling that I was pretty much here to stay and that I was just going to have to deal with it.

I let this sink in.

And then somebody hit me.

As far as first impressions go, this one had to suck.

And since this was *THE* first impression, I guess you could say it set the tone for most of my life.

I started crying.

I don't think I could have been born into a weirder age if I'd tried. The history books tell us that things weren't always like this, that life was once... clean. The records state that natural valleys, forests and grasslands once existed purely on their own, without the need for giant underground TerrainReGens. The human race once spent more time outdoors than they did indoors and animals of all shapes and sizes once charged across lush green plains.

But that gradually changed over the period of a few hundred years and a major war, and before we knew it we'd killed more than we could possibly hope to save, fucked up the weather and holed ourselves up in giant cities of concrete and steel. To sulk.

I grew up in one of these cities. A place called Shillian.

Anyway, that's also exactly where Dex was headed when I called through.

"How did it go?" he asked.

"Yeah, not bad. Except for the vBomb in my apartment," I replied.

Dex looked at the dashboard screen in his hov, an expression of disbelief on his face.

"A what? Hold on; I'm coming back. Gimme an hour."

"No, keep going. I'll meet you in Shillian. At that place with the thing. Tomorrow at three in the whatsit," I said.

"What...." Dex began.

"Tomorrow. Three. See ya." I ended the call, trying not to stare at the expensive, metallic-grey hov that had been tailing me since I left the apartment, taking all the turns I'd taken, remaining always one or two cars behind me.

Hmm...

I slowed down to a crawl and gestured to the hovs behind me to overtake. Two did. The tail, however, slowed as well and pulled into the berth of a mega gym I'd just passed.

"Great," I said. "They know this game too."

I checked the lanes, waiting for a gap, found one, hit the gas (pulling a pretty damn impressive one-eighty degree slide) and roared off in the direction I'd come from, giving a little wave to the grey hov as I went tearing by.

I checked the mirror, looking for signs of pursuit.

The tail had pulled out of the berth, and was heading my way.

Shit, I was hoping the traffic would have held them for a bit.

I accelerated and pulled back on the wheel, shooting up through two lanes of hovs and levelling out on the third, pulling a tight left at the next street, another left at the one after that.

I was beginning to worry that there might be more of these bastards, and realised that my chances of getting out of town would be greatly improved if I wasn't in this particular hovcar. Which was a bit of shame because, as I already mentioned, it's a fucking great hovcar.

I looked around. No sign of them yet, but if there were more of them, I was in trouble. And if they were serious, they'd have the bridge covered, which is the only way off Tanis unless you want to get shot out of the sky by the cops.

I've seen it happen.

Unauthorised entry is a pretty serious offence nowadays, and the same applies on the way out. They just assume you've done something wrong.

So getting the cops involved would basically put me in exactly the same situation I was already in – only the cops are more trigger-happy.

Of course, there was always a chance...

No, I thought, I have a better idea.

I pulled into the parking building of a shopping mall, told the hov to take care, and crossed the glass tube connecting the parking to the mall. I looked out at the skyway, hovs shooting past above and below, checking to see if they'd caught on. No sign of them. I was beginning to wonder if I had been a bit paranoid this time.

Then I saw it, swinging around the opposite corner of the block, moving slowly. Shit, they knew I'd come in here. But why hadn't they followed me in? As the hov passed slowly beneath me, I turned my head, pretending to stare up at the buildings. It moved on and I bolted for the tube exit, into the mall, picking my way through the throngs of people.

I stopped in at a clothing shop that appeared to specialise in all-weather gear, and picked up a nice hooded black jacket with built-in climate control and a communicator screen sewn into the left sleeve. I thought it would be cool to give the com a try, so I called a cab service and arranged a ride.

I made my way to the mall entrance berth and searched for any sign of the bastards who were after me.

Nothing.

My cab pulled into the berth, and I got in.

"Where to, bud?" said the driver.

I gave him the address, and we were off.

About fifteen minutes later we pulled into a berth on the sixty-seventh floor of a fairly swanky apartment block, opposite the beach and about two blocks from the city bridge.

I rang the bell and looked up at the sky while I waited. Clouds were massing, dark, vicious-looking bastards. Rain was close. Sun never shines for long nowadays.

The door was opened by a gorgeous, raven-haired woman in a towelling robe, drying her damp hair with a towel.

"Yeah?"

"Yeah hi, I'm looking for Dante."

She looked me up and down, "Who's calling?"

"Tell him it's Ash Corben."

I could see through to the living room from where I was standing, and as I said this, a man came into view. He was huge, muscular, with skin the colour of ebony and a head devoid of hair, except for a little orange pony tail that cascaded down his back like some bizarre alien waterfall.

"Ash! Waddup man, you in trouble again?" he said, coming forward and grasping my hand, shaking it with force.

"Yeah, you could say that," I looked at the woman.

"Nah man, she's cool. We can talk in front of her. Sheia, this is my ole hombre, Ash. We go waaayy back."

Sheia smiled, and Dante led the way into the lounge.

He offered me a seat. I sat on one of four lavish leather couches, put my feet up on the coffee table (mahogany), and generally made myself at home.

"Mind if I smoke?" I asked.

"Go ahead."

I lit up, indicated the furnishings, "Business good?"

Dante grinned, taking a seat across from me.

"Booming," he replied, brightly. "So what can I get for you? Gun? Drugs? Want someone offed?

"Drink?" Sheia said from the bar.

"No, no, no and yes, thanks, vodka straight," I said. I looked at Dante, "I need a ride."

"You need to get out?" he said, surprised.

"Yeah, fast," I replied.

"Cops?" he asked, still grinning.

"Don't think so, but you never know."

I told him about the vBomb and the grey hov that had tailed me. At this he looked a bit uneasy.

"Don't worry, I lost them."

"Thought never crossed my mind, man," he said.

I took the vodka that Sheia was offering me, thanked her, downed it.

"How soon, Dante?"

"Where you gotta be?" he asked.

"Shillian."

"Give me ten minutes."

He made a few calls in his office and came out a few minutes later, sucking on the end of a fat cigar.

"Got a hov can meet us at six-thirty, just after nightfall. That good for you?" he said.

I did a quick mental calculation, eight hours to Shillian in the rain.

"Perfect," I grinned.

"Good. Now let's have another drink."

"Let's."

I sat back, Sheia heading back to the bar to pour another round, and settled in to wait for night to fall.

Thirty minutes after sunset I was crossing the Tanis City Bridge in the driving rain, inside a hollow seat that Dante claimed was unscannable. There was definitely a bit of tension on my part when we stopped at the checkpoint, but thirty seconds later we were on our way.

After we crossed the bridge and passed through the entry checkpoint, we drove for a few miles into the woods on the edge of the mainland, then pulled over onto a dirt road and stopped after the first bend.

Another hov was parked there, facing us.

Dante let me out and we strolled over to the other hov. A man got out of the driver's side as we approached, a hood covering his head from the rain. He was small and wiry, tiny in comparison to the colossal mountain that was Dante. He handed over the keys to my friend.

"Nice night for this," he said, hopping from one foot to the other in an attempt to stay warm. His breath created a fine mist in the chill night air.

Dante grinned. "Gotta love this cloak and dagger shit, man."

"Not in the rain, you don't."

"Don't be a girl."

"Moi?"

"Si."

The man grinned, "Yes, sir."

He did a little salute, and walked over to the other hov. Dante handed me the keys.

"Now it's my turn," he grinned, turning to leave.

I stopped him, "What do I owe you?"

He shook his head, "It's on me. Be safe, Ash man."

I said thanks and I hoped so and took off for Shillian at a gallop, headlights cutting white swathes of light into the rain-drenched night. At one point during the long drive to Shillian, I found myself wondering this: If it started with a vBomb, where the hell would it end up?

Dex was waiting when I arrived at The Nova, a nightclub in the heart of Shillian whose owner we were friendly with. Another cheating wife situation. Dex once remarked that if it wasn't for infidelity we'd be out of business.

The place was perfect for meetings of a dubious nature. Great decor, loud music, lots of people, and not very well lit.

He grinned and gestured for me to have a seat at the corner cubicle he'd chosen. My drink was already on the table. Vodka straight.

"So what's going on, Ash?"

I leaned back against the soft couch and told him what had happened, including the job and the experiment at Ciegan's End.

"A *vBomb*, Ash!" he said. " Who the hell are these people?"

"I have no idea," I took a gulp of my drink, "but I'm beginning to regret taking this job."

Some girl wandered over to our table, fucked on something. She downed the rest of my vodka, and waddled off.

"So we gonna hit that orphanage tomorrow morning," Dex said, taking a long pull on his smoke. "See what we can come up with."

I shook my head no, gestured to the waitress for another round, "They're probably watching, the creepy bastards. There's a reason why they wanted me on this alone, and I'll be damned if I know what it is, but for now we should keep it that way."

"Ash, hell with them! Someone put a bomb in your place. You need someone at your back, man. And preferably someone who isn't sneaking up to put a knife in it."

"I'll keep you informed, Dex," I said, "but for now let's play it the way they want. Tomorrow I'll contact Rainer, let him know that I'm taking some flack on this, and ask him nicely if he knows anything about it."

Dex didn't like the idea much, but he didn't have a say in it, and he knew it. He was my best friend, but he knew the score. This was the job. We accepted it on their terms.

For now.

"But if things get hot, you're the first person I call," I added.

"Damn straight."

We sat quietly for a while.

"Anyway," I said when the next round arrived, "even if they were tracking my call yesterday, they know I'm in town, but that's about it. It shouldn't be too hard to stay out of sight."

"The orphanage, Ash. What if they're waiting for you? How much do these fuckers know?"

"Our office Is screened, no one could have heard about that. It should be safe."

The girl came over to the table again, made a grab for my vodka. I pulled it away at the last second, downed it, put the glass back down, and grinned at her. She stuck her tongue out at me, swung around on her heel and wandered off again, her Vodka radar no doubt on full alert.

My eyes wandered over to a wallscreen above the bar.

The news was on. I reached over to the earpiece in its cradle beside my drink, placing it in my ear.

"...which led to the arrest of Juan Enrique, UltimaNet executive and well-known highflier, late yesterday evening on charges of drug abuse and sex with a minor. And ending on a good note, multiple Oscar-winning director of *The Mystery Of The Phantom Vessel* and *The Sands of Tabania,* Tommy Slid has arrived back from his sabbatical on Neptune and is currently in the pre-production stages of his new project entitled: *The Pros and Cons of Marrying a Vicious, Cheating, Money-Grabbing, Devil Worshipping, Psychopathic Slag.* Shooting begins soon on Sandy Island, which Mister Slid has stated to be "the geographical equivalent of the soul of a devious bitch: barren, lifeless and full of quicksand just waiting to pull you under and suck the very life out of you." And now over to Jason, with this week's weather..."

I turned to Dex, "Where the hell is Sandy Island?

Dex raised an eyebrow.

"You're kidding, right?' he said.

"No."

"Ash, it's about twenty clicks off the coast. Christ, we used to go there when we were kids."

I looked at him. "What? No we didn't."

I was watching him carefully.

"Dex, the closest island off this coastline is Tanis."

"How many of those have you had, man?" he asked, pointing at my empty glass.

I looked up at the wallscreen again, just in time to catch the last of the weather forecast, and there, as plain as day, was Sandy Island, lying just off the coastline from Shillian.

"Not enough," I replied.

I signalled the barman for another round. Waited for it to arrive. Downed mine as soon as I got it and looked at my oldest friend.

"Sandy Island," I said, still watching him closely. "When do you ever remember visiting a place called Sandy fucking Island?"

He narrowed his eyes, "Ash, this is ridiculous."

"Humour me."

He seemed to think about it, his eyes glazing a bit.

"I can't seem to... I can't think of an occasion offhand." he said, looking a bit confused.

I gave him his drink.

He downed it.

"Ash, this is crazy," he said, looking at the masses of drugged up people, dancing in the 2G dance cube.

Those things are a mind-job, and they're even trippier if you're on something. About five years ago a nightclub owner who was a bit short on space had an idea. Instead of a dance floor covering x metres in floor space, why don't we build one covering y metres, and build another one directly above it, put gravity generators on the top one, and we've got a dance floor double the size at no extra rental. Put a laser emitter in the centre, floating just out of reach, and bob's your uncle. Later, cameras were added to the thing, which allowed for really great videos to be displayed around the club. He patented the idea and went on to become one of the wealthiest men in Nu Caynan, which pleased his wife no end.

"Yeah," I said, "You're right. Maybe I've had one too many."

No use freaking the guy out.

One freaked-out person was enough for now.

He didn't look convinced.

"You okay, man?" he said.

"Yeah," I replied, rising from my seat. "I just need a bit of rest. Been a long day and a longer night. Just drove from Tanis, remember?"

He nodded, "Where you going?'

"I'm going to book in somewhere and fall asleep pretty fast. Call you tomorrow."

Finding a hotel wasn't hard. This was Shillian, my hometown. On the way there I passed a bulletin board playing an ad for a new property development on Sandy Island. From the images on display, I could see what Tommy saw in the place. It looked pretty bleak. But it's amazing what Terrain ReGens can do. The place would be a tropical paradise in six months. If Tommy didn't object to them messing with his "canvas".

Not bad, I thought, for a place that hadn't existed a week ago.

Three

"I told you already I don't know her full name, only her first name: Sarah."

I was in my suite at The Sands Hotel, one of the nicer hotels in Shillian, staring at the wallscreen, trying to explain to an elderly man (hell with that, a fucking *geriatric*) that I needed to find someone and could he please look in the archives for me, and furthermore, if she'd been adopted, could I possibly obtain the address and contact number of the foster parents?

The geriatric in question was a sour old goat by the name of Fletcher. He was the guy in charge of the records department at St Mary's Orphanage in Shillian, and he was taking his job too seriously. Fletcher was grating on my nerves. He was the kind of guy that demanded to see your ID before allowing you in to see a PG16 movie when you were a kid taking out your first real girlfriend; the kind of guy who told parents how to discipline their kids in crowded malls when all they wanted to do was get the hell out of there. I'd already decided that if he had been standing in front of me and not peering at me from the wallscreen, I may have done something bad, and almost definitely illegal, but certainly a whole lot of fun.

"Detective Johnson, I need the full name. I can't – " he wheezed.

"Yes you can. Here, this is the month and the year. It really isn't that difficult." Trying to contain myself.

He looked at me skeptically.

"Which branch of the SPD did you say you're from?"

Easy does it.

I flashed the badge at him for the third time, "Amber District, Grid 32/118, Shillian. Like I said." He eyed the badge, looking very doubtful, which pissed me off even more because it was *real*.

"You don't *look* like a cop," he said, as if that was going to make me break down and confess to being a lying heathen.

"That's funny because *you*, on the other hand, look exactly like someone I'm about to lock up for refusing to co-operate in a police investigation."

He looked at the badge again.

"You're starting to *sound* like one, though."

"Yup." I agreed.

He shrugged and went into the back of his office, out of my line of sight. Which was great, because the sight of the old bastard was beginning to grate on my retina.

"Computer," I heard him mutter. He told the machine to download all files relating to a "Sarah" during the dates I specified.

He came back into sight, walked up to the screen.

"I'm sending the information to your computer," he paused, looking at me. "If you weren't a cop I'd never do this."

I thanked him, told him that God Was Watching, and expressed the hope that good fortune would prevail in his twilight years. And that, furthermore, when he *did* eventually kick it, I hoped that it would be as quick and painless as possible because I hated seeing old bast – elderly people suffer.

After the call I pulled up the file on the room computer, vaguely hoping he hadn't sent a virus along with it, for the hell of it.

He hadn't.

The rest was easy.

For a start, the Sarah I was looking for was the only one under one year old. Also, there was only one Sarah on the roster, which helped a bit as well. Sarah Jennings. That solved that problem. Next was the matter of making contact.

I tried the phone number, but a completely different person answered, claiming they'd had that number for a few years.

Shit.

First dead end.

I checked the address and decided to do it the old fashioned way.

San Marin was a few hundred clicks up the coast from Shillian, a kind of coastal suburbia populated mainly by EA naval officers who were based in Shillian or retired.

I decided an afternoon drive was exactly what I needed, even if it was raining like all hell out there.

It was a nice place, three storeys, built on a rise, with a garden surrounding the property and a stone walkway leading up to the door. It even had a tree with one of those antique tyre-swings that you see in some of the older "movies".

I swung into the driveway, parked next to a nice, family-size hovcar and got out, flipping on the hood of my jacket and hoping the rain wouldn't short-circuit the jacketcom and electrocute me, sending me reeling, writhing and twitching into the mud.

This was too easy.

I rang the bell, heard a little tune coming from somewhere in the house. I hate that. I mean, really. Whatever happened to ding-dong? Nowadays, you're more likely to hear an entire rendition of Beethoven's fifth.

I heard footsteps, and prepared myself, trying to figure out what I was going to say and how I was going to say it.

The door opened, and a dear old lady stood staring at me.

"Yes? What can I do for you?"

I smiled my most endearing smile. "Mrs Jennings?"

"No, I'm Sally Jameson, I'm afraid you're about three years too late, Mister...?"

My heart sank into my lower intestine, "Detective Corben."

I flashed my SPD badge.

"It says Johnson on the badge."

"Er, typo."

"I'm terribly sorry, officer, but –" she began.

"Yeah, don't worry about it. Tell me, did they leave a forwarding address?"

She grinned at this, "I don't think they have a zip code for the afterlife, young man," she said. I wasn't sure if that was funny or just weird.

Dead end number two.

"Thanks for your time," I said, turning to go.

"I have a forwarding address for their daughter, though, poor girl. Don't suppose that will help any?" the old lady inquired.

I stopped short, swung around.

"Some."

"Give me a second."

She went inside, wrote the information down, and handed it to me.

Willowdale, Serenity.

Sounded like a small, peaceful kind of place. The kind of place you go to when you're ready to settle down and relax. Or die.

I thanked her again and turned to leave.

"Always a pleasure to help the authorities."

I left, stopped at the hotel in Shillian to pack, and hit the road.

"Computer, search for Serenity. Subject type: City or town."

The dashboard screen flashed **Searching,** then I was staring at the words **Serenity is here**, hovering above a 3D map of the surrounding countryside, a red arrow pointing at the exact position amongst the landscape.

"Computer, display a route map from here to specified destination." I said, trying to light up a smoke, drive and stare at the screen without leaving the road and crashing into a wall.

The map zoomed out and indicated with a thin green line the easiest route to the town of Serenity from my exact location.

"Distance to specified destination?"

2859.32 km from current position to destination centre.

Nearly three thousand clicks in a hov.

I sighed and floored it, and it wasn't more than a few minutes before the walls of Shillian were disappearing into the haze like a ghost on the breeze.

Night on the road is quite something. Anybody who has travelled long distance in a hov at night knows what I'm talking about. Cars nowadays have receptors that monitor your heartbeat, your breathing, everything, to determine whether you are fit to be behind the wheel, and if at any time it feels that you aren't cutting the grade, it will tell you.

At night it's worse; the car senses an absence of bright light and starts worrying. After a few hours of this it starts getting paranoid. This is why it is extremely important to disable the speakers in your hov before undertaking a long journey. Either that or mess around with the AI chip, which is easier said than done. The thing was installed as a safeguard against accidents, and every hov is legally required to have one. My own hov's AI chip isn't so bad anymore. Dex is a bit of a whiz with that kind of thing.

He fiddled around a bit and now the car thinks it's travelling in perpetual day and we never go faster than fifty.

Ignorance is bliss.

The hov I was currently driving had a fully functioning AI chip.

Believe me, there's nothing worse than a long drive in pitch blackness, with only the rain for company, lost in your thoughts, when suddenly you hear a friendly little computer voice saying **"An alert driver is a safe driver"** and before you have a chance to react, you're blasted with Kleinhund's latest hit, "Ich Het Ein Long Member", screaming at you at a volume that could make your ears bleed.

A few times that night I almost went off the road. Especially when the Kaos Channel came up on the vid screen with DJ Dogman screaming "I'm gonna fuck ya! I'm gonna fuck ya til ya can't take no more! And when I'm through with ya, I'm gonna put ya in da blender and feed ya to ma dawgs! Yeah, see if I don't!"

That was when I pulled over, ripped all the speakers out, and jumped on them until I felt better.

The rest of the drive passed without incident, and as always happens when I hit the road alone, my thoughts drifted to the past: to another time and another life. And as always happens when I hit the road alone, I wondered why I was still here. I wondered what this world had to offer, what I had to offer, now that things had moved on. And as always, I had no answer.

And then, for the briefest instant, I realised something: something that had been avoiding me throughout my entire waking life. For the very briefest of instants, I remembered something that couldn't possibly be, something from another world, caught in the works between here and somewhere else: a glimmer of hope, a message I felt in the depths of my soul, a purpose, stirred back into life by a memory I couldn't even grasp at.

And then, just as suddenly, it was gone.

And I was left alone in the wilderness of the waking world, in a car in the middle of nowhere, moving through the night with nothing behind me and only the darkness ahead.

Four

Darkness.

A warm bed.

A cool breeze blows through the window in our room, and every so often I catch a glimpse of the Moon, swollen and round like a pregnant ghost.

The rest of the city sleeps, but we lie awake. Holding each other like it's the end of the world.

Her lips brush gently against my ear.

I'll never forget how that felt.

Ash

Yeah

Run away with me

I awoke in pitch darkness, clutching at the sheets, the bedspreads lying in a heap on the floor. I glanced at the wall screen, displaying the time in bright green numerals: 11:32 a.m.

Christ. It was time to hit the road again.

I rubbed my eyes.

"Computer, room service," I muttered.

The wall screen flickered, and then a supermodel was staring at me.

She smiled, teeth as white as, well, extremely clean, healthy teeth.

"Room service, how may I be of assistance?" she said through the smile.

"Coffee, make it a jug."

"Anything else, sir?" Smile still there. I was beginning to think the thing had been surgically implanted.

"No, just the coffee."

"Yes sir, and thank you for choosing Room Service."

"You're very wel –". She hung up.

"Computer, TV"

The widescreen mounted on the wall flashed **Channel?**

"Anything with the news," I replied, "and open the curtains."

The curtains slid back to reveal a rainy Sunday morning.

And an image came on the screen, with an irritating nasal voice giving a report on what appeared to be a desert.

"Mute."

Probably another fallout alert.

Another kid born with six fingers and no eyes.

I tried to gather my thoughts.

Okay, first I had to find them. I could see a few of them grazing not too far away, and one was attempting to hide behind the sofa.

I told my laptop to turn on and locate Serenity on the Net.

"Computer, state distance to specified destination."

A string of text appeared on the semi-translucent screen.

1622.41 km from current position to destination centre.

I lit a smoke, went to stand at the window. Rain streaked across the pane, the wind howling outside. This place had come at exactly the right time, about two minutes before I could nod off and crash into a tree. I pulled in just after dawn, tired and hungry and desperate for a cup of coffee, decided I needed sleep if I was going to function at all for the rest of the trip. It's one of those places where every suite is built separately, and has its own little walkway and everything. I like it because your walls don't thump and bang like an exorcism whenever your neighbours have sex. Also there didn't appear to be any other guests, which suited my mood perfectly.

Something made me glance at the wallscreen again, and as I did, I was shocked to see Mrs Jameson smiling brightly for the camera.

"Computer, volume to five."

"...were found murdered in their bed in San Marin early this morning. There were signs of a struggle, as is evident from the footage taken at the scene of the crime. It is still very early in the investigation, but at the moment there seems to be no motive behind the brutal slaying of one of Shillian's most decorated military officers and his wife. The SPD is conducting intense investigations into this terrible tragedy. All they have to go on at present is the sighting of two men, well dressed in dark suits, who were spotted driving slowly past the house earlier in the day, and a man the witness simply described as "A bit scruffy, nice jacket though." And lastly, a meteorite has been –"

A knock at the door.

I went over to the night stand, grabbed my guns and stuck them in the back of my pants.

Old habits…

"Yeah?" I said.

"Room service," came the reply.

"Open," I said, and the door slid back. Subconsciously, I think I was expecting the supermodel, which is ludicrous because she was computer generated.

"Good morning, where can I place your beverage?" said the waiter, who was quite a few rungs lower on the sex chain, what with being a man and all.

"Over there –" I stopped short, staring over the waiter's shoulder and out the door.

Outside, four men were getting out of a hov.

A metallic-grey hov.

I grabbed the waiter by his shirt.

"What's your name?" I said.

He looked shocked. "M-Mike."

I pulled him with me, yelling at the door to close and lock, pushing him past the minilounge area and dragging him down behind the couch that faced the window.

"Mike, be very still," I said slowly and softly, "or you are going to die."

He swallowed, staring hard at the wall in front of us.

I grinned.

We waited, listening.

Any second now.

Any second...

Bang!

The smell of fried metal.

The sound of a door sliding open...

And then the world around us exploded, a lamp to our left shattering, a picture hanging directly in front of us smashing and dropping to the floor as the room was sprayed with bullets. It seemed to go on forever. And then...

Silence.

I came up with a gun in each hand, firing round after round across the living room.

I hit one suit in the chest before he knew what was happening, hit another in the head an instant later, the former flying backwards out the door and landing hard on the walkway outside, gasping and gurgling, the other dropping like a sack of molten lead, dead before he hit the ground. The other two dived for cover, one behind the bed, the other behind the couch opposite our own.

I dropped back behind the couch, leaning back against it, wondering if it would stop a bullet, let alone fifty.

A few shots, a couple more in the couch.

So far so good.

Silence, except for a wheezing, gurgling sound coming from outside.

I couldn't help feeling sorry for the bastard.

"What the fu –" began the waiter, stopping when he saw the expression on my face.

I turned to face the back of the couch, brought my guns up and fired ten rounds, hearing the shattering of windows from the slugs. Waited a split second, then came up firing, taking the suit behind the couch in the face just as he came up to return fire. His face disintegrated. An explosion of blood, grey mush and razor-sharp splinters of shattered skull.

I ducked down again as the fourth suit started firing, the couch shuddering from the impact of the bullets, the wall cracking and flecks of paint flying in all directions.

And then, silence.

"Odds weren't really fair, don't you think?" I called out. "Maybe you should've brought more of your friends along."

Silence.

"Ah, the strong silent type."

I looked at Mike.

"Having fun yet?" I asked, grinning like a maniac.

He seemed to pick up on that, maybe wondering if he was safer with the other guy.

He probably was, but it was too late to swap sides, and there was no use dwelling on the past. I handed him a gun, he held it like it was alive, staring at it in horror.

"What am I gonna do with this?"

"See that little thingy there," I said, pointing at the trigger.

He nodded.

"That's the trigger. You point the gun at the bad man, give that a squeeze, and a bullet comes out the other end."

I told him The Plan. He swallowed, sweat starting to glisten on his forehead, and nodded.

I shot the ceiling.

Two seconds, then a few shots slammed into the couch.

"Now!"

I gave Mike a shove, he jumped up behind the couch, started firing, a mad expression plastered on his face.

I ran and dove down beside the bed, coming up and training my gun on the other side of the bed, just as Mike ran out of bullets.

There was a second of tense silence, then the suit behind the bed came up to return fire, and I shot him between the eyes.

I got up, walked over to Mike, who was standing staring at the gun in his hand with a look of pure exultation on his face.

I took the gun from him with some difficulty, got my shit together and started to leave.

"Thank you," came a soft voice from behind me.

I stopped, turned around.

Mike was staring at me.

"Thanks, Mike. You helped a lot," I replied.

He grinned, looking overjoyed.

I made a run for the hov, hoping to hit the road before the cops came around, asking questions like what four corpses were doing in my hotel room. I almost tripped over the guy I shot in the chest, stopped to look down at him.

He was still alive, barely breathing now.

In the distance, I could hear the sound of sirens, approaching fast.

"You'll live, I think. Maybe now's a good time to rethink your life." I don't know if he heard me, he didn't appear to be conscious.

"Go, the cops are coming!" This from Mike, now standing in the doorway to my room.

I got into the hov, reversed out of the parking bay, and roared off in the opposite direction from the sirens. Fortunately for me that turned out to be the direction I was supposed to be going in. I didn't have time to fuck around. I had to find someone, had to find her before these bastards did, and they were turning out to be quite persistent.

As rain streaked across the windshield, I found myself playing through the events at the motel. It was evident that these guys were going the same way I was, having probably gotten the address from Mrs J before blasting her brains across the wall, and they were probably hoping to bump into me along the way. Also, I'd been the only guest at the motel, which helped.

I accelerated.

I wasn't worried about the cops. I'd booked into the motel under an alias (force of habit, again) and if and when the cops checked for fingerprints they'd come up with a large African lady called Impundu. It's good to have friends on the Net.

There'd been no signs of any unwanted company, cops or other, since I'd made my escape a few hours ago, and I was beginning to think that Mike had led them on a wild goose chase. Remind me to send him a bottle of something.

"Computer, radio," I said.

Channel?

I thought about it.

"Local area. Music."

A song came on, something by Klor Gotta SmorKa Scorcher. It wasn't bad, by today's standards. Klor had quite the voice, Tommy Slid had even done one of his NetVids.

Something occurred to me.

"Computer, scan for news relating to Tommy Slid and/or Sandy Island."

Scanning...

"... is something that my ex bitch would have loved. This place is desolate and hostile, just like her. Anyway, I'm looking for an actress who's willing to film the final shot of my picture. She's got to be about five nine, blonde, with a great rack. Oh, and she can't take this whole life thing too seriously, because the closing scene is gonna involve that fucking great comet-"

"Meteorite –" The interviewer said.

"Did you just correct me?" Tommy asked incredulously.

"Er, no, Mister Slid."

"No you did, I heard you. You just said 'asteroid'."

"No sir, I said mete –" he stopped short.

"Ha! I knew it! You're fired! You're in the fucking can! Get outta here!" Tommy yelled.

"Sir, I don't work for you, you can't fire m –"

"You bastard! You'll never work in this town again!"

There were sounds of a scuffle, then: "We apologise for the break. We are experiencing some technical difficulties. Now, over to Bill for –"

"Computer, previous channel."

The Scorcher song came back on, reaching the kind of crescendo usually reserved for the leaders of religious cults.

I couldn't help grinning. Same old Tommy.

Neptune hadn't changed him one bit.

"Computer, local weather station."

"... storms in the area, so be on the look out, and don't travel too far from home. The –"

"Computer, stop radio."

Shit.

Electrical storms in this day and age are not to be fucked with, and the last thing I felt like was getting stuck in the middle of one. I had to get to shelter before it hit.

Serenity was still a fair distance away, and the rain was beating down harder than ever. I was going to have to concentrate if I was going to get there in one piece, especially at the speed I was going.

I accelerated.

Five

I reached Serenity just before darkness fell.

About seven hours on the road found me taking a turn off the highway and onto a country lane, winding its way through a forest of evergreens.

The sun, edging slowly towards the horizon, cast dusty golden rays across my path, giving the impression of driving from the ordinary world into a dream. A few minutes later I came out of the forest and into the town of Serenity, out of smokes and hungry as hell.

Serenity was the type of place Hollywood made movies about, back in the days when folks actually used to go to the movies. Giant multiplexes housed cinemas where people used to cram themselves like sardines into a room to stare at an oversized screen in pitch-blackness, elbow to elbow, knee to knee, projected onto a white screen from some place high up and away from the sweating masses.

For a time this was the pastime of choice for mostly everyone, but by the middle of the twenty-first century, the whole thing pretty much dried up. The Net had taken over every other form of virtual entertainment and with the advent of Neuro technology, people were no longer interested in the old magic of the movies.

Plug in, go anywhere, do anything, live the life, subscribe now. Never look back.

Fortunately for arseholes like me, there are still a few places you can go to sit and stare like a mindless zombie for a couple of hours. Call me old-fashioned, but the closest you're going to get to my brain is gazing deeply into my eyes, and even then I can't make any promises.

So Serenity was one of those places, still stuck in the old world, before NetLife became the global norm, before multiplexes and peanut-butter flavoured ice-cream and fluffy robot pets who're smarter than you.

A place of graceful buildings, churches with steeples, tree-lined walkways, and a quaint main street you can still amble down without a twenty-four month contract (first three months FREE!).

I parked outside a pub called The Glod n' Gambit as the sun hit the horizon, light turning to twilight, deep orange fading to deeper blue as I watched. Took a deep breath. Fresh air filled my lungs, air so crisp I could taste it. The only time you'll breathe air like that in Nu Caynan is if you import the stuff from places like this. Most of the Upper apartments have this done on a regular basis, "designer air" being the new cool.

Small towns in the middle of nowhere are making a killing exporting the stuff through companies like AirPerfex, who specialise in the more exotic corner of the market, selling brands like "Glacier Fresh", "Thai Meadow Dew" and my personal favourite, "Desert Dawn."

The air around here wasn't quite so, well, flavoured, but I think that's another reason why I liked it. Sometimes less is more.

I glanced up at the wooden sign, swaying very gently in the evening breeze, wondered briefly what a glod was, and walked through the main entrance. The place was small, softly lit. Cozy. I took a seat at a cubicle by the window facing the main road, watching the people amble past, enjoying the last of the day's light, the coolness of early evening.

A woman, somewhere in her late twenties, wafted over to my table, long dark hair framing a face of exquisitely delicate features. Her skin a light olive in tone. A freshness to her that went completely against the deep sadness I sensed behind those big brown eyes.

She smiled, and her face seemed to light up as if from the inside.

Men have travelled far and wide for a smile like that.

I smiled back, my lopsided grin not cutting the grade under any light.

"Are you my waitress?" I asked.

"No, I'm your accountant, and that man behind the bar is your second wife."

A pause.

"Tell her the cheque's in the mail," I replied.

Her smile widened.

"I'm looking for a place. The name's Willowdale. I need to find it urgently. You know where it is?" I asked, not wanting to waste any time. The sooner I found her, the sooner these other bastards wouldn't.

"Yeah, it's out in the farmlands. But I wouldn't recommend trying to get out there tonight," she replied.

"Why not?" I asked, "Is it haunted?"

She grinned, "No, but in about an hour we're gonna get hit with a storm and the chances of you finding anything at night around here during a storm are zero."

I was confused, "Er, street lights? HoverGlobes?"

"Electro Magnetic storm, power will be out all night, and if you go out in a hov, it'll knock that out too. We don't have EM Distorters round these parts."

No storm lights.

I grimaced.

Of course.

This was the biggest bitch about living in the country, the weather.

As I already mentioned, we sort of fucked things up on that front. The Cities are protected from EM storms by giant walls with EM Distorters (thousands of blinking red lights usually referred to as storm lights) but out here it's you and the elements. Some people seem to prefer it to places like Nu Caynan, and I can see why.

But power failures at least once a week (in the deep country pretty much daily); the need to travel at least two hundred clicks to buy anything worthwhile; not to mention storms of the natural variety, which have become ridiculously bad since the War and ravage the countryside on a very regular basis, are the reason why most people on the Planet have moved into MegaCities like Nu Caynan and Shillian.

"I guess I'm grounded til morning," I said.

"Yup, so are you hungry or what?"

"You could say that."

I ordered.

She nodded and went off to do her thing.

Dinner was served and devoured in half an hour, and when the waitress returned with the bill, I asked about accommodation.

"There's a hotel 'bout three blocks up. Place called The Camberton. Check it out."

I said I would, paid and left.

The Camberton was nice enough, not the kind of place you'd find in Nu Caynan, but charming in its own way.

I checked in, unpacked, showered.

Then I called through to the number I'd been given by the old lady again.

No reply.

I tried again.

Nothing.

This was starting to look like a dead end.

"Computer, activate full encryption and call Dex."

My laptop is one of those new X35 Artificial Intelligence machines – you may have seen them on TV – featuring voice recognition and a really great feature called 'gesture recognition', which is cool because you can program it to turn off when you give it the finger. Had to deactivate the AI though. Bloody idiot had a real mouth on it. *You* try searching for information on the Net for your latest case, only to have your entire bandwidth sucked up because the AI is downloading porn. I have to tell you, though, they're into some pretty weird shit.

The screen flashed **Calling**, then **Connecting**.

And then I was staring at Dex.

"Ash, you still alive?" he said.

"Hey Dex, how're things?"

"Quiet, man. Don't worry, I got it covered."

I grinned, "Yeah, I know you do."

Silence for a while, then, "So what's happened?"

"Just got to Serenity. I have her address," I replied. "We're about to get hit with an EM storm, so I won't find the place tonight. Not out there. I'll go through as soon as it gets light."

"Any more unpleasantness?" he asked.

My mind flicked to the guys at the hotel that morning.

"Nothing worth mentioning," I replied, "You?"

"As a matter of fact, yeah. Sharyn called. Says her hotshot boyfriend's out of commission. Got bust doing something he shouldn't. With someone he shouldn't. And they were both doing something they *really* shouldn't."

The day was looking up.

"How old was she?" I asked, amusement painted across my face.

"Fourteen."

My mind flashed back to the news report at the Nova.

"What was his name?" I asked.

Dex raised an eyebrow, "How the hell should I know?"

I shook my head. "Never mind. So what does my beloved ex want? Or rather, how much?" I asked.

"Twenty thou. She says it's urgent, she's been trying DESPERATELY to get hold of you. Says you're the only one she can turn to."

I thought for a while, then, "Send her five, and tell her to get a job."

Dex laughed at that, "It'll be my pleasure."

"Gotta go, Dex. Call you soon."

"Ash."

"Yeah?"

"Watch your back, man."

"You –" The lights went out and the transmission cut as the storm hit and broke the satellite connection.

I lay back on the bed, flashing my X35 the finger. The AI would have asked me for one good reason, and it would have demanded that I answer in perfect Spanish.

Lit a smoke.

I told the X35 to turn back on, accessed the Net, pulled up an old movie I hadn't seen in a while, took a deep pull on my smoke and settled back to relax.

Outside, the town had gone black, except for the soft glow of portable units like mine in a few windows, running on crystal batteries that cost a fortune but never die and, as I just discovered, are also immune to the effects of a raging EM storm. You learn something new everyday, or at least once a month.

It started to rain.

Sharyn.

We'd met at some big do celebrating the release of a NetStar's new album, entitled 'Life in the Ghetto of the Soul of a Musician 4: Journey to Atlantis and Back Again, With Any Luck'.

Dex and I were freelancing as security personnel at the time, installing cameras, laser perimeters, and overseeing the screening process at the entrance, as well as instructing the guards themselves on how to do it right.

It was a good living.

So I met Sharyn at this party. She was easily the most gorgeous woman in the room, all blonde hair and golden-brown tan and legs up to the ceiling. Dex had made some passing remark in her general vicinity, and I, having had maybe a bit more Jack than was necessary, played along.

She turned around, looked directly into my eyes, smiled. I smiled back. Then she slapped me.

Six months later, we were married. A year and a half later, we were divorced.

That's life. Looking back, I can tell you there was no love there. It was never about love with the two of us. Affection, yeah. Sexual chemistry? Hell yeah! But never love. All she wanted was a good time. And me, well, there's always been someone else in my head. Somebody completely different.

Soft.

Gentle.

With a smile that took my breath away every single time.

Sometimes she's nothing more than half-remembered images, fleeting and disjointed, racing across my mind's eye like a million shards of a broken mirror. Sometimes I remember her so vividly I feel I can reach out and touch her. But the feeling, that feeling of being with her, never leaves me. Sometimes I lie awake, trying to catch a glimpse of her face, smiling at me the way she always did. She hovers there, inches from my grasp, so very close I can smell the warm scent of her skin. And sometimes I can almost hear her. Hear her voice in the deepest recesses of my mind, whispering softly to me, begging me with all the love in her heart to remember, remember, don't let go.

So I lay there, letting the glory of old Hollywood take me away until sleep, finally, came to claim me.

And I dreamed.

And dreamed...

And I'm there now. Looking out over the water. The wind is cool against my face, and I can smell the tang of the ocean out there in the night. She's standing beside me, one finger interlocked with my own. I turn to look at her. Look into those beautiful eyes.

I know she loves me; I feel it in every pore of my bod:. a radiance that engulfs me, bringing light into the darkest corners of my soul. She is all I ever want in this world, the warmth of her body on a cold night, the touch of her hand on my cheek, the soft fragrant smell of her hair as she holds me, so close, rocking me gently to sleep after the death of someone I love. I look away from her, out towards the sea. Something's coming. Far off across the sea a storm approaches., I can feel it rushing across the waves, coming closer with every breath I take and every beat of her heart. I look at her again, feeling warmth wash over me like the rain, and I never want to leave her side.

But I have to go now.

There's something I have to do...

I let go of her hand, tell her goodbye, whisper softly to her, my lips brushing against her ear. And then I turn away, and tiny droplets of ocean spray wet my face, even as hers begins to fade, fading away into golden light, as I'm once more bathed in the soft light of day.

And even as I wake I try to hold on, praying for one more glimpse, praying to once more feel the touch of her hand.

Wiping away my tears as she washes away my pain.

After breakfast I went in search of Sarah's place, rain beating down on my windscreen, making me strain to make out the names of the little tree-lined streets I made my way through. SmartGPS is pretty much nonexistent in a town like

Serenity. You can pull up a topographical map, yeah, but if you're looking for street names then you're fucked. By afternoon, I found myself driving along the outskirts of town. To my right, little plots of land, farming vegetables and the like (real vegetables!) and to my left, farmlands stretching out to the distant horizon. And then I saw it: a farmhouse, two stories high, with a weeping willow flanking one side and a water tower on the other. The name Willowdale inscribed on a wooden board above the main gate, swaying in the driving rain.

This was the place.

I turned off the farm road and onto the dusty driveway leading up to the house, parking in front of the entrance.

I rang the bell.

Silence.

Tried again.

Nothing.

It occurred to me that the bell might be broken so I tried knocking instead. Call me old-fashioned. Everyone else does. Still no sound came from the place.

"Shit."

"Lost your way?"

I jumped, spun around, hand already on the 9mm butt in it's shoulder holster. She stood under a tree, not ten feet from me.

The waitress from the Glod.

"Er, yeah," I replied, looking about as guilty as a drug dealer at a sermon. Who has just done the wild monkey dance with the priest's daughter.

And his wife.

At the same time.

"Why do you carry a gun? Or were you going to offer me a Kleenex?"

"No gun here, just tissues," I replied. I am a truly awful liar.

Silence for a while.

"You found who you're looking for yet?" she asked.

I looked around me, gazing briefly at the farmhouse, the surrounding land.

"Maybe," I replied. "Sarah?"

She smiled.

She walked past me and opened the door, turned to me.

"You coming in or what?"

I followed her inside.

We were sitting at a table in the kitchen, windows facing out at farmlands, swept with rain.

"My foster parents died about three years ago, hov accident," she swallowed, looking away from me. "That was when I decided to find my biological parents. It took a while, but eventually I tracked down my dad. He was in an... institution. I brought him back here, thought maybe this place would help him, help his... condition."

She looked at me, saw the surprise in my eyes.

"Your father is here?" I said. "In this house?"

She shook her head. "He never spoke, never said a word, never even made eye contact with me. Just lay in bed, sleeping most of the time. When he was awake he just kind of stared at the ceiling, never left that room, that bed. At first I used to take him for walks in the chair, but after a while it seemed sort of pointless. He was somewhere else." She took another sip of her coffee, "I just hope it was better than this."

I said nothing.

"You ever dream about another place?" she said.

I looked at her, at her eyes, filled once more with that deep sadness. But this time I saw something else. Perhaps a yearning, a longing.

63

"Every night," I replied.

We were silent a while, Sarah staring out at the rain, myself in a state of inner turmoil. I had to tell her.

Now.

I took a breath, and suddenly found myself wondering what the hell I was going to say.

I was calling it off, that much I knew.

I was going to tell Rainer I couldn't find her, and give him his money back.

But as I looked at her I realised that that in itself wasn't enough.

Some very bad men were trying to kill me, were trying to get at her, and my own (ex) employer was looking more dubious by the second.

What had started out as a pretty straightforward job was looking very dodgy, and somebody completely innocent was the target.

And time was running out.

I took another breath.

Let it out.

"Sarah, there's something I have to tell you."

She looked away from the window, meeting my gaze, made curious by the tone in my voice.

"Yes?" she said.

This was it.

I jumped.

"Someone hired me to find you."

I watched her expression change, soldiered on, "A man by the name of Rainer. He wants to ask you some questions about... your origin."

I told her everything. Everything except what really happened on the habitat, because some things were better left untold. I told her about the vBomb and the tail, the men in black suits who had visited the old lady asking for her address, the double murder, and the guys at the motel. I told her that, because of the fuck-up at Ciegan's End, her dad was the way he was. That they alone were the survivors of some terrible tragedy. I told her because she needed to trust me if we were going to get out of this.

If *she* was going to get out of this.

Hell, I'd died once already.

"So it looks like whoever is after me is also after you," I finished.

She took it as well as could be expected, I guess.

After she'd finished beating me with her tiny fists, she sat back, took a long sip of coffee, and said, "So what now?"

"Now," I said, "you call in sick."

We got back to The Camberton half an hour later and I told the X35 to turn on.

New Mail flashed on the screen.

"Play," I said, and then I was staring at Sharyn. I wondered how she had gotten hold of this number.

"Who's that?" asked Sarah.

"My ex."

"Your ex-wife?"

"No, my ex-toaster."

"Ash honey, please! I need the money! Got myself into a fix and now Juan's accounts are frozen 'coz of that little you-know-what! I'm stranded! After all we've been through together, please help me with this, I –" She turned her head, and a shocked expression came over her face.

"Who the f –"

The scene tilted, swung wildly, the last image being a close-up of a wall.

The screen went blank.

Message Ended. Replay?

"Replay," I said, feeling a heavy weight settling on my shoulders.

I watched it again.

Then I called Dex on the jacketcom, trying not to catch Sarah's eye.

He answered bleary eyed and half asleep.

"What's up?"

"Dex, where are you?"

"In bed with your mother."

He saw my expression.

"Still in Shillian, man. What's wrong?"

"Got a message from Sharyn."

"Yeah, I'm sorry about that. I called her to give her the good news, and she just kinda drilled it out of me. You know how she can be."

I did.

Jesus, did I ever.

"Something's happened to her —" I stopped short. Sharyn wouldn't have put an encryption on the call, even if she'd know how to. If they'd checked her computer, they'd have the laptop number and my communicator number too, and therefore, our exact location. Shit. "Dex, make an anonymous call to the cops, get them to Sharyn's place, then meet me at the old pad."

He nodded, "What time?"

"Leave now, I'll catch you there. Sarah's coming too, we need a safe-house. Oh, and forget the old numbers, you can contact me on this one from now."

He grinned, "You loved that laptop, man."

"Yeah."

"Guess I'm involved after all."

"Yeah," I replied. "I guess you are."

S i x

We packed our stuff, leaving the laptop and my mobile communicator in the room, and left Serenity ten minutes later, roaring through the town and out the other side, crossing a wooden bridge over a river I was pretty damn sure hadn't been there on the way in.

"Where're we going?"

I looked at Sarah, head resting on the window, her jacket bundled up as a makeshift pillow.

"Somewhere safe."

She looked out at the rain.

"Where?"

"A motel, 'bout half way from here to Shillian, off the highway. The place is invisible. Unless you know it's there you'd never even guess it existed. No signs, nothing."

"How do you know about it?"

I didn't reply.

Sarah turned her head to look at me.

"Ash? How do you know about it?" she repeated.

"Long story," I said, not taking my eyes off the road.

She shrugged, "Suit yourself."

I gripped the steering wheel tightly and focused on the storm outside while simultaneously fighting down the one that had suddenly and without warning started up in my head.

Shillian.

With a bit of luck the cops were at Sharyn's apartment by now.

How these bastards had found her was anyone's guess, but now she was involved, and that meant someone else to worry about. Things were moving out of my control, and that wouldn't do at all.

The only reason I could see for this debacle was that they would try to use her to get to me.

And Sarah.

If she was still alive.

Sharyn was my ex wife, but I was concerned nonetheless.

Those poor bastards had no idea what they were in for.

The place was called The Rock Palace. I never did find out whether that was because of the owner's choice of music (fast guitar-driven stuff from the middle to the end of the twentieth century) or because it was built on the edge of a cliff facing out over the sea.

Once, years ago, I actually asked him about it and he looked at me like I was a fucking idiot.

I never brought it up again.

We pulled into the parking area of The Rock Palace just after eight in the evening. The rain had stopped and the clouds had parted enough for us to make out the Moon, hanging low and orange in the night sky. As we got out of the hov, a muscular man with long iron-grey hair and a bushy moustache ambled out of the entrance, coming up to greet us.

"Ashman, Dex said you'd be joining us." He grabbed me in a vice-like bear hug, slapping my back. "Hey, you look like shit. Nice jacket, though."

"I get that a lot," I replied.

He grinned, turned to look at Sarah.

"You gonna introduce us, man?"

"Yeah. Sarah, this is Felony. Old bastard from my glory days."

"Who you callin' old?"

Sarah smiled, and I felt grateful for Felony's easy-going manner. It would make her stay here easier to deal with.

He grabbed my shoulder, "Let's get inside, man. Got some coffee goin'. Dex is waiting."

"Dex is here already?"

"Yeah, he got here about an hour ago."

We moved indoors.

The Rock Palace is just one of those places. It has a life of its own, from the antique guitars on the walls to the original autographed pictures of some of yesterday's most famous artists. This place wasn't as much a hotel as it was a shrine. It was in the air. A smell, something from another time.

Felony led us into the bar area, where we took a seat on some dark red couches placed by the floor-to-ceiling windows.

Sarah looked down at the sea, crashing waves illuminated by giant flood-lights rigged to the cliff face below us.

"Hey Ash."

I turned and looked at Dex, standing behind the bar.

"Hey Dex. You and I have got to stop with these midnight meetings."

Dex grinned, holding up a bottle. "Bourbon?"

"Coffee," I replied.

"Coffee's on its way. Hold your freakin' horses," Felony said from across the room.

I gestured to Sarah. "Dex, this is Sarah."

They exchanged greetings, and Dex came to join us on the couches, followed shortly after by Felony and the coffee.

"What's happening, Ash? Dex told me a bit, but he said you're the one to speak to," said Felony, after a sip of coffee.

I told him everything, leaving out, once again, what little I knew about the events at Ciegan's End, until Sarah had dropped off to sleep. And when she was deep in a fitful slumber, I told him that as well, ending with the message from Sharyn.

"And you got no idea who's behind all this?" Felony asked.

I shook my head.

"Rainer," said Dex, "Him and Mathers are definitely up to shit."

I nodded my agreement.

"I'm going to contact him tomorrow, see what he knows about all of this." I glanced over at Sarah, fast asleep on the couch beside me. "Tell him I'm calling it quits."

"What about Sharyn?" said Felony.

"I'm working on it."

I turned my head, looking out over the waves, giant and luminous out there in the night. This was perfect, we were untraceable now, the laptop at the Camberton hopefully leading the bad guys on a wild goose chase. They needed a number to contact me at for the negotiations involving Sharyn, if that was what they intended to do, but I couldn't risk a trace. As I said, with GPS being what it was, if they had my number, they had our location. All I could do was call Rainer.

And hope for the best.

I turned to face Felony.

"I'm leaving in the morning. I have a few things to take care of."

Felony nodded at this.

"Please take —" I began.

"You don't have to ask, Ash. She's safe here."

I nodded, "Thanks."

"So what's the next step?" asked Dex.

"Rainer. I'm going to ask him a few questions."

"You need backup?" Felony said, his eyes bright.

I smiled, good ol' Felony, always up for a fight.

"For the moment I'm cool, but I'll call through if I do." I took the last sip of coffee. "Time to sleep."

Felony gestured to Sarah, fast asleep on the couch, "You need a room?"

I grinned, "It's not like that, Fel. Besides, the couch is comfier than most of your beds."

Dex got up, "Well, I for one have missed those beds. See ya in the morning."

After Dex and Felony had left, I put a blanket over Sarah, and grabbed the opposite couch. In the darkness just before sleep, my mind began to wander, moving back to a few nights before and the feeling of deja vu that had grasped me on the road.

And the dream of the night before.

Of waves.

And darkness.

In another place.

Dawn broke.

I stood on the deck of The Rock Palace, watching as the sky came alive above the ocean, orange and red streaks blazing across the deepest of blue.

And for once, I was up to see it. Not because I was feeling like an early rising health freak, but because my sleep had been strained and I'd awoken some time before the dawn, unable to keep my eyes shut any longer.

Straight after that most beautiful of sights, I ambled inside, hit the bed, and was out like a light.

Felony rose around ten, strolling through the lounge stark naked and climbing into a bath. I can't tell you how happy I was that Sarah was asleep, or how unhappy I was to have been awoken by the sight.

A short while later Dex brought in some coffee. He massaged his temples, appearing to wonder what he was doing awake at this insane hour.

"Get ready, Dex," I said. "It's time to go."

"Jesus, Ash," he mumbled, "it's *dawn*!"

"It's after ten, Dex."

"Yeah, thought I'd sleep in a bit."

I slid open the doors leading onto the deck area, stepped out into the cool air, the coffee giving off steam in the cold morning air. A short while later Felony came to stand beside me, taking in a deep breath. Letting it out.

"So, what's the plan?" he said.

I turned to face him.

"I want to meet with Rainer. Face to face."

Felony let out a low whistle, "If your interview with him is anything to go by, that might be a bit difficult."

I took a sip of coffee, looked out at the waves.

"I'll figure it out," I replied.

Dex joined us on the deck.

"Ready to go," he said.

"Where is Rainer based?" Felony asked, thoughtfully.

"Nu Caynan," I replied.

Dex raised an eyebrow. "How do you know that?"

"The contact number he gave me is a Nu Caynan number, I tried to put a trace on it but it's protected somehow. I guess we'll have to call when we get there."

"You're not very well liked around those parts, Ash," said Felony. "You sure it's a

72

good idea to go back? Your cover has held outside of Nu Caynan, but there're a lot of familiar faces down there, and word is a lot of our mutual enemies are much higher up on the food chain nowadays. You're taking a hell of a risk."

I grinned.

Felony shook his head, "Watch your back, Ash."

"Yeah," I nodded.

We made our way out to where a black hovcar was parked, a few feet from the entrance to the Palace.

Dex raised an eyebrow. "This isn't our hov," I said.

"Yeah," Felony said with a grin. "I took the liberty of getting you a new ride, just in case."

We thanked him, embraced, and as I got into the driver's side, Felony placed a small card in my jacket pocket.

"He's a friend, one of the few you can still trust in Nu Caynan. If you need anything, *anything*, call him."

I looked at the card, raised an eyebrow, "K?"

He nodded.

"Thanks, man."

"Good luck, Ash."

I gunned the engine, swung the hov around, and roared off.

Nu Caynan wasn't close. Shillian was about one thousand four hundred clicks from here, and where we were going was a further two thousand inland from there. It's a wasteland out there, with none of the beauty the coastal regions still possess. Also, if we were to get there by hovcar, we would be conking out every time an EM storm hit us, and that would be pretty damn often.

Dex, who was obviously thinking the same thing, looked at me.

"We going to take a chance on a jet?" he asked.

"I don't think we have a choice. Up country isn't like this," I gestured to the country side rushing past on our left, the ocean a dark blue expanse on our right.

"The storms will mean it will take at least three or four days to get there." He agreed. "But if we're recognized on entry, there'll be hell to pay."

I nodded, "It's risky, the only people who keep a closer watch on the City Gates than the cops are the robbers. Go figure."

We drove through the day, the rain once again coming down but very softly now. We arrived at last at the gates of Shillian as the sun began to set, making our way at ground level to the other side of town. The sky was black by the time we reached Shillian Airport, a massive structure that, when seen from the air, resembled a giant starfish: runways going off in every direction from the main building, millions of lights twinkling in the night.

As we entered the airport gates, I hoped the hov we were driving was licensed. That was stupid, Fel wouldn't have given us an unmarked hov; we would have been pulled over after five minutes in Shillian.

The security guard checked our ID cards and ran a quick scan on the plates. I leaned over to see the results on his DigiPad and saw my face come up on the screen.

I grinned.

Good ol' Felony.

We got the green light and drove through to the parking area, parking the hov in one of thousands of bays. I got out and stared across at the main building, taking in the cool night air in the slight drizzle, remembering the last time I was here.

I turned to Dex, "Memories here."

"I know," Dex said gently.

In the distance and the darkness, the lights of Shillian Airport beckoned to me, calling for me to remember another time, another life. When things were simple and straightforward and our lives stretched before us like a highway into the middle of tomorrow. When the sun used to shine and the only darkness we saw came from a night sky filled with stars.

I steeled myself.

"Let's go."

We walked in silence, coming eventually to one of the main entrances to the airport complex, the doors sliding away effortlessly as we approached.

We entered and I stopped, taking in the sight of the bustling airport. People were everywhere, moving this way and that. Some exec strolled past us, a designer carry-all slung over one shoulder, speaking into an OptiLens Communicator and gesticulating wildly. At least I assumed it was an OptiLens, if they were an ordinary pair of sunglasses then the guy was barking mad. A family, the mother bent over and clucking at her two young boys like a mother hen, her back to the father, who was eyeing a leggy blonde across the central promenade. He looked at his wife (a good thirty years her senior and a lot rounder) and I could see his eyes glaze over, resigned to the fact that this was what he had.

This was it.

So much for picket fences.

And further off to my left a young couple, embracing, the woman crying, the man trying to pacify her, rubbing his hands gently on her slightly shaking back.

Baby it's okay.

I turned away abruptly, blocking out what was rising to the surface of my mind.

An image.

A snapshot of a young couple, standing close, the man's hands on her shoulders, foreheads touching.

And a sound, soft, sweet: a woman, laughing through her tears.

"Let's go," Dex said, his hand on my arm.

I nodded, activated the jacketcom, pulling up the Shillian Airport Web Page, chose an airline at random, bought two tickets to Nu Caynan, and was promptly informed that the flight was on schedule and would be leaving in just over an hour.

I think it was the longest hour of my life.

As we stood in the queue of people waiting to pass through the gate leading to the boarding hov, an alarm sounded from another gate to my right. I turned sharply at the sound, and saw five security guards approaching a young man, dark hair to his shoulders, in a black jacket. He looked shocked, and started kicking and yelling as the guards grabbed hold of him. He head-butted one in the face, kicked the one holding him from behind in the shin, and tried to run for it. One of the guards swung out with his baton as he came past, connecting with his head with a blinding flash of light. The guy went down like a sack of potatoes. They grabbed his unconscious body between them and dragged him out of the gateway to be "escorted" to some unknown destination.

"You sure this is a good idea, man?" said Dex, more than a little uneasily.

"Our ID's will hold up, Dex. They've never failed us before," I replied in a relaxed voice that was a total facade.

We passed through the gate without incident, our bags going through the scanner beside us. Nothing to worry about there, the guns were in the trunk of the hov where they'd be safe. We entered the boarding hov through a short tunnel, wall screens showing some of the exotic locations the airline could take us to. Neptune looked desolate and cold; being incredibly far from the sun, I guessed that made sense. I wondered briefly why Tommy Slid had chosen that destination instead of, say, Empire Beach on Mars.

No, I thought, the place is definitely getting a bit crowded. The Terrain ReGens that were done out there about thirty years ago are to blame. The place went from a dusty uninhabitable world with an atmosphere that would kill you if you stood there without a pressure suit, to a fucking paradise that could rival anything on Earth, in about three years. Space traffic quadrupled in a matter of months. What can I say? People love new experiences.

I looked out of the window, saw the jet looming ahead, sleek and black. I could just make it out through the rain that was now driving down with force. It was huge, its wings stretching out and back like the wings of a sparrow in a dive. Red lights blinked at the tip of each wing and on the tail, pulsing softly.

We pulled up alongside it and the door ahead of us slid open, giving a view of the interior of the craft, well lit for now, but shedding more of an ambient glow after takeoff.

We boarded.

Took our seats.

They were by the window, and as I sat waiting for takeoff, I looked out over the tarmac, the wind sweeping the rain violently across the hazy buildings of the airport multiplex.

"Good Evening, folks, this is your captain," came a soft, pleasant voice from the speakers. "We'll be leaving for Nu Caynan shortly. The flight will take about an hour, so get comfy. Our stewardesses will be on hand during the entire flight to cater to your needs. Thank you, and enjoy."

Dex turned to me, "What, the flight or the stewardesses?

I grinned.

There was a roar as the turbines sprang to life and we started to move, gaining speed by the second, the rain streaking across the window to my right as we accelerated, faster and faster, and then gently left the ground, roaring off towards Nu Caynan and Rainer and a future I couldn't help feeling was far darker than the night outside.

Seven

We flew above the clouds, through a night sky that had gone from stormy and wet, with winds rocking us this way and that, to the icy calm and inky black night at the edge of space.

Below, far below, I could vaguely make out the roiling mass of the storm, white flashes occasionally illuminating, for a second or two, the ever-changing shapes of the giant shifting clouds.

It was peaceful up here, the jet's turbines a faint rumble, as if heard from a great distance. The lighting inside the cabin was soft, subtle, the harshest light coming from the vidscreen beside my own.

I turned my attention from the scene below, looked over at Dex.

"What are you doing?" I asked, leaning over and staring at the glowing screen.

"Pretending not to notice the guy who's been staring at us for the last forty minutes," he replied, not taking his eyes off the screen.

"Where?" I said, also staring with feigned interest at his vidscreen.

"Four rows down, left row, aisle side, two seats from the entry hatch."

I sat back, positioning myself in such a way that I could see the guy in my window's reflection.

The guy didn't turn around.

I continued to stare into the reflection for a few minutes before I realised that he was doing the same thing, staring at us in the reflection of his blank vidscreen.

"How long, exactly?" I asked Dex.

Since take-off, about forty-five minutes," Dex replied.

Black suit.

But every businessman from here to Empire Beach wore a black suit; it didn't in itself mean anything. I strained to make out his face, but it was useless. All I could see for certain was that from the angle of his face, it was clear that he was watching us.

The stewardesses, of which there were three, had been moving around continuously since we left Shillian, offering food and drinks to everyone. They were obviously satisfied that everyone was happy, and were now in the back of the passenger compartment, talking quietly amongst themselves and waiting for someone to ask for something.

It was then that the guy stood up. He walked casually forward, past the rows of people, some at work on their vidscreens, others staring out of the windows, the guy with the OptiLens still deep in animated conversation. The guy stopped at the boarding hatch, turned to face it, took off his suit jacket to reveal a SlimChute parachute, hit a few buttons...

"Fuck!" Dex jumped up from his seat, started towards the guy.

I grabbed his shirt sleeve, dragging him back into his seat a split second before the hatch opened and all hell broke loose.

The guy was ripped through the hatch in an instant, followed by two of the stewardesses who had spotted him at the hatch and moved forward in a desperate attempt to stop him. A second later an explosion rocked the jet. I turned left to see bright orange flames coming from one of the turbines. One of them must have gotten sucked in. The world around us exploded: carry-bags, papers, objects of every shape and size flew through the air, smashing into windows and passengers as the cabin decompressed, sucking everything out into the night.

An instant later, PlastiGlass from different parts of my seat slid silently around me, encasing me in a completely transparent cocoon, my vision broken only by the computer monitor set directly in front of me, no longer a part of the seat in front but part of the Evacuation Unit I was now inside.

I looked at Dex, who was staring out at the damaged turbine.

"This is your captain speaking! Safety procedures have been engaged. Please fasten your seat belts; we're about to abandon ship. Repeat: Fasten your seat belts; we are abandoning ship. Please don't panic. Your Evac Units are designed to land on the safest available terrain. You have nothing to fear."

He sounded a bit fearful to me.

The roof and walls of the jet burst outwards, and Evac pods shot away all around me. Dex's was one of the first to go, and I watched as his glass -bubble-enclosed seat shot out into the night sky, propelled by three rockets set into the back of the chair. Then I was away.

I looked down and to my left as the jet fell away below me with incredible speed, the rest of the Evac pods darting out from the black bulk with little orange bursts of light reflecting against the pitch-black hull. The left turbine was flaming, and as I watched, the wing tore free of the hull, flying back and hitting an Evac pod, glass shattering and a brief flash as it exploded.

And then I could see nothing, I was surrounded by blackness, and I realised I'd dropped down into the storm. Rain lashed at the glass of the pod and thunder rumbled deeply from somewhere off in the shifting mass of darkness.

I glanced at the vidscreen. It was showing the image of a meadow, grass the lushest green I'd ever seen, against the backdrop of snow-covered mountains.

A soft breeze blew gently over the grass, causing slight ripples on the surface. The camera zoomed slowly in on a pond, previously hidden by a slight incline. The water shimmered slightly in the breeze, and as the camera moved in closer I could make out the shapes of large goldfish in the clear water, swimming just beneath the surface.

Clever, I thought. This had to be the most relaxing thing I had ever seen.

I looked around, found what I was looking for: A NeuroLink. It looks like a three-legged starfish, fitting comfortably over any head shape. Allowing for direct brain stimulation, these things were more popular than air. This is why places like NeuroLOG are so well off.

Neurotainment is addictive.

Yeah, I thought, there were a lot of really relaxed people out in this storm. Some of them had probably even forgotten what had just happened.

Hell, maybe I would have given it a go, given the situation, but I'm not fitted with the Plug. Like I said, it's just not my thing. I'll take a good paperback over Direct Brain Stimulation any day.

I fell through the storm for what seemed like forever. No light but for a flash of lightning far off, no sound but the splatter of rain on the glass, the rushing of the wind, and the occasional flash of lightning followed by the rumble of thunder somewhere out there in the darkness. Just when I was beginning to wonder if I was in fact falling, or breezing along on a particularly strong wind current,

Proximity Detection Active flashed suddenly on the screen, overlaying the peaceful image.

Brace for impact... Brace for impact... Brace for

scrolled across the screen, and one of the goldfish popped it's head out of the water, smiled at the screen, and said in a very slow, incredibly pleasant and reassuring voice, " *Everything is going to be alright.* "

I gripped the sides of the seat as the pod broke out of the storm, the ground invisible in the darkness but coming up fast.

And then a sudden jerk as a parachute opened above me, slowing my descent to a crawl, and the rockets on the pod kicked into life, short bursts guiding me to safety.

Below me I could make out bright blue flashes, homing beacons. The Evac pods were all landing in the same area. I touched down softly, landing on little legs that extended when ground proximity was detected. The parachute fell to the ground behind me.

It had stopped raining, and I disembarked, the PlastiGlass sliding away soundlessly when I hit the exit tab. I stepped out into cold night air. There was an air of desolation all around, inner country is a wasteland, and I remember thinking that if I could see through the darkness out there all that would greet my eyes would be a wind-swept plain stretching from one horizon to the other.

People were mulling around, speaking quietly for the most part, except for the OptiLens guy, who was complaining loudly to someone who was obviously a complete stranger to him.

"I'm gonna have their arses for this! They don't know who they've fucked with! I'm gonna hang them out to dry, man!"

The other guy was nodding, looking away, trying to find somewhere else to be. I wished briefly that the stricken jet's turbine had hit the whining runt's pod instead, but I guess you can't win 'em all.

I removed my carry bag from the compartment above the seat on the pod.

Good thing we travelled light, I thought.

"Ash!"

I turned. Dex was coming up to me, a look of relief on his face.

"You made it," he said.

"Good to see you, too."

"Shit, can you believe that? What a lunatic."

I nodded.

"Dex, we have to get out of here. A rescue craft will be here in a few hours. I think we should avoid that."

"Yeah. They must have spotted us at Shillian Airport. The bastards. Those fucking bastards."

No, there was something I'd missed.

Shit.

"Dex," I said.

"Yeah?"

"Give me your mobile."

He handed it over to me, and I dropped it on the ground and smashed it repeatedly with a fair-sized rock.

"Ash! What the fuck?"

"Sorry. But it just occurred to me that my numbers weren't the only ones on Sharyn's computer. They must have put a trace on your mobile as well."

"This is getting a bit much." Dex muttered.

I nodded. "We need to get out of here."

I activated my jacketcom, pulled up the Net, searching for the distance to Nu Caynan from our position.

I grinned.

Dex raised an eyebrow.

"Four hundred and fifty-two clicks to Nu Caynan. Let's get to it," I said.

Dex groaned.

The Evac pods had landed about a kilometre from the highway between Shillian and Nu Caynan to make the rescue easier. The landscape was desolate, a wasteland, with very little vegetation apart from the occasional clump of bushes.

We took a slow jog in the darkness in the direction of Nu Caynan, trying to put a bit of distance between ourselves and the landing site. The icy wind blew against us with force, cutting like a knife through our clothes, and the only thing keeping our body heat up was the sheer physical exertion. I had called the number Felony had given me and at this very minute a car was speeding out of Nu Caynan to pick us up.

Dex was a big guy, and he wasn't taking the exercise well at all. He had broken into a sweat after the first few minutes, and was now (half an hour later) only moving forward through sheer force of will.

I looked over at him, sweating and puffing, and stopped.

"Okay, this is far enough," I said. "Let's get off the road, keep out of sight, and wait for our ride."

"Thank you, Lord," Dex said to the heavens.

We made our way onto the plain, coming to rest behind a bunch of bushes, and settled down. I set the GPS on my jacketcom to alert us every time something of a certain size came within a kilometre of our position, and lay back against a rock, lighting up a smoke for Dex and myself.

"It'll take them about two hours to reach us, so we might as well get as comfortable as possible," I said, handing him a smoke.

"Yeah, let's just hope they don't get hit with an EM storm."

I nodded.

That was a very real possibility. But I didn't dwell on it. Ninety-five percent of the things you worry about never happen, they say. I wasn't sure whether I bought that, but I decided to give it the benefit of the doubt.

I turned up the heat on my jacket, in the vague hope that it would make a difference, and settled back to wait in the wet and the cold.

The alarm came suddenly, a sharp beeping and an onscreen warning.

Perimeter Breach flashed on the screen of my jacket.

"Shit," I said, pulling up a map of the immediate area.

A red dot came up on a thin green line, moving fast towards our location, which was depicted as a little smiley face. I checked the direction it was coming from.

Nu Caynan.

I called the number Felony's contact had given me, and a face came onscreen, illuminated by a faint green light. A woman, middle twenties, dark hair cropped, eyes dark. One word? Sultry as hell. Okay, that was three, but you get the idea.

"Evening. You boys ready to go?"

"Yeah, you could say that. We'll be on the road. You have our location? "

"I do now," she smiled, hanging up.

We made our way onto the road, spotting the headlights approaching as we set foot onto the tar. The hov slowed to a stop beside us, and the back doors slid open.

"Get in!"

We did. The hov spun around and roared off back the way it had come.

"Sorry to be so abrupt, but time's not on our side. We got a storm coming, a big one."

"How close?" I asked.

"Close."

I looked out the window. The rain was starting again, and I realised that for once timing had worked out for me, as opposed to going completely *against* me, which was usually the case.

"You got a name?" The woman asked, not taking her eyes from the road as the rain lashed at the windscreen.

"Ash Corben, and my friend here is Dex Kellerman."

"I'm Trish," she held her left hand back and we shook it..

Feeling like a child being chauffeured, I jumped into the front seat.

"Ash...Any relation to Ash Carter?" she asked, not really joking.

I was silent a while.

"Yeah, kind of."

"Close relation?" she said, looking at me briefly.

"Pretty close."

"You know," she continued, "you look kinda like him, only older."

"Do I?"

She shook her head, "Never met him, but I saw a photo once. Man, that guy was *out there*! Took out the head of the Streiger gang. In the middle of a cocktail bar! Did a lot of people a favour, and pissed off quite a few as well."

"Did he?" This was beginning to drain me.

"You know," she said, "They never found a body. The guy threw himself clear out the window on the two-hundred and fiftieth floor of the NeuroLOG Building, and they never found a body!"

"Maybe they cleaned it up really fast," I said.

"Or maybe it was you."

Dex cursed in the back.

I said nothing, stared straight ahead.

"Don't worry, Carter, your man Felony was right. You can trust us. You and Fel were allies then; that makes us allies now. Relax."

I nodded, "Good... and don't call me Carter."

"Whatever you say, man."

We sped on towards Nu Caynan in the pouring rain, and I found myself lost in the past.

Nu Caynan, fifteen years ago. Long before I killed Cole in the NeuroLOG bar, and just before I met Melanie. Dex and I had been in training back then. We were eighteen, fresh out of school, and we'd been invited to join an Earth Alliance organisation called Apex. We'd graduated in the top five of our class, the top three I think, and on graduation day two suits had come up to us after the ceremony and taken us aside. They'd given us a spiel on how we were the kind of people they were looking for: young, dynamic, ready to take on the world. That last bit should have sent an alarm off somewhere in my head, but it didn't.

We accepted their offer, and began training a few weeks later at their HQ in Nu Caynan.

That's where I met Felony. He was one of four guys in the organisation who were assigned to train the new class. There were twelve of us: nine guys and three girls, all just out of school and eager to get our hands dirty.

There was one Operative for every three trainees. Felony, who must have been in his late forties then, was assigned to us. I'll never forget the first thing he said to us. Dex, myself and a guy by the name of Cole were standing in front of him, rigid as we could possibly be, on the first day of training. The room we were standing in was Felony's office. It was dark, the curtains drawn, the only light coming from a lamp on the table he sat at, hard at work on some report or another.

He'd looked up briefly, then continued with his work.

Twenty minutes later he finished up, stood, and came around the table to see us.

"Rule number one, The Golden Rule as we at Apex call it, is this: You do not speak to anyone about the nature of the work we do here. You do not speak about the training process you will be undergoing; you do not speak of the missions you will be placed on when your training is complete. There is no chance of failure. If you are slower than the other trainees, we will compensate for that. You will not fail. There is no failure at Apex; you're here because you're the best. We have been monitoring your progress for the last ten years, and you have been chosen from the top five graduates of your year. You two," he motioned towards Dex and myself, "were in the same class, I'm told."

I nodded.

"Good teacher?"

"The best," I replied.

He nodded. "Good."

Felony moved around his desk, had a seat,

"Sit. Have a drink with me." He gestured to the bottle of bourbon on the table, four glasses around it.

That was our first day.

Felony was good, he'd been Black Ops before joining Apex. He was the best. Still was the best. And, as he put it that rainy morning fifteen years ago, he expected the same from us.

He got it.

Training lasted a year and six months. It was tough, we'd get up at four in the morning, do fitness training; weapons training (where I learnt about the origin of the vBomb);increased stamina and cross-country training; diving and underwater skills and techniques; space training and above all, we were taught the complexities of inter-corporate espionage.

Long ago the Planet had been broken up into different Countries, each with their own governing body. This had led to a constant state of war, one Country always in need of the natural resources of another, or territory to place them in a better position tactically. Some Countries were more wealthy than others, and of course wanted in turn to be even wealthier, which lead to the starvation of smaller Countries that couldn't afford to profit from their own natural resources, and sold whatever they were able to produce for next to nothing. The rich got richer and the poor, being about as poor as they could possibly be, stayed poor.

This state of affairs went on for a very long time, until one day it all went a bit mad. A few privileged Countries decided once and for all that it was in the Planet's best interests to create a Global Coalition, with themselves at the head of government. The reason given was simple: a better life for all, Freedom from poverty being the biggest calling card for the Countries on the other end of the food chain. The real reasons were altogether different and for many, quite obvious: global control, and the freedom to plunder the natural resources of the entire Planet unhindered.

But the poorer countries, although starving, were not stupid. They refused the Global Coalition Proposal point blank, and were given a choice: open your borders and join the Coalition, or disregard the Proposal and face the prospect of war. Eighty percent refused to join, and a few weeks later, they were invaded by the Global Coalition.

There were, however, a few powerful Countries who decided they didn't like the way this was going. They pulled out of the Coalition and joined the eighty percent.

The Planet was divided.

On the one side was the Global Coalition, who were at that very moment attempting to take the smaller Countries by force, and on the other was the Alliance for Cultural Protection, the ACP.

The ACP demanded the removal of all ground forces from the invaded Countries. Their request was denied, and World War III began a week later.

The war was devastating, with the larger Countries constantly needing to display a stronger show of force. Weapons of mass destruction were eventually inevitable, since none of the countries wanted to be the first to back down for fear of showing weakness and facing the possibility of invasion.

When the first Bomb fell, the world stood still.

It wasn't nuclear. Since the formulation of the International Weapons Treaty a number of years before and the invention of Cold Fusion a bit after that, atomic power had been banned. Even the smaller dictatorships that had held secret nuclear caches were forced to destroy the lot in the name of Global Peace.

The bombs weren't nuclear, but they had proved powerful enough to wipe out major areas of countries small and large, laying waste to huge regions of populated and unpopulated territories, and after it was over, the only entities that still held any kind of power beyond personal survival were a large number of Corporations, most of them with off-world HQ's. The survivors were removed from the giant underground bunkers in which they'd sheltered from the chaos above, and the business of rebuilding the Planet began.

Over the course of time, an economy was rebuilt, under the ever-watching eyes of the corporations. They formed a coalition of their own, under the banner of the Earth Alliance, and a global government was established. They built on cities that already existed, for the most part. Cities like Nu Caynan, which was built on the ruins of a large city and named after the head of the corporation funding a large part of the building process, the same corporation that first found a way of combating the effects of the EM storms that ravaged most of the inner country.

Occasionally small populations attempted to break away from the Earth Alliance, one example being the Lunar Colony, and you know how OreTech dealt with them. I guess I can explain what really happened now, in context. The Earth Alliance government is basically a global corporate coalition, so if one of the big companies does something really bad, and every one knows about it, there is a very simple way of dealing with the situation: close them down; relocate there staff to another company, and continue without a hitch. That, or reopen under a different name.

90

It probably wouldn't surprise you to know that the incident on the Moon was sanctioned by the EA. And the "suit" who placed the vBomb in the promenade was an Apex Operative. That, it turned out, was what we were training for. Apex was an Earth Alliance organisation that dealt with breakaway factions, more often seeking to become a republic rather than to be traitorous.

Apex didn't see things that way.

If you wanted out, you were a traitor. It was as simple as that. And traitors were dealt with harshly.

Provided you acknowledged the EA as government, and yourself as a citizen operating within its governance, everything was fine. Life was very much like it was before the War. This is where we are now, living well, under the rule of a government that allows incredible freedom in exchange for the ability to govern and make money. To all intents and purposes they run the Planet fine. No better or worse than any other would have. But the end does not justify the means, and instead of looking at the standard of living the average citizen of the Earth Alliance enjoyed, Felony taught me to see the world beneath it.

The means: The systematic destruction of all who wished to leave the comfortable walls enclosing them to break away and fend for themselves.

People live their lives and die with the knowledge that the EA is the only government; that things are the way they should be, and the EA in turn has given them no reason to believe otherwise. Indeed, the only times you will ever see behind the broad, charming smile of our global government is if you try to break away, call for a Republic, or when you're holding a gun to someone's head and you see the fear in his eyes and you suddenly realise you're about to take his life and the only reason you can give him is because he wants to be free.

That was pretty much when things changed for me.

I'll tell you about it later.

I was returning to a place I thought I'd never see again. A place I hadn't seen in quite some time. My thoughts strayed from the face of the young man with the gun against his head to another man, and another gun. In a cocktail bar on the two hundred and fiftieth floor of a corporate building.

Same hand, same finger on the trigger, though.

The walls of Nu Caynan loomed ahead, and behind us the first traces of an EM storm were beginning to form, and all I could think about was the grinning face of a young man who only had a few seconds left in this world.

A man who, above all others, deserved to die.

A man I killed in cold blood and never regretted it for a second.

Eight

Electricity filled the air.

You could smell it.

As we closed in on the City Walls, flashes of lightning illuminated the night, hitting the ground just behind us as the electrical storm closed in. Above us dark clouds pulsing with energy were surging forward, moving and changing within a giant mass like a living thing, electricity spurting from the darkness, shooting across the night.

Closer now, lightning bolts exploding onto the ground all around us as we sped towards the storm lights and the safety of Nu Caynan.

We arrived at one of the portals into the city as the first bolts hit the storm lights far above us, the lightning hitting a deflector and dancing across to another beside it in a brilliant stream, disappearing an instant later.

And then another hit.

Another a second later.

And then the storm hit in force, and above us the darkness was filled with a raging ice-blue phosphorescence as a hundred EM bolts beat at the walls of Nu Caynan.

The hov slowed to a stop.

A guard came up to the window, asked for ID. As he took Trish's card to run the usual check, he asked softly, "How are things?"

"Good," she replied, giving him a brief smile but staring straight ahead.

Nothing more was said, and soon we were moving again. I found myself again remembering the last time I was at these gates, ten years ago.

Time waits for no man.

"You guys can stop looking guilty now," Trish said.

"Friend of yours?" I asked, gesturing behind us.

She nodded, "You guys need a safe-house?"

"Yeah, and a hov."

"Done, I'll book you in. You can get settled and do whatever it is you have to do."

"Thanks," I said.

"Don't mention it."

She shot us up to the ninety-first storey, and we drove through the dark, rainy morning, the reflections of neon signs and advertisements glinting on the windows, bright and alive as ever, the headlights of the few hovs around at this level at this time of the morning blurred as they shot past us. Then she slowed, swung into a docking berth, and stopped.

"Here we are," she said.

She called someone on the hov's computer, connected a few seconds later.

"Trish. Everything go okay?" said a totally bald man in his late fifties, an eye patch over his left eye, a deep scar running down the left side of his face, from his temple over where his eye would have been to his square jaw.

"Yeah, we're at House9. Request access."

"Access granted. Gate code is "Tyrant"."

"Thanks, K," she hung up.

We got out of the hov and walked the few steps up to the entrance. Trish placed her right hand on the metallic panel set into the wall to the right of the door.

"Tyrant," she said.

"Access Granted", said a soft female voice, **"Welcome to House9, Trisha Gale."**

"Thanks." Trish gave the computer instructions, asking Dex and myself to enter voice input.

"Voice Input accepted. Welcome to House9, Dexter Kellerman and Ash Corben."

"Gotta go, you bastards woke me," Trish said, turning to go. "Oh, and you'll find whatever firepower you need in the safe behind the wallscreen, it'll respond to your voices."

Dex and I gave our thanks.

Trish smiled, "See ya around, Carter."

She left, and we went inside to get some much-needed sleep.

I slept fitfully through most of the following day, dreaming as always with intense lucidity, and, as always, remembering little or nothing on awakening.

I awoke a short while after the sun had set, her voice echoing in my head. Saying something. What? I couldn't remember, but I had the feeling if I knew, if I could just remember, it would somehow change everything.

I dressed and went through to the living area. Dex was in the kitchen adjacent to the lounge, wearing a night robe, making coffee.

"Evening. Coffee?"

"Yeah, great. Thanks," I replied, picking up my jacket off the couch and activating the jacketcom.

"What you doing?" Dex asked.

"Calling Felony, telling him we made contact."

Felony picked up on the third ring.

"Ash, what's up, man?"

I told him about the guy on the jet, the decompression and evacuation. And the contact with his people in Nu Caynan.

He nodded, "K's keeping pretty much quiet nowadays, he's getting a bit over the hill. But he still has his finger on the pulse that side."

"Good to know. Have you heard anything on Sharyn?"

His expression changed, and his eyes told me all I needed to know.

"They found her body in the apartment. Nothing was taken. She died from a shot to the head... It was quick... I'm sorry, Ash."

I nodded slowly.

"How did you find out?"

"A friend, NCPD."

"Well, I guess they don't want to negotiate for Sarah," I said quietly.

"No, I guess not."

I said goodbye, and hung up.

Lit a smoke. Took a deep drag...

Then I called Rainer's number.

His face came on screen, looking surprised. "Mister Corben, wasn't expecting to hear from you so soon. What news on –"

"Who the fuck is after me, Rainer?"

He looked confused, "I don't underst –"

"Then listen more closely. I accept this job, and not half an hour later there's a bomb in my apartment. Then I get chased all over Tanis. Then some weird guys in suits kill a nice old lady. On the road four suited men, who weren't as nice as the old lady, tried to kill me in my hotel room. And then another guy opens the hatch of a commercial jet mid-flight to cause cabin decompression. Everything was rosy until I took this job, and now everything is very, very difficult. I've just discovered my ex-wife is dead. Murdered, probably by the same sons-of-bitches who're after me, and I think you know who they are, and what they want."

"Mister Corben, please calm down. I have no idea what you –"

"Enough. We're going to meet face to face. Tonight."

"I really don't –"

"Tonight, one hour from now. At Kaisers'. You know the place?" I asked. Of course he did. Everyone did.

"Yes, but –"

"Be there. One hour. And come alone, or I swear I'll blow something and cause a scene that will end in tears... Yours."

I hung up.

Dex handed me my coffee.

"I'm sorry, Ash."

"I know."

I looked out the window, at the patterns the rain made on the pane.

"It's time for some answers," I said softly. "I've had just about enough of this."

Dex went to get dressed.

Another drag of my smoke.

Sitting in silence.

Thinking.

Dex came through a short while later, dressed and ready to go. He handed me a pair of handguns in black shoulder holsters.

"Shall we?" he said.

I strapped on the guns underneath the jacket.

Nodded.

"Let's go."

97

Kaisers' was on the two hundredth floor of the AiroCom Building. A cocktail bar and restaurant, all glass and steel and beautiful people. We sat at a window seat, a vodka in front of each of us, staring out at the hovs zooming by us.

"What if he doesn't rock up?" Dex said.

"He will. He can't afford not to."

We continued to sit in silence.

And then I saw him, entering with two guys wearing identical dark suits. The guys went over to the bar as I motioned for him to join us.

He approached the table furtively, having a seat only after I insisted.

"I told you to come alone," I said softly.

He looked over at the bar, anxiously.

"Look at me!"

His head jerked back in my direction, eyes focussing on my own.

"Ash, his boys are checking us out," Dex said.

I nodded, "Rainer, tell your guys to get lost."

"Who d –" he began.

"My ex-wife is dead and my life and the life of my friends are in jeopardy and I think your organisation is involved. Signal for them to leave or I'll remove them," I said softly.

He looked over at the bar, motioned for his guys to leave. They looked uncertain, but did as they were told. When they had left, I looked closely at our friend, Howard Rainer.

"Tell me what you know."

He shook his head.

"Mister Corben, this behaviour is unwarranted. You tell me that your life is in jeopardy and I believe you, but I know nothing about it. My employer is searching for the survivor of the experiment in Antarctica. That is all I know. I have to report back to my employer this evening, with news on the task we have paid you very well to undertake –"

"Fuck the money. You can have the money back. The deal's off. I couldn't find her," I said.

He nodded slowly, "My employer will not be happy."

"Tell your employer that if he doesn't like it, he is more than welcome to go to hell," I replied.

Rainer swallowed hard, stopped a waiter and ordered a whiskey. Then he cleared his throat.

"Mister Corben, have you noticed some... strangeness... lately? Weird things happening?" he asked, staring at me intensely.

"You mean like Sandy Island?" I replied, trying to avoid Dex's gaze.

Rainer nodded, "Exactly like that, yes."

"What about it?"

"Mister Corben, we are living in very strange times. I cannot tell you the nature of these occurrences, but I do know that my employer has taken a very personal interest in them. He believes what is happening is somehow linked to the Ciegan's End disaster. And Sarah. Any more I cannot say. I don't have that information, but I can guarantee you that this girl is too important to allow anything to stand in the way of finding her. My employer is not responsible for the recent actions taken against you. Please, I know you've found her, please give her to us."

I looked at him. He was telling the truth, I could see that. But what did it mean? Who the hell was after me? And why?

"Who is your employer?" I asked.

The man didn't answer me.

I took out my guns, placed them on the table, barrels facing his chest.

"Who is your employer?" I repeated.

"I can't –"

I picked up the guns and aimed them at his face, he flinched but didn't move. The room was quiet.

He looked around.

"If you think your guys will come in to save you, they won't. If you think security is going to try to stop me, you're wrong on that one too," I said.

He looked confused.

"Where did all the people go?" he said.

"They were quietly told to leave as soon as you sat down. Oh, and your guys are out cold. The benefits of owning your own bar."

Rainer went very pale, stared at the barrels of the guns I was pointing at his face.

"Now. One more time," I said slowly, "Who the fuck do you work for?"

His shoulders seemed to droop, he let out a long breath.

"Mason. Trevor Mason," he said softly.

I lowered the guns, replaced them in the holsters, looking at him with surprise.

"The head of NeuroLOG?" Dex said.

Rainer nodded.

"What does he want with Sarah?" I asked.

He massaged his temples, "I don't know, Corben. All I know is what I've told you. Now if you don't mind, I'm leaving. What can I tell Mister Mason?" He stood.

"I want to know what's going on. With Sarah, with Sandy fucking Island. Everything. How can I contact him?" I replied.

Rainer laughed, a short, dry sound. "That, I'm afraid, I could not tell you. I speak with him only when he calls through to me. None of us at NeuroLOG have any idea where he operates from."

I nodded, "Alright, when you speak with him again, tell him he doesn't get the girl until I speak with him face to face. If he doesn't like those terms, then he can have his money back, and the deal's off."

"How can I contact you? You haven't answered your laptop number."

"You can't. I'll call you when it suits me," I replied.

He nodded and left.

I called the bar's entrance.

"We're open for business. You can let the old guy leave. Oh, and how are the guys who came in with him doing?"

"When we closed the doors, they tried to go through to the bar area. We had to use force, sir," the doorman said, looking guilty.

"That's fine. Are they alright?" I said.

"Yes sir, just a bit bruised."

"When the old guy gets to the entrance, please tell him I'm sorry for the unpleasantness."

"Yes, sir."

I hung up.

I looked at Dex.

"What now?" he asked.

"Now," I said, motioning for one of the waiters who were re-entering the bar, "we have another drink."

Dex grinned. "And *after* that?"

"We wait."

"It might be a while."

I shook my head, "No. Mason will call tonight or sometime tomorrow."

"How do you know?"

"Because, for his own reasons, he's very anxious to get hold of Sarah, willing to pay a small fortune to find her. He's in constant contact with Rainer, you can bet on it."

"So, we wait," Dex said, raising his new glass.

I raised mine, took a slow sip, replaced it on the glass table.

"We wait. I'll call through tomorrow evening."

"But tonight, we drink," Dex said.

I grinned.

"Yeah," I said, "Let's get drunk."

I tossed down the vodka. Looked at Dex.

"You're not really going to hand her over to Mason, are you, Ash?"

I shook my head, "I don't care how badly he needs to get hold of her. Way I see it, that's not her problem. It just wouldn't be right handing her over to them, no matter how good they claim their intentions to be."

Dex nodded, "Ash," he said, looking out at the rain.

"Yeah?" I said, signalling our waiter.

"Sandy Island..."

Shit.

I was quiet as he continued.

"I can't remember... I mean *really* remember... ever actually *being* there."

I nodded, "I know. There is some weird –"

"Sandy Island?"

I turned at the sound of a third voice. Our waiter was standing beside our table, holding a tray with two vodkas.

"Er, yeah –" I began.

I noticed he was shaking slightly.

102

"I went there once... It's not... It's..." He began to shake more violently, the glasses on the tray starting to rattle. "This isn't right..." he said, "...nothing works..."

I stood, moving to take the tray from him before he dropped it.

He shied away as I moved forward, looking directly into my eyes, "You're far away!"

I stopped at the outburst.

"What?" I said.

The waiter was shaking more violently than ever, starting to sweat.

"What did you –?" I started.

"You're... Sandy Island...It's..."

He flung the tray at the window, Dex ducking just in time. It smashed against the window, the glasses exploding as they hit the windowpane. And in the same instant, he swung his head down, smashed his face against the table's glass top. Again. Again. Cracking it on the third attempt, smashing through it on the fourth.

He came up as the glass shattered, blood pouring from his torn face, mixing with a white froth that was coming from his mouth.

He screamed, an inhuman sound.

Security, came forward, I motioned for them to stop.

The waiter fell to his knees, hands to his bloody face, screaming still, but quieter now, more of a deep, animal cry. He rocked forward and back on his knees.

I moved forward, wanting to pacify him in some way.

And stopped short when I saw what he was doing.

He had his fingers to his eyes, trying to gouge them out, groaning and rocking back and forth, back and forth.

"Jesus!" I moved forward again, grabbing at his arms, trying to pull his hands away from his face. I struggled with them, succeeded eventually at pulling them away, and recoiled from him when I saw what he had done.

His eyes were gone.

Nothing but empty sockets stared back at me, blood flowing freely from two gaping holes just below his eyebrows. He stopped groaning, started to smile. He held up his hands, palms up, showing me the blood covering his fingers as if showing me some kind of prize.

"Christ," Dex said softly.

"I..." The waiter began to speak, his voice thick, "I can... see you..."

He got slowly to his feet, reached into the shattered table and pulled loose a large shard of glass, moved toward me.

I backed away, not wanting to pull out my guns.

"Stay where you are, Stan," one of the security guys said.

Stan continued to move toward me, ignoring the guy, grinning like a maniac through his torn and bloodied face.

Crooning, saying over and over in a singsong voice, "I can see you...I can see you... I can see yooouuu..."

"Don't move, Stanley. I don't wanna shoot ya, man," the security guy said again; moving to intercept him; pointing his gun at Stan's head; coming around to stand in front of me.

"Get back, sir," he said to me.

"Don't shoot him, Nick," I said softly.

He shook his head, "I won't."

Two other security guys were coming around, moving as if to grab him from behind. They jumped forward, an instant too late.

Stan lunged forward, stabbing outwards with the shard of glass. Nick jumped back, gun still trained on his face, avoiding the edge of the glass blade by millimetres. The two security guys lunged again, Stan swung around with the shard, slicing one guy in the throat. He fell to the ground, gurgling and clutching at his neck, dark red blood flowing out onto the white carpet.

"Okay," I said, "shoot him."

"Yes, sir."

Nick squeezed a shot off, taking Stan in the right shoulder. He jerked back, dropping the piece of glass, his shoulder exploding. The two remaining men moved forward to grab him.

He turned, seemed to see the wall-to-ceiling windows, and ran straight at them.

Nick tried to grab him but it was too late, and the last I saw of Stan the waiter was as he threw himself through the glass window pane, falling outwards into the rain-drenched night, screaming not with horror, or any kind of fear, but with delight and what sounded like a child-like wonder.

Dex and I left right after, the cops would be swarming over the place in a few minutes, and neither Dex nor I felt like drawing attention to ourselves. The bar was owned by a guy called Mister Gabriel, who was a totally fictional character I created in order to stay untraceable back when things were heated. Before they became all calm and peaceful like they are now.

When they arrived they'd be wanting to speak to the owner, who was unavailable, so management would deal with it. If they insisted on speaking with him, they'd have to call up Mister Gabriel's details on their CopNet, which would leave them exactly nowhere.

Either way, Dex and I were clear.

We drove back to House9 in silence, until Dex finally spoke, airing a sentiment that was on both of our minds in his usual refined way.

"What the fuck was that?" he said.

I shook my head, "I don't know. But I think we must speak with Mister Mason... Yesterday."

"He said he could see us. After..."

"Yeah."

The rest of the trip passed in silence.

We arrived back at House9. I declined the offer of a stiff drink from Dex and we went into our separate rooms,

I needed to clear my head.

Sharyn was dead, Stan had lost it in a serious way and I was beginning to think things were going a bit badly.

I lay on the bed.

Breathed a sigh.

Closed my eyes, and immediately the image of Stan's bloodied, smiling face sprang into my head, and it didn't leave me until I fell at last into exhausted sleep, sometime just before the dawn.

Nine

I'm standing alone on an empty, desolate road in the dead of night. A traveller, walking alone on a highway. A thousand shades of black swirl above me and the stars, scattered far and wide, beckon me from the dark and endless mass of space with promises of a warmth I know I can never reach.

Around me nothing but a barren, windswept plain stretching from horizon to horizon. The wind rushes across this lifeless place, the dust rising from the ground and dancing like ghosts on the night. And the wind lashes at my face, as I try to see the way ahead, but all I see is this strange, lonely road, winding its way through an ocean of dark and empty desolation.

And the stars, for all their brightness, cannot light my way.

Yet I move on through the darkness,

Searching for someone.

Someone who should be with me.

But is no longer.

I don't know where she is. But I have to find her.

Because I love her.

And I can't lose her.

Not again.

Remember!!"

I awoke with a jolt, the sound of my own voice bringing me to full consciousness in seconds as the morning sun filtered through half-closed blinds.

I checked the time. Just after ten.

I lit a smoke.

Remember...

"Computer," I said to the wallscreen, "Access the Net."

Accessing Net... Connected.

"Search for Ciegan's End, news reports. Twenty-six years ago. Also, any related articles."

Searching... Please Wait...

The first page that came up was the article I had seen during the interview with Rainer. It was bullshit.

"Search for related articles, keyword: Survivor."

Another page came on screen.

"Blah-blah-blah were unfortunately no survivors...Shit."

I could get a list of the entire expedition, but considering the amount of people involved, it would be pretty useless. I had no choice but to call Sarah and ask her where I could find her father. I didn't want to, because that would involve explaining what was happening, and I still didn't have an answer as to why the head of NeuroLOG wanted her. I leaned over and grabbed my jacket off the chair next to my bed, activated it.

"Computer, call Felony. Full encryption."

Calling...

Connecting...

Felony's face came onscreen.

"Ash, waddup?"

"Hey Fel, I need to speak with Sarah."

"Gimme a sec."

Felony's face vanished and a minute later I was staring at Sarah.

She looked tired, but alert.

"Hey Ash, you found the bastards yet?"

"Getting there. You okay?"

She shrugged, "Not sleeping well."

Yeah, that makes two of us.

"I need to find your father," I said, cutting to the chase.

She didn't look surprised.

"Ciegan's End?"

I nodded.

"He's catatonic, Ash. What do you think you'll gain from this?"

I thought about it.

"I don't know," I replied, "but it's worth a try. I want to know what I'm facing, and the best way to find out is to go back to the beginning. Sarah, I don't think Rainer and his boys are trying to kill us. I've learned who commissioned me to find you. Trevor Mason. The head of –"

"NeuroLOG?"

"Yep. I'm waiting to make contact with him, probably sometime today."

Something seemed to occur to her.

"So, if NeuroLOG isn't behind this, then who is?"

"I don't know, but I'll find out. Do you have your father's address?"

She nodded, "It's in Shillian, an establishment that cares for people with his... condition. "

She gave me the address, and we said goodbye.

The place was in Shillian.

I'd just been to Shillian. Yet another wonderful example of my unerring sense of timing. I decided to call through.

An elderly lady in a spotless white uniform answered.

"Our Lady of Tranquillity Care Centre, how may I help you?"

"Yeah, hi. My name is Detective Johnson, SPD."

I flashed the badge.

The lady raised her eyebrows, "What can I do for you, officer?"

"I would like to know if you have a gentleman by the name of Darrel Thompson in your care."

She nodded, "We do."

Good. Next question.

"Is he. . . Er, how is he?" I said lamely.

"In the same condition as he was when he was admitted, he's in a state of catatonia. May I ask what this is in connection with?"

"No. Thank you for your time."

I ended the call.

Sarah had asked a valid question. How was talking to a catatonic old man going to help my case? Did I think that I could somehow bring him out of it?

Maybe...

...or maybe not. At any rate, if Trevor Mason wouldn't give me what information he had, Mister Thompson was my only other link. I decided to launch a more thorough search on the net, due to a complete lack of any other ideas.

The day passed quickly in front of the wallscreen with no results worth mentioning and early that evening, just after sunset, I called Rainer.

He answered almost immediately.

"Good evening, Mister Corben."

"Evening, Rainer, has your employer made contact?" I said

"What happened at Kaiser's?"

"You heard?"

"I couldn't help but hear. It's all over the news. The police are in hot pursuit of Mister Gabriel as we speak," Rainer said.

I grinned, "You wanna keep that between us?"

He held up his hands, "I have no proof anyway. But, I think you are starting to appreciate the urgency of the situation."

"Yeah, but I still don't see how Sarah can help."

Rainer nodded, "My employer has agreed to speak with you."

I raised an eyebrow.

"Really?"

"Yes, however he is not in Nu Caynan, very far from here in fact. In the interests of privacy, he will be speaking to you via his personal line here at NeuroLOG. Only I have access to the suite, and the line is totally untraceable."

I nodded, this explained why I wasn't able to hack a line to his number. This was pretty heavy shit they were using, not even a full-time hacker could've put a trace on him.

"What time?"

"Tomorrow morning, ten sharp."

I hung up, went through to the living area. Dex was lounging on one of the couches, drinking coffee.

"Evening," I said.

He looked up, "Hey. Look at this." He pointed at the giant wallscreen opposite him. The screen was showing the interior of Kaiser's, panning over the floor and zooming in on the window Stan had thrown himself through. A pretty blonde was speaking to the camera.

"Turn it up," I said, taking a seat next to him.

"...at Kaiser's, the stylish, up-market venue that for years has been *the* meeting place for many of Nu Caynan's high society, when a waiter apparently had a psychotic episode while serving the owner of the bar, a Mister Gabriel, and an unnamed patron who shared his table. The exact nature of the episode has not been revealed, but we do know that it culminated in the waiter falling through the

111

window pictured here and plummeting to his death. The owner, who left shortly after the incident, has up until now been unavailable for questioning..."

"Yeah, chances of that happening," I muttered.

Dex grinned.

"...and on a totally unrelated topic, there has been another report of a what has been termed Dead Man Walking Syndrome. The as-yet unnamed man was brought in to a Shillian hospital after arriving at his brother's front door claiming to have come from 'another place'. This is the third case of its kind in so many weeks. Here follows a brief testimony from the man's brother, courtesy of our reporter John Jacobs."

The screen showed the form of a man, facial features digitally blurred, voice slightly distorted, sitting next to a slick-looking, dark-suited man. Jacobs, I guessed.

"So, he is alleged to have been dead for how long, exactly?" the slick guy asked.

"Alleged my bollocks. He was dead. Stone-cold dead. And on top of that, my wife and I were both present at his cremation."

The guy seemed quite sure of himself.

"Yes, but are you sure it was his body?" Jacobs pressed.

"Am I sure it was my own brother? What do you think?"

The camera zoomed up to Jacobs' face, and he said with just the right amount of dramatics, "Three people, three weeks, three legitimate death certificates... A bunch of clever hoaxes, or are these people really back from the dead? You decide. I'm John Jacobs for KKP News."

"Bizarre," I said, lighting up a smoke.

"Bizarre seems to be the order of the day," Dex replied.

"...and lastly, Tommy Slid has at long last found an actress who is willing to shoot the final scene, involving the collision of Earth and the giant meteor that is currently heading this way... Is this right?" The blonde held up her palm screen, speaking to someone off screen. There was a reply, but I couldn't make it out. She turned to face the screen, "Um, which is heading this way... and... What the fuck? I don't –"

Some guys in grey suits came on screen and attempted to get her off her chair.

She started screaming, ripping at their faces, her face turned briefly to the camera, her eyes staring in horror and containing a glimmer of something else.

"Do you see?" she said, her voice husky and low, "Can you see them?"

And then she smiled.

"They can see us, they can see –"

Her face contorted, jerked back as if of it's own volition, and she started screaming.

The screen went blank, replaced a second later by a picture of a meadow, snow-covered mountains behind. A few seconds after that the news reappeared, this time with a man's face set against the backdrop of Earth, spinning around the sun.

"We apologise for the break in transmission, folks, we were experiencing a few technical problems. The actress is Mercury Red, who has confirmed to our field reporter, Christine Forbes, that she will be accepting the part."

The news guy was replaced by the image of a beach at sunset in a tropical paradise and two women, one in a smart black suit, the other in an incredibly small red bikini.

"High folks, and welcome to Paradise Beach at Tora Sera, where I'm interviewing Mercury Red, star of the new Tommy Slid film *The Pros and Cons of Marrying a Vicious, Cheating, Money-Grabbing, Devil Worshipping, Psychopathic Slag*. How do you feel about the part, Mercury?"

Mercury Red turned to face the camera, her platinum blonde hair flowing in the breeze.

"Vell, ees good, ja? Da money ees right an Tommy ees good director, so I do eet."

"But of course, you understand that you will be shooting the final scenes in front of a few remote cameras while the earth gets hit by a giant meteor. Everybody else will be either off-world or in the giant bunkers that were previously used during World War Three. Doesn't that worry you a bit?"

"Da money ees *really* good, know? An' Tommy said eet will be okay."

"Er, yeah...but..." she shook her head, and Mercury went off somewhere with a little wave, "I'm Christine Forbes for KKP News, here with Mercury Red, star of *The Pros and Cons of Marrying a Vicious, Cheating, Money-Grabbing, Devil Worshipping, Psychopathic Slag* reporting live from Paradise Beach, Tora Sera."

I looked at Dex, "We have an audience with Mister Mason via satellite tomorrow morning at ten... At NeuroLOG."

"You sure that's a good idea?"

"No, but our options are limited."

"Okay," he shrugged.

I took a seat next to him, lit another smoke, "I had another dream last night. One of *those* ones."

"Yeah? Remember anything this time?"

"Just a highway."

"That's it?"

I nodded, "Dex, things are going to get much worse. I don't know what's happening, but you gotta understand that we're facing something big. I don't know what's going to happen."

"I'm with you on this, man. You know that."

"I know."

We sat in silence, the wallscreen showing images of some Net site or other.

An image of an old house came on, and I suddenly realised it was Willowdale, Sarah's place in Serenity, and an instant later her face came up on the top right hand corner of the screen. The cops would be looking for her, and calling through to let everyone know she was safe was too risky, considering we had no idea exactly what we were up against. Felony knew the routine, he wouldn't let her make a call unless it was safe.

She was a woman, a beautiful woman in fact, and she could be quite persuasive.

But so could Felony.

I went back to my room, nothing more to do now but wait for morning, and hope that Trevor Mason could answer some of the questions that swirled around my brain.

Morning had never seemed so far away.

I sat at a desk by the window and leaned back, watching the rain-drenched night outside. A hovtrain shot by a level below me, faces, nameless and emotionless, staring back at me, ensconced in a soft and sickly yellow glow, watching as life passed them by.

A woman.

Early twenties.

Blonde.

Pretty.

Sitting alone, clutching her bag in her lap.

Our eyes met.

I looked away first, I don't know why.

Something about her eyes.

Or perhaps something in them.

Haunted. Cold.

Hopeless? She seemed to watch me as if wondering if I was the same.

115

As If I too were looking out into the night and wondering where this life would take me, deep down fighting the slow but inevitable realisation that life was not what I wanted it to be, and for all intents and purposes, never would be.

And you know what?

She was probably right.

Ten

We stand facing each other, cloaked in darkness and drenched by rain, outside a deserted way station on the edge of the highway.

He stares at me, his eyes hidden from me in the darkness of this night and the shelter of his hood.

You've lost something, *he says, voice measured.*

I'll find her, *I reply.*

He nods, slowly. **No doubt.**

Who are you? *I say.*

Just a friend, *he replies.* **Someone who is still around.**

Do I know you? Show yourself.

A soft laugh, **My face will make no difference to you now, Ash. Just know that you're not alone.**

He turns then, the rain coming down, and he pulls his coat around him. The wind springs up, ripping at my own, and I'm forced to pull back as the rain lashes at me with a ferocious strength.

He walks away, dissolving into the darkness and the storm, and I enter the dusty, quiet sanctuary of the way station. A knock sounds, from somewhere in the darkness.

Another.

Knock...

Knock... knock...

Knock... knock... knock...

I awoke in pitch darkness, the slow rapping on my bedroom door bringing me to full alert in seconds.

I checked the time.

117

3:37 a.m.

"Dex?"

Silence.

I got up, pulled on my pants and grabbed the guns off the bedside table, training them on the door. I left the lights off. If it was someone unfriendly, it would be harder to see me.

"Computer," I said softly, "Open the door."

The bedroom door slid open.

There was a figure standing in the doorway. A figure, black against the glow coming from the hallway light behind it. Slightly slouched on the left side, breathing heavily. It extended an arm out toward me, slowly, making a noise. It sounded like a keening, a soft crooning in some guttural tongue.

"Who the fuck are you?" I said.

The figure took a step forward into the room, its breathing dry and raspy, ceasing its previous attempt to communicate, if that's what it had been trying to do, and moving forward.

Another step.

"Any closer and I shoot."

The figure stopped, started to chuckle.

A harsh, dry, wheezing sound.

"I shoot... I shoot.." Voice like sandpaper on steel, followed by more laughter.

It took another step into the room, and I fired.

One shot.

Into it's knee.

It jerked back, fell to the ground.

"Put your hands where I can see them," I barked.

No reply.

"Computer, lights –". The thing got up, a black bulk against the brightness outside the room.

The lights came on, and I could see it clearly now. It was cloaked in black rags, tattered but seeming to form some sort of whole. The same seemed to cover its head, almost like a cowl, only wrapping all the way around its face as well.

"I shoot... " It wheezed.

"You get the idea. Good. Now –"

And then the thing came at me. Tearing across the room with a violent velocity that couldn't have been human, it came at me, hands reaching for my face.

I started firing, taking it full in the chest.

It flew backwards, somersaulted, landed face down in a crumpled heap by the door and lay dead still.

"Dex!"

Still no response.

He should have heard the gunshots.

Something was wrong.

I walked over to where the thing lay, guns trained steadily on its unmoving figure.

Kicked it.

Nothing.

Again.

Nothing.

I backed out the door, guns still on it, and made my way to Dex's bedroom, not letting the thing out of my sight.

"Open, "I said as I got there.

The door slid open to reveal a pitch black room. No sound came from inside.

"Dex?"

Silence.

I hesitated a second, then, "Lights."

The bedroom lamps came on.

The bed was empty. The blankets had been slept in, but no one lay there now.

Something caught my eye. I moved quickly into the room, over to the bed, leaned over and picked up a piece of dirty, tattered black fabric.

"Computer, is Dexter Kellerman in House9?"

"Dexter Kellerman cannot be located within the specified parameters."

I went back to the doorway, guns ahead of me, turned my head to check on the thing in my room.

It was gone, where it had been lying there was now just an empty patch of floor.

No blood.

I'd hit the thing seven or eight times and there was no blood.

That bothered me a bit.

It was impossible that the thing could have come past this doorway without me seeing it, I'd looked away for only a split-second, and even then I would have caught it in my periphery.

Therefore, it had to still be in my room.

As I slowly made my way back to the room, I found myself wondering how the hell this thing got past House9 security. It wasn't only a question of how the bastard got in undetected, but how he got in *at all*.

Security here was pretty tight.

I got to the door, stopped. I was going to face this thing, find out who or what the hell it was, how it got in, and what the hell it wanted.

But first, I had to beat it.

I decided to use the element of surprise, since the guns alone obviously weren't going to be enough. I stepped back a few paces, took a deep breath, and threw myself headlong through the door, doing a roll as I came through, flipping sideways as I came out of the roll and landing on my back on the bed with a gun trained on either side of the room.

"Hoo-AAH, motherfucker!" I yelled.

"*You can't kill it.*"

Silence.

"What?"

More silence.

"Hello?"

I shook my head, looking around for the source of the voice, or any sign of the thing.

Nothing.

"I must be losing it," I muttered.

A gentle laugh sounded, fading away as if carried on a breath of air.

I knew that voice.

I knew it well.

And then I saw it, a shadow moving across the wall to my right. Moving of its own volition, across the wall and then up on to the ceiling, drifting over to hang above my head. Two arms extended out from the main mass of the shadow, and all of a sudden the glOlamps on either side of the bed burst and the room was plunged into darkness.

I trained my guns on the ceiling, unsure of what to expect, but taking no chances.

Silence.

Pounding heartbeat.

And then it was on top of me; I don't know how. I saw no transition from shadow to solid form. One second it was hanging above me, a dark shifting patch on the ceiling, the next a massive screaming weight on my chest, grabbing the guns from

121

my hands like candy from a baby. Standing then, lifting me from the bed with one hand.

Christ, it was strong!

It grabbed my neck with its free hand.

Squeezed.

Choking me.

Panic took me and I started struggling against the hand around my throat, trying to pull it away.

I couldn't.

Kicking, thrashing wildly with hands and feet.

It was useless.

My vision started to blur.

The world seemed to swim around me, lucid and light and mixing like a water-coloured dream. I was suffocating to death and there was nothing I could do about it and all the military training in the world wasn't going to save me now.

There was a large window directly behind me, at the head of the bed, and through the mists of my fading mind a plan started to form.

I brought my arms back, grabbed the curtains. Took a fistful in each hand, brought my legs up into the foetal position, and kicked forward into the thing's chest with every last shred of strength I had left.

It worked.

The thing let go of me, stumbled a few paces back as I hit the bed. I dived for one of my guns, but too late. It swung up with one filthy arm, connecting with me mid-scramble, sending me backwards, up off my feet, flying into the curtains and through the window, glass exploding all around me.

I thrashed out desperately, trying to grab hold of something, anything, to keep me from falling ninety-one storeys into the night. My hand caught hold of the curtain, I clutched at it with all my strength as I swung around and my body hit the side of the building below the window.

I fought to gain my breath back.

Gasped, pulling air back into my lungs.

"Warning. House9 security is breached. Please give vocal disarm command and password."

It was raining, as always in Nu Caynan, and soon it would be difficult to maintain my grip on the curtain. This would be a problem. I looked down, searching for somewhere to climb down to.

Nothing, there were no balconies on this side of the building.

And then, out of nowhere, I was hit with an ice-cold gust of wind that knocked me across the wall, spinning around and around as I held on for dear life.

"House9 Auto-Destruct active. To deactivate, please enter vocal disarm command and password immediately."

A mad, inhuman scream sounded from above me, and I looked up to see the creature standing above me in the remains of the window, arms outstretched as if crying defiantly at some unseen adversary.

It looked down, saw me.

Oh bugger.

So much for unseen.

I thought now was probably a good time to survey the situation.

Okay: No way down, and up definitely wasn't an option. Sideways didn't really have much to offer either. So much for that, then.

Above me the thing uttered it's dry, scraping "laugh" again.

And then I heard it:

A sound.

Coming from a distance.

Closer now.

Closer.

The thing reached down, grabbed the curtain, started to pull me up.

Slowly, one hand over the other, I was being dragged up the side of the building. The thing laughed again, reached down to grab hold of my arm.

"Fuck you," I said nicely. I kicked away from the ledge and threw myself backwards, out into the rainy night, twisting in the air and the darkness and falling...

...falling...

...landing hard a few seconds later on the roof of a hovtrain that came tearing by. I rolled over, coming to lie on my back, watching as the thing screamed another inhuman scream, infuriated and enraged and totally powerless to stop me. I watched as it disappeared into the darkness, the scream staying in my ears until at last it was dissolved away by distance and the dull droning of the hovtrain's turbines.

And then the night was lit up by an explosion, the sound a roar in the distance, an orange glow visible even from here. The flames would consume everything in the apartment.

Everything.

I lay back, soaked, exhausted, and wearing nothing but my pants. No shoes, no shirt, no jacket and no guns.

Damn.

The roof of the hovtrain was hard, but it provided a hell of a relief after the struggling against the Thing, and then hanging ninety-one storeys up with nothing but a damn curtain between me and the devil. Slowly, my body started to relax. Muscles unclenching as the rain soothed my skin.

Everything had been in the apartment.

Which meant everything was toast.

And then it hit me.

I checked my back pocket, pulled out my wallet and grinned like an idiot.

Well, it wasn't all bad.

If I was going to be lost in the depths of Nu Caynan at night in the pouring rain wearing nothing but a pair of pants, then at least I was going to do it with my wallet.

Eleven

I got off the hovtrain at Spire.

Fuck Ya'll! EA Pigdogs Must Burn Station. The station had been called something else at some stage, but now the original words on the board were completely incomprehensible beneath the graffiti. In fact, I suspected there were so many coats of spray paint on it that if the metal were ever to dwindle away due to rust or whatever, the sign would remain in a state of perfection forever. Well, I thought, it wasn't too serious.

Hell, it had a ring to it.

A vagrant tried to hassle me as I climbed off the roof of the train, but I told him to get lost. I wasn't in the mood for shit right about then. I was cold and wet and I'd just lost my brand-new jacketcom to a House9-fire.

I made my way along the walkway in darkness, trying to hail a cab. This wasn't easy during the day in a place like Spire. At *night* it was close to impossible, even if I had been fully clothed. Spire was not a nice neighbourhood, in fact it ranked as one of the very worst neighbourhoods not only in Nu Caynan, but on the entire Planet.

Spire had been an incredibly prolific neighbourhood in the early days of Nu Caynan, when we were still building up the city after World War Three. The area had been designed as an entertainment area, with five-storey shopping malls, restaurants and cosy walkways for families and couples to stroll down, but they ended up going really wild with the place.

Because the whole city is technically indoors, by virtue of there being no actual ground (except, of course, for the *ground*, which is too far below to really give a damn about), people increasingly felt the need to walk in the grass, take a dip in a pool on a sunny summer's day, watch their kids play in the park, and the wasteland beyond the City Walls wasn't really an option. So they just built parks and meadows and grassy fields inside giant, interconnected buildings and warehouses, and built the restaurants and malls around the indoor landscape, next to the walkways and winding streams.

Spire was born.

Ambient lighting inside these giant, interconnected buildings ensured the environment was always cosy and warm, making shoppers feel relaxed and comfortable even if outside the temperature was below freezing. Which, in the early days of Nu Caynan, it could very well have been.

Spire was beautiful, technically brilliant, a feat of modern engineering.

And its popularity soared.

Anyone who was anyone wanted to be seen eating in its excellent restaurants, picnicking in its grassy little meadows or strolling along one of the many meandering, tree-lined walkways.

And then, about fifty years ago, that all changed.

I don't know exactly what happened.

I guess it just got outclassed over time. Some of the malls in the newer buildings in the city are twenty storeys high, and the gardens in Helvetica became nicer and better tended than the gardens of Spire. I guess people just started to lose interest.

And eventually the place just went to hell.

And stayed there.

Now it was an overgrown mess, dirty and tired, its buildings derelict for the most part, and considering the type of scum living in Spire these days, better off for it. The place was home to some seriously dodgy taverns and clubs and pretty much nothing else in the way of retail, and the one I was heading for was, although better than them, still in Spire. Which speaks volumes.

I wasn't even sure if it was still there, but if it was, it was a source of back-up, a place to crash the night, and maybe a change of clothes.

As it turned out, I was in luck.

The place was called SkyN. It was the best club Spire had to offer (not that that says much), back when Nu Caynan was still my home, and in the twelve years since then I have never found anything to match it for sheer *personality*. The proprietor was a guy called Neth. He, it must be said, was not what you'd call a man of calibre. Unless of course you were referring to ammunition, in which case he was a man of extremely high calibre indeed. But if you were tight with the guy, he was a useful contact to have. He had the run of most of the lower levels of Nu Caynan back when I knew him, ran the whole show pretty much single-handedly.

We weren't tight, not like Dex and I. But we had an understanding, always had. The guy was a fucking lowlife when you came down to it, but not complete scum. He viewed the "business" of drug dealing and prostitution as just that: a business. And if a kid occasionally ODed while partying at SkyN, well hell, no-one forced the stuff on the guy.   Shit, he probably paid top dollar for it.

But if someone hurt one of his girls, there was hell to pay.

That was Neth.

It was now twelve years later, but when you were cool with Neth, you were cool. Time wouldn't be an issue. He was the guy who organized the D/Type when I needed it. I'll tell you about that later.

The question was, did Neth still run SkyN?

Well, two hours later, after consistently failing to hail or even spot a cab, I found out.

I rocked up at SkyN just before the dawn.

The party was just getting started.

The club was located in the middle of a dry, very dark and dodgy field, what obviously used to be a meadow, the entire area lit by spotlights and giant controlled fires raging further out in the field.

SkyN was the most popular club in Spire when I used to go there, and judging by the amount of people hanging around the courtyard by the entrance to the place, that hadn't changed much. The courtyard used to be a parking area for hovs, back when Spire was still frequented by anyone other than dealers, users, whores, johns, or stupid people looking for a party. Of course there were no hovs there now, just dealers, users, whores, johns, and stupid people who'd found the party and were beginning to regret it.

I made my way through the crowd, passing a dingy looking queue full of extremely dingy looking people (at this time of the morning everyone looks dodgy, even if you are just a stupid kid looking for a party, which it was clear to me most of these people were). It was sad to think that about three quarters of the people in the queue would end up completely fucked on something within minutes of entering the club, and the other quarter would probably have their drinks spiked a short while after that.

Addiction was a fact of life at a place like SkyN; it wasn't a matter of if, it was a matter of when. I had been one of the lucky ones.

The bouncers wouldn't allow me access when I eventually made it to the entrance, telling me to stand in line like everyone else. I told them that this didn't really work for me, that it was cold and I was half-naked and could they call Neth for me please before I lost it and killed them all.

"Tell him it's Ash Carter."

The one raised an eyebrow at this, spoke briefly into his headset, the glimmer of murder in his eyes but not taking any chances.

He went pale.

Then he nodded, "Yes, sir."

He turned to face me, "Neth says welcome back. I sincerely apologise for keeping you waiting, Mister Carter. Please, come in. If you would just follow me, I'll escort you to the VIP room-"

"I know where it is," I replied, stepping past him and through the doorway.

"Of course, Mister Carter."

And then I was in, and the dance floor stretched off into the distance and hundreds of sweating bodies writhed before me, dancing beneath pulsing strobes and lasers that cut through the darkness and the smoke. I looked up and to my right.

The VIP room.

I made my way up, and was greeted at the top of the stairs by two more armed thugs.

"I'm Ash Carter. Get the fuck out of my way."

The older of the two looked like he might have known who I was. News travels fast in the underground, and twelve years ago I hit instant celebrity status when I removed Cole from the fold, taking away Neth's only competition.

I was right.

"Yes sir. Welcome back, Mister Carter," he said, as the other guy looked on incredulously as some half-naked nutcase with very bad manners walked right past his superior and into the VIP room.

The interior of the VIP room looked like something out of ancient Rome, scantily clad young ladies hovered around a few men sprawled out on giant cushions on the floor, bringing plates of food, drinks, drugs. Seeing to their every need.

Yeah, this was pretty much how I remembered it.

"Carter!"

I turned from the scene, looked to my right.

130

A giant, overweight behemoth with flowing blonde hair in a toga was approaching me from a private bar in the corner, a vodka in each hand. He came over to me, handed me the drink, and grabbed me in a one-armed bear hug.

"Hey Neth, how the hell are you?" I said, grinning as he took a step back to look at me.

"Life's good." He raised an eyebrow, "I see you've come dressed for the occasion."

I grinned, "Yeah, is there any way I can get hold of a shirt –"

"Say no more!" Neth snapped his fingers and one of said scantily clad ladies bounced up to us.

"Rachel, baby. This is Ash Carter," he said.

She smiled, "Hi, Mister Carter."

"Hi."

"Mister Carter will be requiring a..." He looked at me enquiringly.

"Whatever," I said.

"Get him a suit. Black, wasn't it?"

"Yeah," I replied. "And two guns with shoulder holsters. Nine-millimetres."

Neth grinned, "The man has a plan! Gonna be needing any people?"

I shook my head, taking the vodka down in one swig.

"No, not for this. I have a meeting."

"You always take guns to the business table?"

"Don't you?" I replied.

Neth laughed.

"So when is the meeting, Carter? Got any time to get roaring drunk, maybe pop a few, what was it, D's?"

I sat on a long black couch overlooking the dance-floor. The couch's other occupants were a lesbian couple having a make-out session at the other end. Neth hadn't changed much in twelve years, it seemed.

"I'm gonna pass. Need to lie down. Meeting's the other side of town, NeuroLOG building. Ten sharp."

Neth nodded, took a seat beside me, "No problem. Rachel will take you to a room when she gets back. Would you be needing any company tonight?"

I groaned, "That's pretty much the last thing I'll need tonight."

He got up, took my glass, and went to the bar area to refill it, came back and crashed on the couch again, handing me my drink.

"Quite a view," I remarked, taking a sip.

"Yeah," Neth replied, sitting forward and looking out at the colourful, shifting mass below us.

"Business looks good."

He looked at me, becoming serious, "It's not what it should be, Carter."

I raised an eyebrow, "How so?"

Neth dropped his voice, his eyes becoming intense.

"It seems I have some... competition."

"That shouldn't be a problem for you, Neth."

"No, under normal circumstances, you'd be right," he replied, face grave. "But this is different."

This surprised me. Neth didn't really have a problem when it came to business. Either you were with him, or you were floating down a river.

I mentioned this.

He nodded, "This new guy on the block is pretty jacked. He has effectively, how shall we put it, resisted my advances so far."

"You tried to make friends?"

"Well, no, first I tried to kill him. When that didn't work a few times, and I started losing one too many boys, I tried for peace. Thought we could come up with some sort of business arrangement."

"He didn't go for it," I said.

Neth shook his head, looking out at the dance floor again.

"He wants the whole lot," he said, quietly.

"The whole —"

"Nu Caynan underground, yeah. And so far, I've had three attempted hits on me."

"Shit."

We were silent for a while. And then, "Carter, whoever is trying to take me out is good. Really good. He seems to know this place. The underground. And he's got an outfit going, an outfit that's growing in size by the fucking *minute.*"

"Neth, I've never seen you —"

He looked at me sharply.

" – concerned like this, before," I finished.

He shook his head, "And here I thought I was going to spend my twilight years in peace and quiet. Instead, I'm going to war!"

I nodded, "A man your age should be relaxing on a beach in Tora Sera."

"Yeah, so much for fucking retirement."

Rachel returned a few minutes later, and at Neth's request she led me to one of the suites SkyN was famous for. She unlocked the door, gestured for me to enter. I did, and she followed me in, dropping the suit and holstered guns on the chair next to the massive double bed in front of us.

She turned to me, putting her arms around my waist, "You want some company, babes?"

"No, thanks, Rachel," I disentangled myself from her limbs.

She was gorgeous.

133

Young, soft and I was sure she was pretty damn supple, but I just wasn't in the mood. All I wanted was sleep.

She smiled, "Maybe some other time, then?"

"Maybe."

She blew me a kiss, and left, shutting the door quietly behind her.

I was left to my thoughts.

Dex.

Shit.

I hit the bed, "Computer..." I gave it Dex's mobile number and waited patiently as it dialled through.

Calling...

No reply.

I waited far longer than was necessary before eventually hanging up.

Where the hell was he?

My thoughts wondered back to House9, and the thing in black...

Dex's room...

The shreds of black fabric on his bed...

But there was no body, and I really didn't think the creature would have gone to all the trouble of hiding it if there had been. What the hell would have been the point? Besides, the creature in House9 had had a problem stringing a few words together. So, my rationale went, if said creature was experiencing difficulties expressing itself with more coherence than a couple of howls and grunts (not to mention the occasional fragment of sentence and the more occasional piercing, inhuman scream), the chances were it hadn't really thought past its nose.

I hoped.

No, Dex was fine. He could take care of himself.

Apex had made sure of that.

And anyway, there was nothing I could do about it now.

I lay back, closed my eyes.

Jesus, I was tired.

I wondered how Sarah was, if Fel was keeping her comfortable since I barged into her life and took away everything that meant something to her. Also I wondered how long it would take me to fall asleep...

Five seconds later I was out like a light.

Twelve

The NeuroLOG building.

09:56am.

I stood in the main lobby, waiting for Rainer, having a smoke next to a 'No smoking' sign, messing around with the new jacketcom2.0 I'd picked up on the way here. It's not that I have a complete disregard for the health of others. Nothing could be further from the truth. It's just that in the particular state of mind I was currently in, I couldn't have given a flying shit.

Besides, I just kind of felt like being contrary.

You know what I mean.

So I stood there, smoking and thinking.

Dex had disappeared.

I'd called his mobile number again.

No reply.

This was worrying, but at least he hadn't been in House9 at the time of the attack, which meant the freak I'd had a fight with hadn't killed him in his sleep.

This was a Good Thing.

True, I didn't know where the hell he was, which could probably constitute a Bad Thing, but at least he wasn't dead.

Or I didn't think he was, at any rate.

As far as intelligent rationale was concerned, that was about the extent of it. The rest would have to wait until after the call from Trevor Mason. I'd called Trish and she had promised to launch a surreptitious search for him, using every agent available to the K-Foundation. I wondered how far that spread, and who else exactly had access to the information on their system, and was dragged from that line of thought by a hand on my shoulder. I turned to see a huge black man in a black suit and headset standing beside me.

"Mister Corben?"

"Yeah."

"I am Mitchell. Mister Rainer has sent me as your escort. Please follow me."

I nodded, "Let's go."

Mitchell led me to one of nine elevators standing in a row against one wall, to the one in the centre, number five. He hit a button and the doors opened immediately.

We entered.

The elevator itself was almost completely made of glass, affording what turned out to be quite a view of the city. Around us other lifts were moving up and down, as ours continued its journey upwards into the sky. The buildings dropped away one by one, the distant horizon becoming more and more vivid and clear as we left the city air far below us, replacing it with the crispness of altitude.

We eventually passed the cocktail bar on level 250, and I looked away, out towards the city skyline.

Up and up we went.

And then we stopped.

"Welcome to level three hundred and seventy," Mitchell said, as the doors slid silently open.

I stepped out into what turned out to be a small but extremely well appointed lobby.

Exceptionally big and heavily armed men stood on either side of a large, black door.

"Morning, boys," said my escort, stepping out of the lift.

"Good morning, sir!!!"

Mitchell spoke briefly into his headset, and a few seconds later the huge black doors slid effortlessly open.

"Welcome to the top of the world, Mister Corben," he said.

"Thanks."

I walked through the doors, into a massive, marble-tiled room. Windows extended along the entire circumference of the place, and a pond stood at its very centre. A child, a small boy, no older than five, was playing in it, splashing water around, laughing and giggling.

"The child is a hologram."

I turned at the sound of a familiar voice.

"The pond is real, but the little boy and the water aren't there," said Rainer, watching the scene intently.

"Who is he?" I asked, staring once more at the projection in the pond.

"Mister Mason's dead son. Daniel."

"I'm sorry," I said.

Rainer nodded, "Come with me, the call will be coming through presently."

He led me to a sitting area, plush white couches and a large low coffee table overlooked a view that Shakespeare would have had a hard time describing.

I had a seat. Mitchell hit a button on the table and a wide glass screen slid up into view.

"Would you care for a drink?" Rainer asked.

"No. Thanks."

He nodded, "Very well, then we shall leave you to it, Mister Corben."

Rainer smiled, turned and left with Mitchell.

I stared out at the sprawling mass of Nu Caynan, and beyond at the barren wastelands surrounding it, and something flickered in the back of my mind.

Just enough time.

For what?

You'll see. Come

Across the desert the wind blew, the dust swirling and rushing across the ground, bringing to the surface of my mind memories I had thought long buried and so very far away.

Incoming Call...

This was it.

"Answer."

The message was replaced by the face of a man, somewhere in his sixties, hair slicked back, clean-shaven, eyes as cold and blue as a glacier at midnight.

"Mister Corben," he said, his voice deep, gravelly.

"Yeah."

"Where is Sarah?" he said levelly.

"What the hell is going on?" I replied, just as evenly.

A beat.

"I've been targeted by someone," I continued, "and I have been since I accepted this job. People have been going crazy all around me, my ex-wife is dead, my best friend has disappeared, I was attacked last night by a fucking *thing*, and I'll be damned if I'm going to hand over the only person I've been successfully able to protect without the full knowledge that it's in her best interests."

Mason looked surprised.

"Who is trying to kill you?"

"Who isn't?"

"Mister Corben, it is imperative that you deliver Sarah to me safely, I –"

"Not before you tell me why."

He sighed, "Mister Corben, did you know that you are one of the only people on the planet, most of my staff included, who has seen my face?"

I didn't reply.

"This entails some form of trust. Surely you could extend the same courtesy to me? Your situation is perilous; you've made that abundantly clear. I understand, really I do. You and Sarah will be safer here with me than out there; I can guarantee you that. You will have all the protection you need until this has blown over –"

"I don't need protection–"

"And Sarah? How long can you hide her for? Do you even know who you're hiding her from?" Mason said.

"Let's just say I'm trying to keep her out of harm's way."

Mason nodded, "I understand, Mister Corben. Believe me, I wish to do the same."

I thought about it. Mason saw that he was making progress, pushed the point.

"Mister Corben, NeuroLOG is a very large corporation. I have all the resources necessary to keep Sarah safe from harm. And you will be coming along as well, along with whomever you wish."

My own back-up.

"Okay," I said. "Where are you?"

Mason smiled, but I really didn't catch much humour in it.

"Far away, Mister Corben. Mister Rainer will make the arrangements. I assume you don't have any particularly pressing engagements on your schedule for the next few weeks?"

"Well, not dying, for one."

Mason laughed, "I think I can help you with that one. You and Sarah will receive a full armed escort from Nu Caynan through to where I am stationed."

"Sarah isn't in Nu Caynan, "I said.

Mason nodded," Very good. You're smarter than you look. You can pick her up on the way."

"Thanks. But remember, Mister Mason, this only happens if Sarah agrees. I will need to contact her now to ask her."

He nodded, "Very well, I shall call back in ten minutes."

He hung up, and I called The Rock Palace from the new jacketcom.

Felony answered.

"Hey, Ash, how are things?"

"Still okay. Oh yeah, we had a break-in. House9 was destroyed and Dex has disappeared."

"What?"

I explained what had happened, along with the conversation with Mason, as quickly as possible.

"Neth says hi."

Fel groaned, and put Sarah on the line.

"Hey, Sarah. I've spoken with Trevor Mason. Considering the seriousness of things right now, I think you'll be safer with him."

"What? No –"

"I'll be coming with you. And Felony too. We'll get the answers to this," I said. "Sarah, I know that Mason needs you, and I also know that he is genuinely interested in keeping you well protected. Considering the type of creepy shit that has happened in the last forty-eight hours, I think it's in your best interests that we go."

She looked very uncertain.

I didn't blame her.

"Can we trust him, Ash?"

"He's a corporate executive, so my first thought would be 'No'," I replied. "But I do believe he has your best interests in mind. And he's the only lead we have on this thing. What do you say?"

She shrugged, "Let's do it."

She put Felony back on, and I told him to pack for a journey.

"Where we going?" he asked.

"Somewhere far away, apparently."

"No problem, where you wanna meet?"

"Shillian. Sands Hotel. I'll book in under John Smith."

"Original."

"What can I say?"

We ended the call and a few minutes later, Mason called back.

"We're on," I said.

"Excellent. I look forward to our meeting, Mister Corben."

"Yeah."

The screen went blank.

I sat back, lit a smoke, and wondered what the fuck I was getting us into.

Whatever it was, it could be no worse than what I was getting us out of.

Or so I hoped.

In my world, things had a funny way of not working out according to plan.

Well, I thought, I guess we're safe then. Because, as far as I was concerned, there was no plan.

The NeuroLOG jet roared off into the stormy sky, rain streaking across my window as I looked down at the sprawling city of Nu Caynan, already fading into the haziness of the torrential downpour.

We were headed for Shillian.

Sarah and Felony would be on their way by now, and from there we would start the journey to visit Trevor Mason and finally find out what the hell was going on.

I didn't completely trust Mason, but I trusted the fact that he needed Sarah, and as long as that was the case, this would work out fine.

I sat on a couch in the softly lit cabin. Rainer, seated directly across from me, was deeply involved in some financial report or other. I had to admit, the guy had a lot of energy for an old man.

An image on the wallscreen just behind him caught my eye, the familiar sight of the Tanis coastline, the camera zooming down the coastal street where my offices were located, palm fronds swaying slightly in the breeze.

"Computer, volume up a bit."

"...where the bodies of the sisters, twins aged eleven, were found, decapitated, and their heads placed on poles at the entrance to these offices."

"What the fuck?"

Rainer looked up, pushed his glasses up his nose, staring at me intently.

Mitchell came over, had a seat on the couch beside me.

"What's happening?" he asked.

I pointed at the screen, "That's my office."

He looked at the screen, Rainer turning to stare as well.

"No shit?" Mitchell said.

"No shit."

It was a message, a warning.

Had to be.

From the same psychos who were after me.

"Looks like you might need our protection after all, Mister Corben. As much as you might dislike the idea," Rainer said, eyes not leaving the screen.

Mitchell nodded his agreement.

I hated the idea of being under the cover of a corporation, but I had to admit, it felt good to have a bit of weight behind me. Also, no-one would be decompressing *this* fucking plane.

I stared at the news report in horror, not believing the depths these sick, crazy bastards had sunk to in there efforts to –

To what?

What were they trying to do?

I caught the names of the little girls, below their images on the screen. Natalie and Jennifer Reilly.

Natalie and Jennifer.

Two more completely innocent casualties in my battle against Christ-knew-what and no signs of slowing and now they weren't even targeting people I knew anymore but complete fucking strangers.

I turned to face the window to my right, staring out at the blue sky, the blanket of clouds below. So peaceful up here. So calm. Down on the ground World War 4 could be in full swing and up here you'd never know.

I sat back, closed my eyes, still exhausted from the night before. I hadn't gotten nearly enough sleep, and the freak in House9 hadn't exactly helped me conserve energy either.

I cleared my mind, letting my thoughts drift away, relishing the opportunity to relax. Everything, *everything,* was a problem I would deal with later.

I drifted off with no trouble at all.

About three quarters of an hour later, the pilot's voice came on over the intercom, "Gentlemen, we will be touching down at Shillian Airport shortly. Please engage your seatbelts. We'll make this one a smooth landing for you."

Rainer grunted, "Best he does."

The NeuroLOG jet dipped, flying through the clouds, and eventually came out into a dark rainy day. I could just make out Shillian far below in the rain and haze, lights twinkling in the half-darkness that comes with a good thunderstorm.

Lightning flashed around us.

We hit a bit of turbulence, the jet vibrating and rocking like an exorcism gone wrong.

"Quite a day," I muttered, uneasy about the weather outside.

Mitchell turned his head, about to reply, but he never got the chance.

From over the intercom came the pilot's voice again, this time sounding a bit strained, "Gentlemen... There is no reply from... Shillian Tower... Er..."

Rainer stood, "This is ridiculous."

He walked up to the cockpit, rapping on the door.

I stood as well, joining him there.

The door was opened by the co-pilot, whose face was looking a bit pale.

"Mister Rainer," he said.

"What's the problem, James?" he asked, not unkindly, but with a definite briskness to his tone.

James glanced into the cockpit, then back at us, "Please come in, sir."

We entered the dim, cramped cockpit, filled with glowing lights and dials of every shape and size. Ahead of us the pilot was attempting to make contact with Shillian Airport Tower, but to no apparent avail.

Rainer went to stand beside his pilot, guy by the name of Tom, and I stared down at the city below us.

That's odd...

Was it maybe a trick of the light?

I leaned closer to the window, staring out more intently now, trying to determine if what I thought I'd seen was actually there.

145

Straining to see through the haze of rain...

Straining...

Yeah. There it was. I turned to the captain.

"You sure this is Shillian?" I said.

He looked at me briefly, nodded, "Without a doubt, Mister Corben. Same coordinates, and you can see it down there, even through this ghastly weather. Shillian Tower, this is NeuroLOG one-four-five, do you copy, over?"

I nodded, looking out the window again, "Yeah, you can. But look a bit closer. Isn't something a bit... wrong?"

Rainer stared out at the city below while the pilot continued his attempts to make contact, "Just what are you driving at, Mister Corben?"

"Don't you think it's a bit... *green*... for a MegaCity?"

He looked out at the streets and buildings, brow furrowed. Deep in concentration. Then it struck him. His eyes went wide.

"Oh my God."

"Yeah," I said quietly.

"What's happening?"

I shook my head

Below us, far below us, the city of Shillian was changing.

One second I'd be staring at a large corporate building, soaring up into the sky. The next it would blur, shimmer, distort. And then I was looking at a fragment of a mountain, trees hanging on its side, rock in some places, grass in others, ending in thin air in one place and fused to the side of a building on the side, as if God went someplace green, and went crazy with the cut and paste.

I looked up, looking for Shillian airport.

146

Where I knew it should be there was a grassy meadow with a spattering of trees, a stream running through it, and a couple of cows just sort of standing around for good measure.

That would explain why we couldn't contact the Tower.

It wasn't there anymore.

The more we watched the more the city started to resemble a giant garden town, with fragments of buildings/mountains/buildings all over.

It occurred to me that we weren't in the safest of places. If we got caught in one these shifting areas, who knew what would happen. There was also a pretty good chance of us flying into something that hadn't been there five seconds before. I decided to share that sentiment with my fellow aviators.

"We have to get the hell out of here, " I said to Rainer.

He nodded, turned to look at the pilot, "Tom, get us out of here."

"You bet."

The jet arched to the right, Tom engaging the emergency turbines, and we shot off through the rain.

We probably would have gotten away, too, if it hadn't been for the giant bird that materialized right in our path, smashing into the cockpit windscreen before Tom had a chance to react, smashing through the glass and crushing our pilot, sending our cabin into complete windy chaos and our jet into a spin through the hazy, crazy sky.

I looked in horror at Tom, his body crushed by the weight of brown feathers on top of him, blood trickling from his mouth.

He was unconscious.

Or dead.

I didn't have time to find out.

The co-pilot had darted forward, "Oxygen masks on the wall!"

147

He grabbed the controls, fighting desperately to get the jet under control, to bring us to a safe altitude as Rainer and I grabbed the closest masks, breathing in deeply, hanging on for dear life. Christ, I couldn't believe it. If it wasn't a lunatic with a parachute, it was a giant fucking bird.

I couldn't win with planes.

Eventually, after much struggling, James stabilised the jet, righting it at an altitude where we could breathe comfortably even with the gaping hole in the windscreen.

Rainer moved over to check on Tom.

Dead.

We were okay, though. Yes, we had a colossal bird sticking out of the front of our plane and we couldn't gain any altitude, but at least we could get the hell out of here, out of this bizarre, shifting dreamscape.

That thought brought me a lot of comfort, right up until the left wing of the NeuroLOG jet clipped a mountainside that hadn't been there five seconds before, ripping away and sending the jet spinning out of control and hurtling towards the ground once again.

PART TWO
Another Place

Thirteen

I was eighteen when I first met Melanie.

It was nearly six months into my training at Apex, and this was one of the very rare occasions when Felony had given us the whole weekend to ourselves.

It was Friday night. Dex and Cole had gone some place fancy to get shit-faced and pick up women, and I'd decided to go out alone and think about things.

I ended up at SkyLounge, an observation lounge built high up in Nu Caynan's city wall, staring out through huge floor-to-ceiling windows at the most phenomenal electrical storm I had ever seen.

Melanie stood a few feet away.

She was so beautiful. Dark hair falling across her face and down her back, eyes watching the lightning intently as it hit the storm lights and bounced around like a new kind of life.

She was so beautiful.

I've never been particularly hot with the ladies. It's not that I can't be charming.

I can.

And it's not that I'm ugly.

I'm not.

Some women have even gone as far as to say I'm handsome.

It's just that when it comes to making the first move I'm totally bloody clueless. A woman has to pretty much hit me over the head, rip off my clothes, drag me into her bed and straddle me like a wild bronco before I'll take the hint.

Mainly, it has to do with interest, I think.

Or rather, lack of interest.

Before you question my sexual orientation, let me justify that.

150

It's not that I am disinterested in women. The opposite is true. A beautiful woman is a truly wonderful thing. It's just that I've always been attracted to a certain something in a woman, and if she doesn't have it, I just can't get interested.

I have no idea exactly what it is. Maybe it's a smell. Or a glimmer, something in her eyes. I don't know. But whatever it is, Melanie had it, and I could not take my eyes off her.

The first time our eyes met is something I don't think I'll ever forget.

An incredible burst of energy hit the storm lights, and the entire lounge was ensconced in liquid blue-green light as the electricity outside danced and played across the giant observation window. Melanie turned her head, her eyes following the flow of energy outside, moving like a living thing across the glass, and our eyes met. I, of course, had been staring at her like a caveman studying an origami bird.

I remember her eyes so vividly.

Excitement.

Wonder.

I fell in love with her the second I saw her, and that look in her eyes would keep me there forever.

I had to say something. We were a few feet apart and I'd just been caught staring like an idiot.

"Pretty, isn't it?" I said.

On a scale of one to a hundred, one hundred being the height of intellect and suave, mysterious masculinity, and one being an idiotic monosyllabic grunt uttered by some primordial cave-dwelling Neanderthal he-beast, I think that rates about a five. And maybe that is, in fact, being too kind.

Anyway, she smiled at me. And not one of those half-arsed attempts people usually dole out when faced with someone they don't really want to speak to.

A *real* smile.

And then her eyes were pulled from mine as another burst of energy hit the glass, and I watched her as her face was bathed in radiant aquamarine light.

She knew I was watching her, but it didn't bother her. Much later I would discover that she had been watching me too. When my eyes had been caught by the fantastic display outside, she had stolen a glance here, another there. Never letting me catch her at it. In fact, I had had no idea she had even given me a second thought at that first encounter, much less been at all interested, until months later when, after making love until close to dawn, she had rested her head on my chest, tilted her face up to kiss me, and whispered softly to me of how she had felt on that first night.

After the storm had subsided, I went over to the bar, had a seat and ordered a drink. That was me in a nutshell. Didn't even try any further. In my defence, if *you* had said something like "pretty, isn't it?" to the most beautiful girl you'd ever seen, you'd probably want to go and get drunk as well.

As it happened, I wasn't destined to drink alone that night.

No sooner had my drink been placed before me than I became aware of someone taking a seat immediately next to me. I turned my head, and nearly fell off my stool.

"Hi, I'm Melanie."

"Yeah." Christ.

She was smiling, hand outstretched.

Christ.

I took it.

"Ash. Ash Carter," I attempted a smile. I don't know how that worked out, but she didn't run screaming, which was good. That's the thing about smiling when you're nervous as hell, most of the time you end up looking like either a homicidal psychotic mental hospital escapee with a penchant for the jugular or someone with a very unfortunate facial twitch. However mine came out, she stayed, and I offered her a drink.

We talked all night. She knew things about the world, about life, that I'd never been able to discuss with anyone except Felony. And when she spoke, it's like life opened up and carried her voice, her thoughts, up into the sky and made them real. She had passion, her whole being seeming to glow with some inner light as she spoke, her voice washing over me in waves, moving me, bringing me to life as her smile and the soft glow of her skin and the beauty and depth of her big brown eyes penetrated straight to my heart, through my heart and into my soul.

At one stage during that magic night she asked me what it was that I did.

Apex had a strict ruling on that.

Felony's golden rule:

Don't tell a soul.

But I didn't want to lie to her either, so I went for broke.

"I'm in training at a government agency."

Melanie raised an eyebrow, "Training? To be?"

"A field agent. I can't really talk about it."

I wasn't ashamed of what I was getting involved in, not at that stage. I was still of the opinion that what I was training for was in the best interests of not only the EA, but all the citizens of the EA worlds. The greater good, fighting terrorism and fringe factions intent on destroying the EA and the freedom it represented. It would be a while still before I realised the truth.

"You can't *really* talk about it? Or you *can't* talk about it."

"The second one." Jesus, I liked this girl. I prayed she wouldn't get up and leave.

She got up, took her coat off the bar counter.

"This place is closing. Time to go," she said.

Shit.

"Yeah," I replied.

Silence.

"So you wanna get some coffee or what?" she said.

I grinned.

"Yeah, I think I do."

We spent as much time together as possible, meeting whenever I had some time off from the rigorous training I was undergoing at Apex. Every day I had to myself, I spent with her; every night I could get out of the Apex complex belonged to her. The days filled with light and love. The nights with deep passion and a happiness I'd never until then even realised existed, and have never found since.

Yet for all of this I still kept completely focussed on the training, so much so that a year later I graduated top of my year, and was honoured with my first mission two weeks later. Melanie and I had been seeing each other for a year then, and it had gotten to the stage where we wanted to live together. We found a place in Helvetica, Nu Caynan. It was a beautiful area, a lot nicer than what most nineteen-year-old couples could afford to rent. But Felony and Apex pulled some strings, and suddenly this fantastic, high-rise apartment was ours for the taking. We moved in two days before my first mission, and I'll never forget Melanie unpacking our first lounge suite. She squealed with delight, tore off the plastic, and dove onto the couch, grabbing me as I came past and dragging me down to her.

"I love you."

She said it so sweetly.

"You're lying."

She kissed me all over my face, as I lay back on our new couch, stroked the hair back from my forehead.

"I love you," she repeated, softly now.

"Prove it."

She did.

Two days later we stood at the departure gates at Nu Caynan Airport. Outside night had fallen, and the endless rain lashed at the windows facing the runways, branching out from the centre column like the arms of a giant, blinking scarecrow. The airport was located about twenty clicks from the outer wall of the city, and was only accessible from underground lines running from Nu Caynan.

It soared up into the night like a giant monolithic tower, lights blinking, with the runways at the very top, ten on level one, eight shorter ones above it on level two, four even shorter private ones above those on three, each with a large landing pad at the end, and a giant landing pad for private jets and the like on level four, out of the centre of which protruded the Airport HQ tower.

The place was spectacular.

I stood directly in front of her, holding her head in my hands, kissing her softly.

"Baby, don't go," she said, a tear gliding down her cheek, onto my hand.

"I have to. This is what I've been training for, Mel. You know I have to do this."

She looked down, her face still in my hands.

"What if you don't come back?" She said quietly, not looking at me.

"I will," I moved my head down to hers, looked into her eyes. "Mel, I'll come back. I promise."

The jet blasted off twenty minutes later, headed for the Moon and my first hit and nothing after that would ever be the same again.

A giant dome, invisible to the naked eye. A force-field, housing within it a city of soaring skyscrapers, each with the most incredible view money can buy:

the earth, a blue-green bobble hanging in the sky, bright against the blackness of space, luminous and clear and perfect.

High up in one of these skyscrapers there is a man. Advancing in years, but holding himself well. Hair iron-grey. Powerful in stature. Eyes dark. Intense.

He sits at the window, staring out at the radiant earth, deep in thought.

Lost in his own mind, he believes he is on the brink of something. He thinks the negotiations are working, and the thought fills him with, if not happiness, then at least hope.

This man is Dr. Edward Moore.

He is the man who has been fighting for the rights of the Alpha6 research and development facility on Neptune to work outside of the jurisdiction of the EA government. The research taking place there is of vital importance and, having secured private funding, he believes it will be in everyone's best interest to leave them to it. This situation is worrying to some of the suits in charge. They understand the importance of his work, but for that very reason they cannot allow the Alpha6 group to continue "unsupervised."

A deadlock has been reached, a decision has been made, and the EA have notified Dr. Moore that an envoy will be meeting with him on Lunar Colony Damascus to discuss the new terms for the continuation of research at Alpha6.

I was the envoy, and my negotiating skills were not going to be in use that night.

I rang the bell, showed my ID to the door camera, flashing my most endearing grin.

He opened the door for me, and I entered.

I looked around, didn't remove my gloves. He didn't notice. If he had, things may have turned out quite differently.

He smiled, introduced himself, offered me a chair at a table by the window, asked if I'd perhaps like a drink. I accepted with a smile, he turned to mix up a couple of drinks, and I shot him in the back of the head, dropped the gun on the floor, and walked out, closing the door quietly behind me.

I thought I was a fucking hero.

I really believed it.

It wasn't until much later in my career at Apex that I learned of Dr. Moore's wife, of his young daughter, and of the true nature of the research at Alpha6. Information that had been kept from me, deliberately hidden from me. Information that would have changed everything.

And eventually did.

I arrived back at Apex HQ the following morning and Felony held the debriefing in his office. He congratulated me, told me that I'd done well, that I'd saved lives.

I think he was having doubts even then, but would say nothing for a while to come. I thanked him, said goodbye, and gave the job no more thought.

It was over.

Done.

And there was someone I had to see.

Someone very special.

Someone who had waited for me all night.

I sped through the rainy morning, arriving at our apartment in what had to be record time.

Melanie opened the door, looking like she hadn't slept much.

She smiled, her head turned coyly to the side, eyes lowered to the floor.

"I'm sorry," she said, "It's too late. I've found someone else."

"But I've been gone for less than twenty-four hours!"

Eyes moving slowly now, up from the floor to meet my own.

"Felt a lot longer to me."

I was about to reply, but I didn't get the opportunity. Because at that moment she threw herself at me, wrapping her arms around my neck and kissing me all over.

We went inside, slammed the door behind us, fell into bed, and stayed there for three fucking days.

That was the way our life was for the next year and a half, spending all the time we had together, making love and laughing and speaking about the future, and occasionally getting a phone call. Giving me the time, the place, the target.

Melanie never asked me where I went, in the middle of the night, in gloves and a coat, and I never made any move to tell her.

I loved her, she knew that.

I loved her more than anything in this world, and that was enough for her.

There was a place she took me to once, far beyond the walls of Nu Caynan, out in the desert, out in the dead of night. The Moon was low on the horizon, dark orange and huge and burning in the night sky, and the wind blew with a warmth and substance I couldn't understand. Almost like it came from another place, another world, another lifetime.

We came eventually to a stop, and I stepped out of the hov onto a desert plain on the very edge of night. I gazed out towards the distant horizon, where storm clouds, dark and foreboding and so very beautiful, were massing, bringing once more the promise of a stormy night.

Dex, who had accompanied us, swung the hov around and shot off back towards the walls of Nu Caynan, whose dark shape and glittering lights could be seen vaguely in the distance and the gathering dark.

Melanie came to stand beside me, took hold of my hand.

"Just enough time," she said.

"Enough time? For what?"

"You'll see. Come."

"Where's Dex going?"

"Home. Follow me."

158

She led me out into the desert, and eventually we came to an ancient, ruined skeleton of a motorcar, only the bonnet sticking out of the ground, the manufacturer's logo still attached to the front, a sort of three pointed star, rusted and faded and worn away from years spent at the mercy of the elements in a desolate wasteland.

I don't have any idea how she knew this ancient motorcar was there, but this was one person who could always surprise you.

She opened the hood.

My face cracked into a smile, I almost laughed.

A birthday cake, twenty candles on top, all lit. To this day I don't know how she pulled that off.

"Happy birthday, baby," she said, and there was love in those eyes.

After I blew out the candles, she led me around the motorcar to where a tent had been erected, the soft light of candles coming from inside shining through the slightly transparent material.

"Oh, Mel..."

She smiled, "After you."

I went inside the tent.

She followed.

We lay on soft blankets, ensconced in candlelight and surrounded by a dark and dusty plain and, later that night, engulfed by the forces of nature, the desert was hit with the second most phenomenal electrical storm I had ever seen.

And we made love all night, safe from the lightning and the thunder and the howling wind and the rain drumming down outside. Safe and secure and at peace with the world, knowing only the glow of love inside our tent, and the warmth and closeness of each other's bodies, and the softness of each other's lips.

159

If each of our lives has one defining moment, one perfect moment, when you could look back someday and point and say, "There... that's what made it all worth while", then that would be mine.

Everything that came to follow that night on the desert would pale in comparison. The world spinning on its axis, the corporations that governed it, and all that would come to pass and all that had come before existed to me as a pale grey when compared to the deepness and vibrance of that one night on the desert.

And, as with every piece of perfection you will find in your lifetime, it couldn't last.

It couldn't endure.

That's the nature of things.

That's the nature of life, and certainly the rule that has governed mine.

Nothing lasts forever.

Fourteen

On the outside, everything remained the same.

Everything was fine.

Mel went to work; I worked on our garden in the Helvetica apartment.

She cooked, I washed up, and above all, we loved each other.

. But inside, something was changing.

It wasn't Mel; she was amazing.

It was me; it was Apex. I was a field operative, lying dormant for months, and then called upon to act at a moments notice. That was my job, why Melanie and I enjoyed the lifestyle we did.

But something was wrong, and Dex saw it too, and it was he who eventually came to me, laid his cards on the table. I fought against it, told him it couldn't be, even threatened to turn him in as a traitor. I refused to accept the possibility that our targets had been innocent people, that we had murdered innocent people at the whim of some EA exec with a fucking grudge.

Dex and I lost contact for a while after that. He left Apex with the help of Felony, and I continued to work as an operative, trying to fight the gradual dawning of insight that was lighting up the inside of my head until one night I just couldn't fight it anymore and I had a revelation that nearly tore me apart.

The operation had been simple:

Infiltration under cover of darkness. Access to the main building with a DNA sample, voice recording and retina (encased in plastic) courtesy of Apex. I went right through the front fucking door, passed security (asleep at the desk thanks to some clever planning by a man inside), down the corridor, and into the guy's office.

His name was Jason West.

He worked for a company called GlydeNet, a Net-based company dealing with flight simulator software for Net holidays. He was one of the head programmers of their newest product, Glyde7: Soar With The Eagles.

He was also the head of a fringe group who believed the EA were an evil bunch of capitalist tyrant bastards who were keeping the good people down and, together with two of his colleagues, was implanting a subliminal message within the simulation. A collage of images and phrases. The message obvious:

Be free.

Fight the EA oppressors.

Lift yourselves up and take control.

Down with the Corporations.

Down with the EA.

Be free!

I walked right into his office, where he was deeply involved in something on his computer workstation in the corner of the room, and used the fake retina to lock the door.

West swung around on his chair.

Scruffy guy, beard, unruly blonde hair hanging to his shoulders. Shirt out, tie lying on the floor to his right. He reminded me a bit of Dex.

"How did you –" he closed his mouth when he saw the gun.

I aimed it at his head.

Our eyes met.

"I could call security," West said softly.

"They're asleep."

A beat.

"Oh."

A moment of silence.

162

Gun trained on his face.

He just stared at me, saying nothing more. No begging. No pleading. No family photos.

Just silence and a calm, cool, stare.

He knew who he was dealing with, the role I played in it.

He knew what he was up against; he'd known from the start.

It had only ever been a matter of time.

"Do it," he said quietly. "The message won't end here. You bastards can't control us forever."

I said nothing, kept the gun trained on his face.

"Do it!"

"What are you involved with?" I asked.

West looked surprised. He hadn't expected a conversation with his hitman.

"What?" he said.

I repeated my question.

He told me about Glyde7 and his "unofficial work" on the simulation.

"And?" I asked.

He nodded, "*And* I represent a group of people who believe the EA is suppressing us. The Glyde simulations are our way of sending our message out to the people."

I lowered the gun.

"You're no terrorist," I replied softly.

West laughed, "A terrorist? Is that what they told you? I'm a fucking computer programmer!"

I told him to run. Pack his shit and go. *Don't look back.*

That was the very last time I went on a field operation for Apex.

I had my answer.

I was a government-sanctioned murderer, and no matter how hard I tried, I couldn't justify that to myself.

So I did the only thing a young man could do under those circumstances, the only option I thought I had.

I let go.

I let the fuck go and spun away into the darkness of my mind and my memories and all of the things I wanted to forget.

SkyN was packed that night.

Neth had taken one look at me as I entered the club and pulled me into the VIP room.

"I need something," I said, deadness in my voice.

"No, you're clean, Carter –"

"I fucking need something!!"

He went silent, watching me intently.

"What you want?" he said finally.

As I said, Neth and I weren't what you'd call friends, but we had an understanding. He was a kingpin in the Nu Caynan underground, and I was an Apex Assassin, but we shared the same sense of humour and we'd had a few laughs and he didn't want to see me get fucked up.

But that wasn't for him to decide.

"Something strong. I need to... relax. I need to forget."

Neth gave me something called D/Type.

I got lost.

And I didn't come back for a while.

D/type is a drug.

Some people call it a hard drug, and they would be dead on.

The stuff was designed to align your brain impulses during "high band" Net interfacing. Basically, Net technicians only had one way of working on broadband lines, and that was to plug in using a NeuroLink. Problem was, with that kind of data traffic, the chances of a neural overload were pretty high.

Enter D/Type, a drug that kept your brainwaves running at the same speeds as the information around you. Take D/Type outside of the Net, however, and it's the most intense rush you can imagine. Lasting three to four hours, it has been called 'The Virtual Off' by DanzerO, author of *Drugs+Life+onedeadPeach*, who says in his novel, "D/Type, man... It opens your brain, man... lets you see past all the bullshit... this stuff takes you *home*, man...It pulls your 'nads in ways your bitch could never do..." The stuff is also highly addictive, which is why most Net technicians never seem to be in complete control of their faculties.

I doubled up, popping two D/Types at once, and the next few days were a blur.

People.

Places.

Blood and laughter.

Spinning and forgetting and clutching my hair in my hands.

Distress gave way to joy and joy gave way to pain and the pain was my friend and it really loved me.

At one point a pony came up to me and asked me for my autograph.

"Why me?" I asked it.

"Because you are the one."

"The one what?"

The pony said nothing, just smiled at me, and then trotted off over the rainbow.

And then I was at a river in the middle of a forest of pines.

Fishing.

There was an old man on the other side of the river, about twenty feet from me.

165

His name was Jack.

He loved fishing.

I cast a line out, taking in the cool morning air, the fragrance of nature and the wild. Jack had a cottage out here, a tiny little place up the steep side of the valley. The place had a view that took your breath away, of treetops and other valleys and far off mountain peaks covered in snow against a slowly setting sun.

"Nature doesn't care about my sins, Ash. Nature doesn't give a damn."

Yeah, Jack could fish for days, just lose himself in nature, forget about his troubles and become one with the river. The only problem was, Jack was a fish, casting his line into a river full of people, splashing in and out of the water.

I was trying to catch a Dex, but I couldn't see him.

"That's a rare one," said Jack the fish. "Don't find those every day."

I looked up into the darkening sky and saw myself on a starship, on my way to Empire Beach, the stars streaking past me, blurring in the infinite blackness of space. I placed my hands to the cool, smooth wall of the ship, rubbing it softly, and then everything morphed, swung around inside out, and I was sitting next to Melanie in our lounge, my hands on her large, round, naked stomach.

She was pregnant, and really, really happy about it.

"How long now?" I asked, not surprised for some reason.

She laughed, "Soon enough."

She turned her head, face to me.

She was about to say something else, but as she opened her mouth to speak the front of her face exploded and I was covered in her blood and bits of her brain and skull.

I screamed.

And screamed and screamed and screamed...

...and I came out of it on the floor of some seedy restroom, curled up in a ball and shaking violently and clawing at my face, the iron-grey light of dawn a vague promise seen through a tiny, filthy window above me.

I picked myself up off the floor, dusted off my trousers.

It was time to tell her.

I needed to tell her.

I left the club, stumbled home to the one person in the world who I knew loved me no matter what.

Melanie opened the door, eyes wet from crying.

"Where have you been?" she screamed, hitting me with her tiny hands. I had been gone for three days and three nights.

I broke down.

I was a young man, not yet twenty-one, and I'd suddenly realised I was personally responsible for more innocent deaths than I cared to remember.

She came to me, cradled me in her arms, and I cried like a baby.

I told her about Apex, I told her about my position in the organisation, about my late night missions, and what I'd done.

We lay on the couch together, my head cradled in her lap. She was silent the entire time. She never said a word, just held me, and let me speak, softly stroking my hair.

Because she loved me, and that's all she could do.

Afterwards, I stood up, walked over to the window, looking out at the rainy morning. Melanie came to stand just behind me, wrapped her arms around my waist.

I turned around, pulled her closer, kissed her for a long, long time.

God, I loved the way she smelled.

I made my decision, pulled myself together, grabbed my coat, and went to meet my mentor.

Felony's office was dark. It was always dark, even at this time of the morning.

It was eleven a.m.

He sat at his desk, going through some field reports, looked up briefly as I entered.

"Ash, what can I do for you, man?" Back to the paperwork.

"We need to talk." He stopped, looked at me.

Raised an eyebrow.

I nodded slowly, aware of Apex's policy on privacy. There was none. Senior officer or not, the room was bugged. You could bet on it.

"Problem?" he said.

"Moral dilemma," I replied, quietly.

"Over coffee?"

"Definitely."

We went to Ginty's, a coffee place in Helvetica, around the corner from our apartment. We took a seat at a cubicle by the window, the rain lashing against the windowpane, water streaking down the glass.

We ordered coffee, and I waited for it to arrive before I spoke.

It arrived, and I took a sip, thinking through what I was going to say.

"Apex," I said.

Felony nodded.

"I want out."

Felony shook his head, "I can't do it, Ash."

"What? Why the hell not?" Jesus, I was angry.

"Calm down, Ash. Take a fucking breath."

I took a breath.

Had another sip of coffee, regained my composure.

"Why can't I get out?" I asked evenly.

"Because they're watching you."

This surprised the hell out of me.

"What? Me? Why?"

"Do you remember Dr. Moore?"

"My first hit."

Felony nodded, "He was head of R&D at a research facility on Neptune: Alpha6"

"Yeah, I know."

"Alpha6 were involved with pharmaceutical research and development. medicine, which they were going to give to the Global Health Organisation for free. The EA disapproved, and sent you in to make sure this didn't happen. The drug is now available on the open market, for a price. Thousands can't afford this treatment."

"You told me in the mission brief that they were developing biological agents used for military purposes –"

"I know... That's not all. The man left behind a wife and a young daughter, a little girl called Julia –"

"Christ, Felony! Why are you telling me this?"

"Because Apex won't let you go because they think you know the truth, and now I guess you do. And they'll never let me go because I know everything they have to hide. And they can't touch either of us because I have friends, some of them ex-Black Ops, some of 'em ex-Apex, who'd like nothing better than to take out a few EA suits."

"So why don't we just walk. Let them know that if we turn up dead, so will they?" I asked.

Felony was silent.

169

"Because I've done some very bad things, Ash. And so have you."

I nodded, "I need to atone, Felony. Badly."

"You will, Ash," said Felony, "And Apex will burn."

And over the months that followed, Felony and I made plans, putting the wheels into motion. We would put together the facts, incriminate every high-ranking member who had willingly played a part in Apex's reign, and take the organisation down. Felony saw to it that I didn't receive any further assignments, sending them all to Cole, who appeared to be enjoying his job a bit too much, and slowly but surely we built enough evidence to put before the Free Press, media being the only way the bastards would really pay. The public would want to see heads roll for this, Alpha6 being one of the bigger calling cards, the proverbial ace up our sleeve.

But the plan wasn't foolproof.

We were being watched, probably from the start.

Probably even from that first conversation at Ginty's.

Apex didn't know exactly what we were doing, but they had an idea, and that was more than enough.

Things got intense, a game of cat and mouse intelligence followed, with information becoming misinformation and everyone trying to prove they were in the right.

I started spending less and less time with Melanie, as I became more and more deeply caught up in the storm that Felony and I were busily and intently whipping up.

And what's worse, the time we did spend together I was either very quiet, deep in thought on some Apex espionage, or we would argue because she didn't see me enough or because I was still disappearing in the middle of the night. I didn't tell her why. I never told her that now it was for information, meeting secretly with members of the media and K-Foundation, a group Felony was affiliated with through K, who along with a group of ex Ops people, kept a finger on the pulses of most of the corporations operating in Nu Caynan, not to mention the dealings the EA was getting involved in. Basically, K ran the corporate while Neth ran the shade.

Apex knew what we were doing, and they decided to do something about it.

It was supposed to be a warning.

Nothing more.

It was supposed to be a message: Back off from this, leave it be.

But it didn't turn out that way.

Not at all.

Fifteen

She was alone that night.

I'd left her at Ginty's, needing to be by myself, to clear my head, leaving her alone and bewildered and sad. I don't remember what we'd been arguing about, but I'm pretty sure it had been me who'd instigated it. It was probably some bullshit I'd made up, brought on by exhaustion and Apex-fuelled paranoia. I'd stormed out, leaving her sitting alone at the cubicle we always sat at, a tear rolling softly down her cheek even as I got up to go, grabbing my jacket without another word.

She'd tried to stop me, putting a hand on my arm.

Baby, don't go.

I'd pulled away, my anger blinding me. All I could see was the door, and that's exactly where I went.

She didn't call to me, made no move to go after me. At the time, I remember, that made me even angrier. I didn't think for a second that maybe she was crying, crying her beautiful, gentle eyes out. I didn't think for one fucking second that she would sit there, at the cubicle where we always sat, looking out of the window until the sun began to rise. I didn't realise what I was doing to her until Dex hit me in the face.

I washed up at his place just after sunrise, after spending most of the night drinking myself half-blind and then dropping a D/Type on top of that. I was now sobering up at a hell of a rate, but I must have looked like shit, because he'd taken one look at me, grabbed me by my jacket collar, dragged me into the lounge and thrown me on the couch.

I got up, ready to take him on, and he decked me.

I landed heavily on the couch, rubbed my jaw.

"Dex –"

"Shut up, Ash! Shut the fuck up!"

I was silent, shocked by his outburst.

He sat down on the couch opposite mine, lit me a smoke, handed it to me, then lit his own.

He took a deep drag.

I did the same.

"Ash, you're close to losing the only two people in the world who give a damn about you."

I stood up again.

"Relax, I've got it under cont –"

"Sit down! You're gonna hear this."

"Dex –"

"You're taking D\Type. You're on it. Melanie came to me three days ago. I know what you're doing, Ash."

"Dex, I'm clean! Look at me! I'm not on anything!"

Dex went silent.

"Okay, yeah, I dropped last night. But it's not a habit, man."

"Last night?"

"We had a fight."

Dex shook his head.

"You have to believe me, Dex," I said, "Felony and I are taking down Apex. How could I operate if I was hitting D\Type every night?"

Silence.

Then he nodded.

"I'll take your word on this for now –"

"Thank you –"

" – but Mel's going crazy, Ash. She thinks you're losing it. The midnight meetings, the phone calls, disappearing 'til five in the fucking morning. You've got her worried, man. And me too."

I nodded, "I know, Dex. But I've done some really bad things, for some really bad people, and this is my way of atoning. I have to finish this. I have to."

"You're not gonna lose me, Ash. But I'd worry about Melanie if I were you."

I nodded.

Dex and I talked for a while longer, easing over the wound we'd put in our friendship several months ago, healing it in our own way. And then I left, going to find Melanie and tell her what was happening. I hadn't told her because I didn't want her to worry. She thought I was already out of Apex. If I'd told her that two of us were attempting to take them down, she would've freaked out on me.

I arrived at our apartment in Helvetica just as the rain was beginning to fall, assuming she'd be home.

I rang the bell, thinking it would be the right thing to do after staying out all night.

No answer.

"Computer, open the fucking door!"

The front door slid open, **"Welcome home, Ash."**

"Thanks. Any visitors since I've been gone?'

There was a brief silence, then, **"Ash Carter at two forty-two am. Access Granted. Melanie Portman at seven twenty-three am. Access granted."**

Christ...

Oh Christ no...

I rushed through to the bedroom, noting the door was closed.

I stood there, took a breath.

174

"Open," I said, my voice little more than a whisper.

The door slid quietly open in front of me.

And there she lay on our bed.

Naked.

Hands tied to the posters behind her.

There was blood everywhere.

"No! Jesus! No!"

I scrambled over to the bed, putting my hands over the gaping wound in her neck, trying to save her. But it was way to late, the blood had already started clotting, she'd been dead for hours.

I untied her hands, removed the underwear that had been stuffed in her mouth, cradled her in my arms, rocking her back and forth, her arms falling limply down her sides.

Baby, don't go.

You can't leave me here.

Baby please don't leave me here...

Apex had given Cole the order:

Stop them digging. Scare them. Use Melanie.

Scare her, and Carter will back off. Only he went too far. He broke into our apartment using my DNA and voice-print, waited there all night until Melanie came home, alone and sad.

He'd tackled her.

Pulled her onto the bed.

Gagged her.

Tied her hands to the posts.

Ripped off her pretty blue dress.

Tearing at her clothes until she lay completely naked beneath him.

He'd caressed her soft breasts while she pulled futilely at her bonds, tears in her eyes.

He'd kissed her neck, she'd tried to pull away.

He'd slapped her. Slapped her again. And again until she bled.

And then he'd received a call.

He'd nodded, told them it was done, that she was crying. He'd got off her, grabbed his coat.

Patted her cheek.

"Ciao, babes."

Walked towards the door, leaving her bound and gagged.

He'd stopped.

And, almost as an afterthought, he'd turned back, walked up to her and casually slit her throat.

She'd struggled only slightly against her bonds as the blood left her beautiful body, a dark crimson stain spreading over the pristine white sheets she had dragged me out to buy with her.

I know it happened this way for the same reason I know it was Cole who did it: because I watched the whole thing.

A security cam hidden in one of the corners of the master bedroom had recorded everything, and I had had to watch it.

And she'd known it was there, had looked up into it even as the life left her body, her eyes saying to me words I would never forget.

I love you, baby.

Those were the last words she said to me, although the words themselves were not said. And she lay there in the silence of our room, staring into the invisible eye of a security cam she knew was there, telling me goodbye.

My last words to her had been *Fuck you.*

I held it together for Melanie's funeral, her parents not being able to look at me the entire time. Afterwards, back in the apartment, I lost it.

Went crazy and wound up eventually at SkyN some time in the early hours of the morning.

Neth was more than helpful.

I triple-dropped on D/Type that night.

And went away for a while.

Dex found me a few weeks later, dragged me out of SkyN by himself, threatening to kill Neth in front of his guards.

"If I see you again you're a dead man!" he'd roared, "A fucking dead man!"

I was only semi-sane for that, and don't ask me what happened before or after because I won't be able to tell you. In the three weeks I'd been in SkyN I'd taken so much shit I'm surprised I survived.

So Dex came in like a bat out of hell, took me out of Spire and Nu Caynan, knowing full well that I'd have killed myself on D/Type or some other shit had I stayed there.

We left town, and for nearly six months after that I was catatonic, completely out of it, dead to the world.

He took us to Tanis, got us an apartment in one of the nicer areas, and took care of me like I was an invalid (which, to all intents and purposes, I was).

Apex, in the mean time, crashed and burned.

Felony saw to that.

He executed the man who had given the order for the hit on Melanie.

The guy had cried, pleaded, sworn that Cole was only supposed to scare her.

Fel had, I'm told, nodded, said he'd believed him.

And then promptly shot him in the face.

The rest of the organisation went down in flames with the information Felony and I had gathered together.

We got away with a Corporate Commendation.

The Press loved that. They called us the People's Heroes.

Everyone else burned for their sins in Apex.

Everyone except Cole, who, by that stage, was already too big a player in the Nu Caynan underground to touch. He had had enough protection around him directly after the fall of Apex to invade a small country, and it didn't take the bastard long to manoeuvre himself into a position where he rivalled Neth in the Nu Caynan underground.

Even the K-Foundation couldn't touch him.

It took me two years, with Dex's constant help and support, to build myself up again. I wasn't fine.

Far from fine.

But I was okay.

Dex and I had our names and documents changed courtesy of Dante. We opened a detective agency, which we ran from Tanis, and for two years I lived with peace of mind in the belief that Cole was dead. That it was over.

Until one evening I happened to spot a news report featuring the new head of the Streiger Gang, one of the biggest gangs in Nu Caynan at the time, while I was in Shillian.

The guy's name was Forbes.

But I knew better.

The realisation hit me like a brick wall.

And I knew what I had to do.

I returned to Nu Caynan, planning to finish what he started. I killed Cole in cold blood in a cocktail bar on the two hundred and fiftieth floor of the NeuroLOG building exactly two years to the day after he murdered my Melanie, and fell through the window, not really caring whether I lived or died.

But someone had.

I'd called Dex from the hotel in Shillian, told him I'd seen Cole on TV.

Told him I was going to kill him.

He'd asked me to wait until he got there.

I'd said okay.

I didn't.

Not for one fucking minute.

I sped out of Shillian that night with no thought for the storms that ravage the wasteland that makes up the inner country.

Dex must've known I wasn't going to wait, because my old friend took a jet from Tanis and got to Nu Caynan before I did, putting a trace on my mobile as soon as I arrived, following me in a rented hov as I moved through the skyways of Nu Caynan toward my arranged meeting with Cole, hovering outside in the rainy night as I spoke with him in the NeuroLOG bar, his guns trained on Cole's henchmen, ready to start firing around me as soon as was needed.

It was needed...

But I don't think he expected me to go flying through the window in a hail of bullets and glass, plummeting down into the darkness and the rain.

He floored it, brought the top down (luck or destiny that he'd hired a convertible?) and connected with me somewhere around the hundredth floor, catching my head on the bonnet before the rest of me.

We returned to Tanis, and I continued my life as Ash Corben, and things were good for quite a number of years, right up until some old bastard came to my door and gave me an offer I couldn't refuse.

Sixteen

People play games.

We just do.

Sometimes we do it on purpose, trying to gain the upper hand, trying to gain some kind of advantage over someone. Maybe it's someone you just met, and you don't want them to know how much you like them. Or maybe you're already together, and you're afraid if you give too much, they'll somehow lose respect for you, maybe stop loving you.

And sometimes we don't even know we're doing it, have no idea how much we're destroying even as we try to build it up.

Don't tell everything.

Don't show yourself completely.

Open up, but not all they way.

Hold back a bit, just enough.

Keep them guessing.

And never, never say I love you until it's safe.

But it's never safe. And one day you meet someone who knows you better than you know yourself, and you know there's something special there even though you just met, and all of that bullshit goes out the fucking window and you remember what it feels like to be alive.

For a while.

Because nothing lasts forever.

After a while, something changes, and one will feel more than the other, and the games start, and we say things to hurt each other, and we do things we shouldn't be doing just to get the upper fucking hand.

Humans are like that, always fucking things up. Build them up to see them fall, and it's truly amazing how much easier it is to destroy something than it is to create it.

But sometimes you find something different.

Something beautiful.

No games, no advantage, no well-aimed blows and no upper hand. Sometimes that's all you ever wanted.

And then some stupid evil son of a bitch comes and takes it all away.

Seventeen

Shillian was deserted.

Or what had been Shillian at some stage, anyway.

There was no sign of anyone besides myself, Rainer and Mitchell among the grassy meadows, hillsides, fragments of forests, looming half-buildings and skyways that ended in the middle of nowhere.

The NeuroLOG jet had crash-landed in a large field, hurtling through the trees on its edge and ploughing through the grass before coming to rest near a grove of pines beside a stream. The three of us had emerged from the wreck wired and out-of-it, with a few nicks and cuts, but otherwise pretty much unscathed. James, sadly, had died from massive trauma to the head after struggling to bring us down safely.

We buried the pilots in silence in the grove of pines.

None of us knew any 'official' prayers, so afterwards we each said a brief eulogy praising their bravery and flying skills.

Then I used the jacketcom2.0 to call through to Felony.

There was no signal.

Rainer glanced at the screen on my sleeve.

"Shit," he murmured.

I pointed to a building about a kilometre from where we stood.

"Maybe from higher up?" I said, thinking that whatever was happening was probably affecting the signal, and if we could get to a 'normal' position, we'd probably have a better chance.

Rainer and Mitchell agreed.

We made our way across the field to the building, looking above and around us for any sign of human life.

Nothing.

Not even another giant bird.

The air was hazy, almost seeming to shimmer, and a soft breeze brushed gently against my face. Not cold, but fresh.

I looked up. The sun was shining, hazy clouds occasionally wafting across its face.

It wasn't raining!

In fact, it felt like a perfect Spring morning.

"This is all very strange," Rainer muttered to himself.

I had to agree.

We stopped when we came to an open patch of concrete, about twelve foot squared, upon which stood a shiny red convertible hov.

I jumped into the front seat and was surprised when I didn't hear a snooty little computer voice telling me I was in the wrong hovcar. I reached under the dashboard, ripping out the appropriate wires, trying to hot-wire the thing.

Nothing. No sparks.

No power.

The thing was a dead weight.

We moved along, coming to another hov. This one was the same, no power. Although on closer inspection we discovered that it was, in fact, missing most of its back end and where the tail should have been was in fact the trunk of a very large tree. I glanced off to my left, staring closely at a few hovs parked together near another building, watching to see if anything would happen, wondering if maybe they'd transform into a couple of huskies and a German Shepard and would bound off on some great adventure.

This didn't happen. For now, at least, whatever was happening to this place seemed to have stopped, leaving all of Shillian's electrical systems fried and its geography fucked.

Well, it looked like any journey we were going to undertake would be, at least for the time being, on foot.

We reached the building, and I walked over to the entrance, checking the jacketcom2.0's screen until the words **signal acquired** appeared. I dialed through to Felony's mobile number.

This time it rang.

Felony picked up, "Ash! You there yet?"

"Yeah. Listen, there's something very weird happening here. The place is deserted."

"What? The airport?"

"Er, no. Shillian, by the look of things"

Felony's look said it all.

"Man, have you taken your medication today?"

I told him briefly about the changes we all saw, about the bird and the crash and the stark contrast between what remained of Shillian and the strange greenness that had sprung out of nowhere around and within the city.

While I spoke I looked through glass doors at the entrance, raised an eyebrow. I moved up to the building wall, walked around the corner, along the wall, until I found what I was looking for. The building wall melded seamlessly with a wall of rock and moss that made up the base of another fragment of mountainside.

"Where do you want to meet?" Felony asked.

"I'm not sure how safe Shillian is right now," I said softly, my hand running across the point where the two worlds met, "I don't think it's very stable at the moment. Don't even know how long the signal's going to last"

Fel nodded, "Cool, then where?"

It hit me. Shillian Airport was close enough from here, two hours' walk at the most. Rainer would just have to keep up.

"Shillian Airport has its own gateway. We're going to head out in that direction, get the hell out of the city, travel along the highway. It's the closest gate from our current position, so it shouldn't take too long. Fel, for chrissakes don't enter the city gates," I said, "If we're not on the road from Shillian when you get close then we will be eventually. Stop as soon as things get weird on your side."

"I'd rather come in and get you –"

"No! You guys have to keep safe. I'll see you in a few hours."

He nodded slowly, "Define 'weird'."

"You'll know it when you see it."

I ended the call, walked back to where Mitchell and Rainer stood looking out at the strange, deserted city.

"What's the plan?" Rainer asked, more than a bit of tension in his voice.

"From here we walk to Shillian Airport, or where it used to be, anyway. Then we exit through the city Gate on that side and meet up with Felony and Sarah on the road.

"How far is your man from Shillian?" Mitchell asked.

"About nine hours from here. But he'll be moving much faster now, I think."

"That's a lot of footwork for an old man –"

"You'll be fine –" I started to tell Rainer.

"*Fine*? *You'll* be fine, Mister Corben. You'll have to keep up with *me*, however!"

I grinned.

"Very well then. Shall we?"

"Let's get to it," Mitchell said.

Rainer gave me a wink.

We hit the road.

It was the strangest walk I had ever taken.

The city was outlandishly beautiful.

Very occasionally we spotted one of those giant brown birds, like the one that brought down the NeuroLOG jet, flapping lazily in the sky.

The buildings (or in many cases fragments of buildings) soared up into the sky all around us, while city streets stretched off into the distance, only to end at the edge of a grassy field or a cluster of trees. I looked into the windows of some of the buildings as we passed them, trying to see if there were any people (even dead ones) inside.

No-one.

"Not a soul," Mitchell remarked, as we beat our way through a particularly dense area of foliage.

It was as if everyone in Shillian had just suddenly upped and left.

We came eventually to the place where the airport used to be. It was quite a sight, a rolling green meadow stretched out before us, a giant wall to our left running from way behind only to stop at the grass, disappear for a few kilometres, and reappear further down the way.

We walked out onto the meadow and towards the huge break in the wall, towards where I thought the entrance would have been.

The sun was sinking lower and lower in the sky, and by the time we reached the left edge of the giant city Wall, it was hitting the distant horizon.

Sunset was breathtaking.

And bizarre beyond comparison.

The sky lit up like fire, the hazy clouds going from white to orange, orange to pink, and pink to the deepest, deepest red, as the sun dipped below the distant horizon.

We briefly caught sight of a small flock of the brown birds as they passed across the glowing red sky, but they disappeared after about thirty seconds, probably going back where they came from.

And then, off in the distance, I saw it.

"The road!" I said, pointing.

"Where?" Rainer asked.

"Follow my finger."

Rainer strained to see, "Yes! Good, let's go."

Jesus, for an old guy he really *did* have a lot of energy.

We walked on quickly, making our way towards the distant highway in the gathering dark.

We'd made good time since setting off from the crash site, and we would have gotten to the road a lot quicker if we hadn't suddenly been attacked by a gang of marauding psychotic mutants.

It was dark now, the only source of light coming from the beam of Mitchell's glOlite, helping us negotiate the uneven terrain between here and the vague and indistinct orange radiance of the street lamps of the highway ahead.

I heard a sound to my right.

Stopped.

"Hold," I said, quietly.

The other two stopped.

"What's wrong?" Mitchell asked, barely more than a whisper.

He'd obviously received military training as well, because something about his stance in the darkness told me he was on full alert.

"Company," I replied softly, drawing my guns.

He did the same, pulling two guns from shoulder holsters.

I grinned, gesturing to his guns, "I like your style."

"You too."

And then they were on top of us.

Seven or eight of them.

Surrounding us.

"Who the fuck are you?" I asked nicely, levelling my guns at head-level, not really having a lot of time for people who make their appearance in pitch blackness in the middle of nowhere without a sound.

They didn't reply, just circled slowly around us.

One of them behind me muttered something. I couldn't make it out.

Another one, opposite him and circling past me, replied. The second appeared to have only one arm, but I couldn't be sure.

"You have three seconds to speak or go away. If you don't comply, we shoot," Mitchell said, his voice strong and assured.

"One," I said, evenly.

"Two," Mitchell said.

"Thr —" I began.

One of the circling psychos let rip on a chainsaw he'd been holding, revving it over and over, a manic grin on his face illuminated by two small lights that protruded from his neck, making him look like the world's ugliest disco queen.

"Hell with this," I said, and shot the guy in the face.

He hit the ground, one hand reflexively clutching at the grass, his feet kicking and thrashing out wildly as his blood flowed out of his body and onto the ground. The chainsaw spun away doing crazy somersaults, finally coming to rest some distance away.

Mitchell started firing into the gang. He dropped two before one jumped him from behind, forcing him to the ground. I glanced around for Rainer, hoping he wasn't dead yet. He appeared to have one of them in a choke-hold.

188

I could not get over this guy.

The remaining two closed in on me, one brandishing a long curved sword, swinging it at my face. I jumped back, barely avoiding the tip of the blade.

As he came closer, I realised it wasn't a sword. It was his entire forearm. Someone had soldered a piece of sharpened steel to the elbow joint, and done a pretty shoddy job of it at that. You could see the rust patches even in this light.

I shot him in the chest, and he dropped like a rock.

"Everyone alive?" I called to my comrades as the second of the two moved in on me, swinging a ball on a rusty chain.

A grunt from Mitchell, as he struggled with one of the mutants, rolling around on the ground.

"Quite alright, thank you," Rainer replied before snapping his guy's neck with one sharp, swift movement.

This guy was really something.

I ducked as the ball flew over my head, came up a split-second later and shot him in the head.

The bullet glanced off the guy's cheekbone.

He grinned.

I could clearly make out the glint of steel beneath the freak's skin.

"Ugly," I said.

He laughed.

Good.

A sense of humour was an important thing.

"Okay, pretty boy. Let's try that again –" I brought up my guns, shooting him in the knees, and a split-second later they were smacked out of my hands as an iron pole swung up out of the darkness, knocking the guns up into the air.

A roar sounded from my right, and a massive weight collided with me a second later. We collapsed in a heap on the ground. Pretty Boy's insane laughter sounded again.

The guy was beginning to irritate me.

The thing on top of me smelt really bad, but I didn't really have time to worry about that, what with being choked with a fat metal pipe.

Its mouth was open as it tried to force the life out me, its rotten teeth clenched, it's breathing heavy, harsh. I stared up into its ugly, stupid, uncomprehending eyes, attempting to say 'Go to hell' with my own. I wasn't going to show it any fear. Besides, I wasn't afraid. Not at all. I was mildly irritated that I was going out like this, instead of while humping some gorgeous blonde at the age of ninety-eight.

But I wasn't afraid.

It occurred to me as I began to pass out that none of these circus freaks had in fact *said* anything intelligible since this confrontation began. Not a word. Well, there'd been the grunt, and the reply to the grunt, but I refused to consider that a language.

And they didn't seem to have any firepower either, which made my current situation more or less inexcusable.

The world, dark as it was, began to fade around me. Pretty Boy's laughter sounding further and further away from me. I could feel someone pulling at the giant weight on top of me, but it was useless

I started to lose consciousness.

I'm coming baby.

It got darker.

Darker.

Complete blackness enveloped me.

The last thing I heard was the harsh breathing of the thing on top of me. Harsh and steady and hot against my face.

At least, I thought, the laughing has stopped.

.

I awoke with a start.

My right cheek was stinging. Rainer and Mitchell were staring down at me intently.

"Did someone just slap me?" I asked, rubbing my cheek, attempting to sit up, collapsing back down with a grimace.

"I'm afraid that would be me," Rainer said.

"Be thankful he didn't have to give you the kiss of life," Mitchell said.

This was true.

I took a few deep breaths, tried to sit up again, succeeded this time.

"How long have I been out for?" I asked, tenderly touching my throat.

"A few minutes. You lost consciousness, but you didn't flat line," Mitchell said.

I nodded, came slowly to my feet with Mitchell's help.

I looked around us, dead mutants lay all around.

"Who were they?"

Mitchell kicked the one closest to him, who turned out to be Pretty Boy.

"I have no idea... freaks, all of them," He replied, disgust in his voice. "That one over there has three eyes. The one next to it has a steel blade coming out of his forehead. That's one guy I wouldn't want to head-butt me... "

"Vicious bunch," Rainer muttered.

"Any still alive?" I asked.

Mitchell nodded, "Yeah, the one you shot in the knees. I knocked him out. We had to kill the one who was strangling you to get him off of you," Rainer said, offering me a smoke.

191

I accepted it gratefully. Mitchell lit it for me, and I took a long, deep pull, releasing the smoke from my lungs into the chill night air.

"What say after the smoke we wake him up?" I said.

"Excellent idea," Rainer replied, grinning.

"Let's tie the bastard up first," Mitchell said.

I nodded.

Mitchell tied him up while Rainer and I finished our smokes, then I kicked Pretty Boy in his head until he woke up.

He peered up at us with eyes full of a leering smugness.

"Who are you?" I asked, quietly.

No reply. His head moved in jerky movements, looking at one of us, then another.

"Okay, where are you from?"

Again, no reply.

I shook my head, handed the interrogations over to Mitchell and Rainer, and went off to find my guns. I heard low-pitched screaming come from behind me as I searched, and decided not to go and see what Mitchell was doing.

The guns weren't far from where I'd fallen, and I dusted them off, checked them and replaced them in my shoulder holsters before sitting on a rock and lighting up another smoke. I checked the time, realised we still had a while before Felony and Sarah rocked up, and decided it would be a good idea to put as much distance between ourselves and the city of Shillian as possible.

After my smoke, I returned to the others, who had gotten exactly nothing out of Pretty Boy. Mitchell had settled for putting a bullet in his head, another in the head of the thing that had tried to strangle me.

I thought that was a bit harsh, but they *had* tried to kill me, so I couldn't really complain.

His reasoning was pretty straightforward when relating to the Thing that was already dead: "It has two arms and two legs. But I'll be damned if it's human. Best to be safe rather than sorry"

I was inclined to agree with him.

My thoughts strayed back to House9, and the thing that had attacked me.

That, too, had been far from human.

We gathered together the bodies, piled them up, and set fire to them, turning away as the heat became intense and the burning flesh began to smell.

It was time to go, the highway beckoning to us with its soft orange glow.

I looked out towards the city as we walked, black buildings and towering mountain fragments soaring up into a blacker sky.

Something was wrong with the world.

Very wrong.

And I had the sneaking suspicion that, for some reason, I was the one who was going to have to fix it.

Eighteen

The highway was dark and cold, stretching ahead of us into endless night, the warm glow of the streetlights having fallen away hours before as we left the limits of the city of Shillian far behind us.

Kind of reminded me of some place I'd been before.

A wind had sprung up at some stage in the evening, an icy wind that seemed to blow right through us. We walked on for hours, putting ground between ourselves and the city behind us until, at last, Felony rocked up, screaming down the road like a bat out of hell, missing us completely and sliding to a halt somewhere behind us.

"Looks like our ride's here," I said.

"Thank God," Rainer said through chattering teeth.

Felony's black hov sedan pulled up beside us, and the back door slid open, a dim light shining out.

"Need a ride?"

I grinned, getting in, "Hey Fel."

"Evenin'."

Rainer and Mitchell climbed in after me.

Sarah gripped me in a tight embrace as soon as I opened my mouth to greet her. When I eventually untangled myself from her, I made the introductions, and asked her how she was faring.

"I'll be better when all of this is over," she replied tiredly.

"Soon enough, young lady," Rainer said kindly, "soon enough."

I nodded my agreement.

"Where to, Ash? Wanna hit the Palace for a while?" Fel said, putting the hov into first and pulling away from the side of the road.

I thought about it, fighting the temptation to check out Sandy Island, which wasn't far from where we were. There was nothing we could do until Mason made contact with us, anyway.

"If I may?" Rainer interjected.

. "Yeah?" I said.

"NeuroLOG has offices in Tora Sera. And a jet, of course. San Marin doesn't even have an airport and Tanis is way too far away. I say we head for Tora Sera and wait for Mason to make contact."

I nodded, "Alright, Tora Sera it is," I paused, "Fel, you see the news lately?"

"Yeah, the little girls?"

I nodded.

"Harsh one, man. Connected to all this, obviously."

"Yep. I think so."

Felony shook his head, "Things are getting way out of control."

"You could say that," Mitchell agreed.

The hov sped off into the night, following the highway along the coast in the opposite direction from Tanis, going through San Marin without stopping, the rain catching us as we moved further and further from the strangeness that was Shillian.

We were silent for the most part, everyone in their own world. I fell asleep after a time, having had very little sleep since the episode at House9.

We came eventually to a highway roadside motel, where we decided to stop for the night, booking into two double rooms. Me, Sarah and Felony in one (with me on the couch, of course) and Rainer and Mitchell in the other. I can't speak for the others, but I slept like a baby that night.

195

The following morning I was the first to rise, awake as the sun began it's slow ascent into the sky. I went into the motel diner, had a seat at a cubicle by the window, and stared out at the ocean and the morning sun.

The waitress who came to my table was quite something.

"Get you some coffee, hon?"

She was the usual highway truck stop type, close on fifty, broad at the hips and sagging at the chest. Wearing clothes from a time when the fashion police must have been disbanded. Showing more cleavage than leg (and pulling off neither), she had made it clear on booking us in the previous night that other services were available here at Cammy's. I had passed, opting rather for a vodka and some rest as opposed to a night of dubious sexual positions with the Venus of Seaworld.

I looked at her, pulled reluctantly from my mesmerized state.

"You want coffee or what?" she said. "I ain't got all day"

I got the feeling she was pissed about the missed opportunities of the night before, not that I gave much of a damn.

"Yeah."

She poured me a searing cup of rather scary smelling brown liquid. Maybe I'm wrong, but coffee isn't supposed to go gloop. Sarah joined me at the table a few minutes later, ordering a coffee as she took a seat across from me..

"Good morning," I said.

"My self-appointed protector. How did you sleep?"

"I slept."

She nodded, "Yeah, sounds about right."

We were quiet for a bit.

"You know," she said, gesturing to the cigarette in my hand," those things will kill you."

"They can stand in line."

196

Fel, Rainer and Mitchell joined us a few minutes later.

We ordered breakfast, which turned out to be an incredibly greasy plate of sausages, eggs, bacon and fried onions and tomatoes. The waitress glared briefly at Sarah as she served the food, then enquired icily from me if we required anything else.

"No."

She left us to eat.

"Charming woman," Rainer said dryly, pushing a piece of sausage around the plate with a fork.

"How far is it from here to Tora Sera?" Sarah asked, not bothering with her breakfast, having a sip of the highly dubious coffee instead and regretting it immediately afterwards.

"About five hundred kilometres from here," Mitchell said, through a mouthful of food.

"Good, then we'll be there in time for lunch," Rainer said, putting down his fork without having had a bite to eat.

We finished up, and I asked Venus for the bill. She took her time, eventually bringing it and placing it on the table.

We paid and left.

Tora Sera.

My number one favourite place on the Planet.

White beaches, tanned blondes, crystal waters and all that.

The city looks like a holiday resort, only a lot bigger. Ridiculously tall, high rise skyscrapers tapering off lazily down the coast. In fact, the entire stretch of it is built solely along the beaches and the citizens of Tora Sera pride themselves on the knowledge that the ocean is *always* no more than five minutes from your room, even if you live on the top floor of the last building from the beach. The city was built on an incredibly steep hill, and the only way to avoid building back down the *other* side of the hill (the side *without* a view, in other words) was to start building up pretty early on, while cities like Nu Caynan and Shillian were still expanding horizontally.

For this reason Tora Sera boasts the second highest buildings on the East Coast (Shillian being the first), and the fourth highest on the Planet, next to Nu Caynan and Shillian (MegaCities that had to catch up eventually) and Kai'San
(this last because of one building in particular: The Kai'San Rising Sun, the biggest hotel on the Planet, and pretty damn impressive at that). Also, for some obscure reason, Tora Sera seemed to suffer from Perfect Weather. Half the year was summer, the other half an intense and concentrated variety of Spring, Autumn and Winter, all of which were extremely pleasant for their own reasons.

The place was the closest to paradise I've found on this planet. Only Empire Beach can really even compete.

NeuroLOG had a building here, naturally, and it was across the road from the beach. The place was a hotel, no doubt every executive in NeuroLOG having brought a mistress around at some stage or another (a nice place where they could play while they were out of town) but for the right amount of money it was open to the public as well, which made it not entirely secure, but a step up from the roadside motels, at any rate.

Rainer had been right. We arrived in Tora Sera at around one, just in time for lunch, and after booking into the executive suites – each getting our own room –
and freshening up, we met at the restaurant on the one hundredth floor for lunch. It was quite something; Rainer was a Big Cat in the NeuroLOG corporation, second only to Trevor Mason, and everyone who approached *any* member of our group did so with such reverence that I was beginning to feel like a star or a perhaps even a

member of royalty. And our waiter at lunch, as professional as he was, was obviously nervous as hell. The guy was a wreck.

I mentioned it to Rainer.

"Really? I hadn't noticed," he replied innocently.

He'd noticed, alright.

And he was enjoying it.

Oh well, I thought, why not? The guy's worked hard to be where he is. Might as well bask in it a bit. I hadn't really figured Rainer as much of a celebrity type, but I guess it just goes to show.

After lunch, everyone went off on their own, arranging to meet back for dinner at seven. I took the opportunity to take Sarah for a walk on the beach, to unwind a bit, take in the cool ocean breeze, watch the waves breaking lazily on the shore.

It would have been a lot more relaxing if we hadn't bumped into Tommy Slid.

"Ash fucking Corben!"

I turned, just in time to see the slickest bastard you can imagine throw an arm around my neck, pull me forward and kiss me on the head. He was about my height –just under six foot – dark glasses, skin tanned a golden brown, dressed in tan slacks and an open white shirt, showing off a few gold chains and a ridiculously smooth chest.

"Tommy Slid, how ya been?" I said, disentangling myself from him.

He flashed me a grin, "As you see me, man." His attention drifted over to Sarah, who I have to admit was looking gorgeous in a flowing cream dress. "And who is this lovely young thing?"

"This is Sarah. Sarah, this is Tom –"

Tommy Slid's hand shot out like a snake, "Tommy Slid. Direc-tor." He kissed her hand in a way he obviously felt was incredibly suave, "A pleasure."

"Oh my! Tommy Slid!" Sarah said, batting her eyelids, "I've seen all your films!"

"Really?"

"No."

Tommy flashed another of his grins, "A difficult woman. I see nothing's changed, Ash."

"What can I say?."

Sarah punched my arm.

A six-foot tall platinum blonde in a black bikini came and stood beside Tommy.

"Ash, Sarah. This is Mercury Red."

We said hello.

"Why don't you ladies go on ahead? Ash and I need to catch up," Tommy said, earning himself further Asshole Male Points in Sarah's book. She agreed, though, and she and Mercury went off down the beach. I think she was happy to have some female company, having spent so much time recently in the company of men, even incredibly handsome and charming men like myself.

Tommy watched them go, "She's nice."

"We're not together."

Raised eyebrow, "Is that so?"

I decided to change the subject before it went any further, "How's your new picture doing?"

Tommy rolled his eyes, "Don't ask. Sets keep fuckin' out because of the weather, I've got the Net Actors Guild on my case, some company wants to stick Terrain ReGens down and build some fuckin' *condos*, and Mercury is demanding a pay increase because she's going to die at the end."

"I can understand that."

"Well, *yeah*, but it's not like she's going to be able to *spend* it or anything."

I nodded, "This is true."

Tommy kicked at some white sand, accidentally catching a small child in the face. The child started screaming.

"Shut up, you little bastard," Tommy said under his breath, going over to the child and attempting to bribe him with money.

"Hey man, who the hell do you think you are?" yelled a big ugly man, obviously the little boy's father, coming over, pushing Tommy away and putting his arms around the child, "You kick sand at my kid, now you propositioning him? What kind of sick, twisted –"

Tommy removed his sunglasses.

"Shit! Tommy Slid! Damn! I love you, man!" The guy said, letting go of the kid and coming over to shake Tommy's hand.

"Yeah, hi. Sorry 'bout your kid. Accident –"

"Whatever, man. Little bastard had it coming. Can I have your autograph?"

Tommy complied, signing the guy's towel with flair, and we moved on.

"Christ, children are so stupid I'm surprised any of them make it to adulthood," he said.

I didn't say anything.

"Oh yeah! And that's not the worst of it!" Tommy said.

"Yeah?"

"My ex-bitch wants a percentage of the profits for *Pros and Cons*! Says she's the original creative driving force behind it. Says it's based on her character and she wants half of everything I earn from it!"

"What did you say?" I asked, quite taken with that.

"What do you think? I told where she could put it."

I nodded, "Good man."

We walked on, catching up. Next to Dex and Felony, Tommy was one of the few people I got on with naturally, and it was good to unwind for a change, considering the madness that comprised my life at the moment. We talked briefly about our respective exes, and Tommy was shocked to hear of Sharyn's death.

"Who was it?" he asked.

"I'm working on it."

He adjusted his sunglasses, "When you find out, let me know."

"I will."

The women joined us shortly after, and we went up to Tommy's hotel room for a drink.

He had the penthouse at a hotel called The Sera Winds, probably the best hotel in Tora Sera. We walked in, Tommy going straight to the bar and offering us a seat in the expansive lounge area by the balcony. Sarah and I did, and I noticed the lawn and pool outside as Mercury walked right through the lounge, onto the patio and dived into the pool.

Sarah let out a girlish squeal when she saw the pool, and, having changed from her beautiful dress to a sexy little number, ran out to dive-bomb into the cool water, popping up next to Mercury a few seconds later.

"Nice place," I said to Tommy.

He flashed me a grin, "Thanks," he gestured to the women, "they seem to think so."

He finished making the drinks, brought over my vodka and had a seat beside me, sitting back and putting his feet on the coffee table with a long sigh.

"Ash."

"Yeah?"

"I think I might be burning out, man."

"Crap."

He was silent for a bit, then, "It's Sandy Island; it's the strangest thing."

He leaned toward me.

"Maybe I'm losing it, but I can't remember ever hearing about the place until I started scouting for locations not two weeks ago. I've lived on the East Coast my entire life and I've never heard of Sandy Island before then."

I nodded, "Neither had I."

"In the beginning, when I first heard of the place, I was like 'Yeah! Sandy fuckin' Island. Why didn't I think of it before?' But, since I've been on location there, I started wondering what the hell I'd been thinking. I swear, I could almost *remember* going there as a kid with my folks. But when I tried to delve into it, to really *get in there*, the memories just kind of slipped away."

He took a sip of his drink, an insanely coloured cocktail with so many umbrellas and toys and shit in it I found myself wondering how much room there was in there for the actual alcohol.

"There is something severely wrong with that island, Ash."

I agreed, deciding to hold back on all that had happened since Rainer came to my door. The state of Shillian, alone, was enough to get the guy worried, "Just keep your head, Tom. Keep it together."

Tommy downed his drink, went over to the bar.

"Another vodka?"

"Er, no. Got dinner at six with, well, my employer."

Tommy's interest was sparked, "Really, who?"

"You know I can't tell you that, Tom."

"Yeah, policy, I know," Tommy said, "So who is it?"

"Trevor Mason."

"Shit, you're kidding! The head of NeuroLOG?"

"Yeah."

"Why? What's his problem?"

"Long story."

Tommy grinned, "They always are."

We chatted a bit longer, the women coming in from the pool to join us, and all talk on the nature of Sandy Island was dropped. This place, the people, were exactly what I needed right then, after all that had happened. The strangeness. The violence. The deaths. Yeah, if there was one place I really needed to be right now, it was Tora Sera.

Sarah and I resolved to get drunk and miss dinner with the others. I called through to Rainer, told him we were occupied for the evening.

He grinned, "Enjoy it, Ash. To be honest, I don't know when next you will have the opportunity."

"Thanks."

I ended the call, and Tommy, Mercury, Sarah and myself proceeded to get completely smashed, and it was only much later in the evening that I realised that that was the first time Rainer had ever called me by my first name.

Nineteen

I'm standing on a hill overlooking the many fires of a large encampment at dusk. Two men stand beside me, one on either side of me. They're friends, trusted above all others in this time of chaos. The one to my left turns to me.

The winds of change blow with strength.

I look at him **I feel it too.**

Time is running out.

I nod.

He looks up into the pitch black sky **Even the stars have forsaken us.**

Silence, as all three of us stare out at the desert night, seeking a sign, perhaps, of the coming storm.

I look down, across the encampment. People sit around camp fires, their worn faces bathed in the soft light of flames, some talking quietly, others alone, just staring into the flames, and then I spot her. All alone, holding herself, rocking gently from side to side. Her raven black hair glinting in the glow, her skin like silk, eyes far away from this place. She looks up, across the encampment, directly at me.

Our eyes meet.

I can't seem to pull mine from her.

She knows something *This from the one to my right.*

I turn to look at him, partly grateful to break contact with the strange angel below.

Her eyes don't leave you *He whispers, staring intently below.*

If only she could speak *I reply.*

He nods his agreement.

She is... very familiar to me. *I say*

She seems to feel the same way.

205

I shake my head. *I don't have time to hold her counsel, there is something I must do.*

You're leaving then?

I nod *In the morning.*

You continue your search?

Yes.

Are you sure she is in this place? he says. *The one you search for?*

The one I search for is one you once knew, I say *One you once called a friend, before all this strangeness.*

He does not reply.

It is useless. It is as if she never existed. No-one remembers her, not even her closest friends.

Rumours are circling around the camp.

What rumours?

He clears his throat, *They are saying you have gone mad.*

I laugh dryly.

So it's not true then? I say

I never said that.

Look around you. The world is changing. Open your eyes

Silence as we survey the camp below.

My eyes find her again. She no longer watches me, just stares into the flames with the same gentle, slow rocking motion.

Watching her now.

Openly.

Her face. I know we have spoken before, I seem to vaguely remember her voice, and rain, and grasslands stretching to the distant horizon.

Perhaps in another place.

Another life.

A dream, perhaps.

Dawn breaks over the desert.

I'm packing, readying myself for the long road ahead.

She comes into my tent, sits by the embers of my dying fire, hugging herself the way she does.

I look at her, surprised.

Hello, *I say, continuing to pack.*

I look up briefly.

She smiles.

You should be resting, *I remark.*

The camps can be a harsh place for a woman, especially one so young. But with most of the cities being what they are, no one really has a choice anymore.

The nomadic way seems, at the moment, to be the only way.

I finish up, shoulder my bag. **Time to go**

I move past her, and she grabs my arm, pulling me towards her and putting a small package in my coat pocket.

I say nothing, surprised into silence.

She smiles again, then she is up and gone as suddenly as she arrived, disappearing into the twilight desert outside.

I pull out the parcel. There's a note on it, tied to the string wrapped around the brown leaf paper.

Not until you have reached the highway, it reads.

Replace it in my coat pocket.

So be it.

I step out into the cool morning air.

Take a deep breath.

Exhale.

The highway lies out towards the rising sun. You can't see it from the camp but it's there. I make my way out of the camp and towards it alone, picking my way around dying fires and tents and bodies in blankets, huddled and bunched around the warm, dying embers.

I have to find her.

I can't lose her again.

Twenty

The call came early the following afternoon, as Rainer, Mitchell, Felony, Sarah and myself were finishing lunch at the hotel restaurant.

Mason wanted to know of our progress, and something in the way Rainer replied made me wonder exactly how far away the guy was, exactly how far we needed to travel to get to him.

They arranged the transport, and Rainer hung up.

Mason hadn't seemed to be too perturbed about the loss of his jet. There were probably more where that came from.

"Where are we going?" I asked Rainer.

He looked at me, but didn't reply.

"Jesus, come on man," Felony barked. "You can tell us where the hell we're going, it's the least you can do."

He was silent a short while longer.

"Ciegan's End. Antarctica."

A beat.

"What?" I said.

Rainer nodded, "We're going to Ciegan's End, Mister Corben."

"I thought the habitat was, how did you put it, 'blown off the face of the Earth'," I said, feeling a bit screwed-with all of a sudden.

Rainer nodded.

"Sooo...Where, exactly, in Ciegan's End would we be going?" I asked, getting more irritable by the second.

Rainer cleared his throat, "Mister Corben, please calm down. The habitat was destroyed. I give you my word on that. I have seen the documents myself. Ciegan's End seems to be the site of some very strange natural phenomena. Incredible and almost too numerous to mention. It has been a source of great interest for Mister Mason and NeuroLOG scientists. He is there because of that interest, and because he wished to inspect what remained of the site of the habitat. He is something of an historian."

"And Sarah's part –"

"Historical. Believe me, Mister Corben, there is nothing to worry about. We are offering you the protection of the NeuroLog Corporation. That is all. Believe me, we have more to lose from this than you do."

The guy made a good point.

I nodded, "Okay. But if things get weird, I take Sarah and go."

Rainer let out a dry laugh, "It's a deal."

"Even if we have to swim back," I added.

"I don't think it will come to that."

I didn't reply.

He wiped his mouth with a serviette, stood.

"Lady and gentlemen," he said, "we have a jet to catch."

He smiled, and promptly left the table.

Felony and I exchanged looks.

"Why do I have a funny feeling about this?" he said.

I nodded my agreement.

The NeuroLOG hovship was impressive.

It was huge, just hovering above the water in the twilight in Steiner Harbour, a corporate harbour about a thousand kilometres up from Tora Sera where a number of companies kept their larger seafaring vessels. It was shaped like a flattened out bullet, turbines on either side extended outwards on thick steel 'wings'. The words

EAV NeuroLOG Crusader were emblazoned on its hull, lit up now as the last of the day's light faded away.

This, I thought with a sinking feeling, would be our home for the next four weeks.

We were originally scheduled to take a hovship from Shillian, but since that obviously wasn't going to happen, Rainer had called ahead immediately after lunch and secured the *Crusader*, then booked the jet for five p.m., allowing us time to do a bit of shopping before leaving Tora Sera for Steiner Harbour. Clothes, toiletries, that kind of thing. You had to be prepared for a journey like this, four weeks in the same pair of pants wasn't really something worth considering.

Felony came to stand beside me.

"Home sweet home," he remarked dryly.

"It's going to be a long trip," I replied.

He moved his bags over to his other shoulder.

"Shall we?" I said, gesturing towards the gangway.

"By all means."

We boarded, found our cabins, and settled in. Shortly after, there was the deep rumble of turbines as the hovship powered up, pulled out of the harbour and started the long journey to Ciegan's End.

The cabins were comfortable, spacious even, the beds decent and each cabin had its own bathroom, kitchenette and bar area. The benefits of travelling on a Corporate Vessel. If the *Crusader* had been a scientific hovship, we'd be sleeping on bunk-beds and sucking our meals through a straw.

I had just stepped out of the shower, dried myself, and slipped into a new pair of pants when there came a soft electronic ring from the door.

"Open," I said, drying my hair with a towel.

The door slid open, and Felony and Sarah came in.

"Hey, have a seat," I said, gesturing to the sitting area. "Drinks?"

"Yeah. Bourbon, rocks," Felony said.

"Make that two," Sarah said.

I nodded, going over to the bar, pouring their drinks, and a vodka for myself.

Then I went over to the lounge area, handing them their drinks, and sat next to Sarah, across from Felony.

"So, we're on our way to Ciegan's End," he said, taking a sip of the bourbon.

"Yeah," I replied, "this should be good."

"We're gonna have to watch our backs out there. I feel like a mouse that's going for a nice big piece of cheese."

"We can trust Rainer," I replied, "and he has the respect of his men."

He nodded, "Respect instead of outright fear. Always a good sign. But Mason?"

"He'll be fine. He's just a curious old man."

I found myself wondering, vaguely, how old the guy actually was.

We spoke for a few hours, and a few drinks, until eventually Sarah went back to her cabin to collapse into another troubled sleep and Felony went off to explore the rest of the hovship.

I sat alone, a vodka in one hand and a smoke in the other, wondering what the hell I was going to do with myself for the next four weeks.

I glanced at the wallscreen in front of me, gave it Dex's number and told it to call him.

Calling...

Still no reply.

I ended the call, took a deep pull of my smoke, got up and walked over to the giant window, looking out at the stormy night. Waves crashed against the huge hull of the *Crusader*, breaking and falling away only to be replaced with others, while far off across the sea a bolt of lightning hit the surface of the ocean, illuminating the black and roiling clouds above.

I told the lights to dim, had a seat on the observation couch facing the window, took another sip of vodka, and settled down to watch the storm.

The journey was long, but far from boring.

For a start, about ten days into the journey, Mitchell lost it, almost killing a member of the crew. It took four of us to eventually get him to the ground. We had to tie him up, drag him to his cabin and tie him down to the bed so that he wouldn't hurt himself. It was the same madness I'd seen in the eyes of the waiter at Kaisers', and the news reporter the following day. Rainer had been in to try to speak to him, but the guy wasn't coherent.

I wasn't very happy about that.

Hell, I quite liked the guy.

A crew member turned up dead two days later, his corpse found in the cargo hold with no eyes and Mitchell had immediately been blamed. I couldn't argue the point, not after seeing how other people (the waiter at Kaisers' in particular) had acted after being bitten by what I'd started to call The Barmy Bug. Besides, it was better to think that the murder had been committed by someone who was now safely tied up and tucked away, rather than someone who was at that very moment stalking through the quiet corridors of the *Crusader*, knife in hand, manic grin and insane ocular glimmer present and correct.

It was a week after that (day nineteen into our journey) and Felony, Sarah and I were seated in the dining area, staring out at the storm clouds and the tossing waves as violent winds lashed rain and spray against the windows next to our table.

It was nearly three weeks into our journey, and the weather had been little better than this since leaving port. Since the first body had been found, three more had been found around the ship and two more crew members had lost the plot and attacked their fellow crew mates, before being tied to their bunks and drugged, to be constantly monitored by the onboard medical staff.

Things were a bit strained on the *EAV NeuroLOG Crusader*.

I held up a mug of coffee, took a sip, letting its warmth wash through me, while outside nature went wild in the darkness. I fingered the mobile communicator the crew had given me on boarding. It was a small black disk, easily fitting into the palm of my hand, with the word 'NeuroLOG' engraved on one side and a button on the other. It allowed for vocal communication onboard the ship.

The thing didn't have much on my jacketcom2.0, but it was good enough. I hit the button on its smooth black face, it flashed a dull red. Hit it again and the light went off. Archaic, but it did the job.

Rainer joined us at the table, taking a seat with a smile.

"Good evening," he said amiably.

"Evening," I replied, "How is Mitchell?"

Rainer had just come from a visit to Mitchell to see how he was doing. I had gone to visit him a few times myself, but it had gotten to a point where I just couldn't do it anymore. The guy had lost it. He'd tried to escape from his bonds, and had succeeded only in tearing at the skin around his wrists and ankles until it bled, forcing the medical staff to secure not only his hands and feet, but his arms, legs and head as well.

Rainer shook his head, "Not good."

"Still yelling at himself?" Felony asked.

"Or at someone we can't see, yes."

We were silent, as dinner was served.

I eyed out our waiter, half-expecting him to suddenly go insane and attempt to stab me with a plate.

"We arrive at Phoenix Outpost in just over a week," Rainer said, trying to up the mood.

"Yeah, thank God," Sarah said, "If I never set foot on another hovship in my life it'll be too soon."

We had dinner pretty much in silence, and afterwards I walked Sarah to her cabin, said goodnight, and decided to retire early. I really didn't feel like company right then, possibly never again, for that matter.

I entered the darkness of my cabin, hearing the door slide softly closed behind me. There was a sharp snapping sound, the pungent smell of smoke. I turned around to see the wall switch for the door burning out.

"Shit... Lights."

Nothing.

I remained standing in pitch blackness.

"Computer, lights!"

Again, no response. Obviously the lights shared the same panel as the door.

And then I heard it, a harsh, dry breathing.

. Very, very soft.

Oh shit.

Not again.

"Hello?"

No response. But the breathing became slightly louder.

Or maybe I imagined it did.

"Who the hell is in my room?"

No reply.

I wasn't about to take any chances, not after the House9 debacle. It was time to act. Not having the option of leaving due to the door being burned out, I dived for

215

the bedside table in the pitch darkness, retrieving my guns, and spun around, pointing them into the darkness.

The breathing continued, soft, but there, and growing louder all the time. I couldn't make out where it was coming from, how far away the source of it was. It just seemed to be hanging in the air. For all I knew it could've been a couple having sex in the next room.

No.

Not very likely, considering there were only two women onboard the *Crusader*. The one was Sarah and the other didn't have a chance of scoring with the Elephant Man at happy hour. I felt for the communication disk in my pocket, found it, and hit the button.

"Call Felony," I said quietly.

It dialled through.

"Yeah, Felony here."

"Fel, got a security problem," I said softly, "and someone fused the door panel to my cabin. Locked in."

"I'm on my way." His cabin was a few doors down from mine. He'd be here in no time at all. I hoped.

I started to move towards the opposite side of the room, making for a lamp I knew was on a side table beside my bed. It would be much easier to aim when I could see.

I got about two feet past the bed when I realised that someone was on it. I don't know what it was that made me aware of this, maybe a sound that my conscious mind couldn't hear but my subconscious picked up loud and clear, or a subtle shift of air, but whatever it was it was bad, very bad. I reacted at once, spinning around and firing four shots into the bed, before my shoulders were seized and I was thrown like a fucking rag doll head-first into the nearest wall.

216

I hit the ground, dazed.

The thing grabbed me by my neck, lifted me up into the air, off my feet.

Oh no, not this time.

I brought both my guns up, pushed them into the thing's chest, and started firing.

It roared, letting go of me and flying backwards to crash back down on the bed, lying still.

"Ash?"

It was Felony.

"Fel!" I yelled. "Get that door open!"

"You okay?" he said, sounding freaked.

"Yeah, for now."

There came a thudding sound from the direction of the door.

And another.

"I've contacted ship security. We're gonna have the door open now. Hang in there, man."

"In there..." The thing on the bed uttered weakly.

I recognised that voice.

I moved towards the lamp again, or at least in the direction I assumed the lamp to be in. I could vaguely make out the crazy bastard on my bed as I trained my guns on the place I hoped his head was.

I took another shot.

And another.

There came a guttural shriek from the bed.

I'd taken the thing in the chest six times, and still it lived. Shot it in what I hoped was the head, and it could still scream. My mind flashed back to House9. The slugs should at least make it docile for a bit, I thought. I'd just have to keep shooting it until they can get the door open.

When this thing had grabbed me my nostrils had been filled with the smell of burned leather, charred... what? But it was impossible. How did it survive the self destruction of House9? Even if it had still been standing at the window when the explosion hit, it would have fallen far enough to break its neck and body into millions of pieces.

Or maybe not.

Either way, the thing was very here.

Couldn't really ignore *that* little bit of truth.

It started to roll off the bed and I squeezed off a few shots. This only succeeded in pissing it off; it rolled the rest of the way off, came to its feet screaming as I gave it everything I had, sending it sprawling onto the bed again.

Click.

Click-click.

Out of bullets, and the rest of them were on the *other* side of the bed! I was in trouble. The creature started with its dry, harsh, sand-paper chuckle again, coming slowly to a sitting position and I realised with a sinking feeling that Ugly and I had indeed tangoed before. Last time I had stepped out, what the hell would I do this time?

The thing got to its feet, breathing harshly.

"I shoot..." it growled.

It uttered another guttural laugh.

"Good memory, Ugly."

It came for me.

Note to self: Shooting Ugly only makes him angry. And making Ugly mad constitutes a 'Bad Thing'.

I dove to my right as he came at me, trying to avoid his long, grasping arms. It worked, the thing stumbled past me and I heard a crash behind me. I looked back but couldn't make out what it was. I saw my chance, got up and made a wild dash for the bed and the precious ammunition. Something tripped me on my second step, and I fell to the ground with a thud, spun onto my back, arms out to protect me.

Ugly stared down at me, leaning in close.

I decked it, my fist connecting with hard leathery material.

It stumbled a step back, then came at me again, gripping my shirt and lifting me up. Not really into the idea of being strangled again, I twisted my legs around his and held on tight. The Thing screeched, trying to pull me up further by my neck but I hung on like a leech, my hands coming up to its face, feeling for its eyes.

Just charred leather and cloth.

My thumbs moved over the place where its eyes should have been, but there was no softness there, no give. Just hard, charred fabric, rough against my fingers. I started feeling light-headed, as Ugly tightened its grip on my neck, chuckling softly to itself, as if enjoying some private joke.

My head felt like it had been dipped in Novocain and left out in the sun to dry.

I started to lose consciousness, my mind slipping out from under me as the oxygen slipped from my blood stream. I heard sounds at the door, someone at work on the panel on the other side, in the corridor, sounding like they came from an unimaginable distance. And a voice.

"Ash? Everything cool, man?"

I could say nothing, my head dipping under the warm waters of unconsciousness even as Felony's words were spoken.

Dipping under...

Under...

Nothing to do now, nothing I could do...

There was a sudden, intense flash of light and someone was beside me, struggling with the thing, pulling its hands from me. I hit the ground, sucking in great lungfuls of air. One after the other. Fighting up from the darkness.

Thank God, good old Felony. I grabbed at the Thing again, and together we grappled with it, wrestling it eventually to the floor. I reached over for one of my guns, lying on the floor beside me, thinking I'd pistol whip the bastard.

"You can't kill it."

I looked up in the darkness, shocked.

"Dex?"

The thing somehow pulled itself forward across the floor, wriggling out of our grasp, got to its feet and ran headlong through the window and out into the watery darkness, it's screaming cut off abruptly as it hit the waves and went under. Icy rain, carried on the wind, came rushing into the room. I went over to the wall to the left of the observation window, felt the cool wall against my hands, and moved across to the left, coming eventually to a side table with a lamp.

I hit the switch, and turned around.

My friend Dex stood a few feet away.

"How –?"

He grinned, "A pleasure. Couldn't let you take it on alone. Once was bad enough."

He stood, walking over to the smashed window to look out at the crashing waves.

I went over to stand beside him, "What was it?"

"It's made up of fragments of negative emotions, sadness, anger, hate...."

"Who –" I stopped, silent for a second, something dawning on me that filled me with dread. "In House9, the voice... That was you."

He nodded.

"Dex," I said softly, "Where have you been?"

I think I already knew.

Looking back, I think, in some deep dark corner of my mind, I'd known all along.

"Another place, Ash," Dex said, a gentle smile on his face. "And I have to go back now."

"What? Where the hell are you going? How did you get –"

"See you around, old friend."

My eyes widened, I tried to speak.

And then he was gone, and I was left alone.

Tired, bewildered and suddenly very, very sad.

Twenty-one

8:30 p.m.

Not that it made much of a difference in this place.

The *Crusader* travelled across a vast snowfield in the twilight of Antarctica, lights cutting intense beams through the hazy gloom as we navigated through a snowstorm that had hit suddenly and without warning early the previous morning just after we'd crossed some invisible line into Ciegan's End.

I stood at the repaired observation window in my cabin, staring out at the near darkness, the snow illuminated occasionally, a flash of white lit up briefly in the darkness.

I found myself longing for the warm sand and sparkling seas of Tora Sera, perhaps having a cocktail with an old friend I wouldn't be seeing any more.

My mind flashed back to just over a week ago

Dex.

The door had opened a few seconds later, and Felony had come in to find me alone, standing by the window and murmuring something about Dex being dead, something about a fragment, something about Melanie. He'd taken me back to his room and poured me a stiff drink.

Another.

Another after that.

Until finally I'd relaxed a bit.

Until finally I'd stopped shaking like a leaf, and told him what had happened.

"Ladies and gentlemen. We will be docking at the NeuroLOG Scientific Outpost Phoenix within the hour. Please make all the necessary preparations, and –"

I touched the mobile communicator, "Call Felony."

"Calling Felony..."

"Ash, ready to get off this rusty bucket of bolts?"

"Yeah, can't wait. Get Sarah, and meet me at the observation lounge. I want to see this place."

We met at the lounge about twenty minutes later, had a seat at our usual table, which afforded us an excellent view of the NeuroLOG outpost as we made our approach.

Rainer joined us shortly after, took a seat at our table, and our waiter brought us coffee, always an excellent idea. The others spoke amongst themselves as I sat staring out at the ice-cold twilight outside, staring out across the vast white expanse that stretched off into nothingness and darkness and the distant horizon.

And then I saw it, coming up out of the darkness, a giant dome materializing out of the shifting storm, an impossibly tall tower shooting up from its centre, up into the night. As I stared out of the window the scene grew in substance and size, blinking lights becoming visible in the distance, a few smaller domes surrounding the main one coming into view, and as we got closer still I realised that those were accompanied by yet other buildings. Smaller, all flat in shape, no more than two or three stories in height. Except for one, one that stood a fair distance from the main dome and right beside one of the smaller ones. It was big, larger than the main dome, in fact. The place was quite a sight.

Something caught my eye.

I gazed upwards.

Searchlights scanned the sky, cutting through the snow-storm, brushing over the *Crusader* briefly as we made our approach. My eyes followed its graceful sweep through the night. Further afield I spotted tiny buildings, circular, with gun turrets, all but invisible if it hadn't been for the sweep of the spotlight.

"Impressive, isn't it?" Rainer said with a smile.

I nodded, "Yeah, you could say that. Ever spend any time in these parts?"

"Yes, when the need arises. Mister Mason has spent more and more time here since we built the outpost twelve years ago, opening it on NeuroLOG's tenth birthday. It's okay for a visit, but I wouldn't want to live here."

I grinned, "No."

"This place looks very secure," Felony said, gazing around the compound as we approached the larger of two buildings standing side by side.

"It is," Rainer replied, a slight note of pride in his voice, "Phoenix is totally impregnable. You don't get in without an invitation. With the type of sophisticated technology we have on base, there is no need for walls."

"Mister Rainer, if you don't mind me asking, what is the need for such tight security if you are situated in the middle of Antarctica?" Sarah asked.

"Yeah, what do you guys have to hide?" Fel agreed.

Rainer smiled, "NeuroLOG has been at the forefront of neuro-technology, hardware and software, since the company's inception twenty-two years ago. Needless to say our R and D is the subject of great interest to a number of people. Industrial and corporate espionage is rife in this day and age, and there are many companies who would go to great, even extreme, lengths to acquire NeuroLOG-level research.

I nodded, "Have you had any surprises in the last twelve years? Any, say, unwanted guests?"

Rainer shook his head, "No. There was one attempt, a number of years ago. It failed. Never even made it through the front door."

I looked down into my coffee mug, blew softly into it, feeling my face bathed in warm air.

Nobody asked what 'failed' entailed to the people who were doing the trying. I think we could all pretty much guess.

224

The Planet is ruled by corporations. Theft of research is, although considered illegal, vital to most companies' development. Get caught, though, and you're toast.

That's just the way it is.

It's law.

Well, not *actual* law.

Shit, you know what I mean.

I looked up.

Giant hangar doors slid open before us as we slowed our speed and the *Crusader* drifted gently into the huge hangar, coming to a stop in its berth.

"Time to go," Felony said with what sounded like joy in his voice.

We got up, grabbed our bags, and went down to the exit hatch, stepping out into the ice-cold air inside the hangar.

I stepped out just in time to see the gigantic hangar doors closing with a dull clang, pulled my coat tightly around me, glancing around. Technical teams were grouped around the vast floor space, working on vehicles and machines of different shapes and sizes. A banging here, a spray of sparks there.

"This way," Rainer said, leading the way toward the entrance to a warmly lit corridor stretching away to our left.

Sarah, Felony and I walked after him.

"Well, here we are," Fel said, looking around, "still cold as a bastard."

He clapped his hands, rubbing them together.

"Yup," I replied, noticing the tiny security cameras dotted around the hangar, and thinking to myself that no doubt there were plenty more outside.

This place was a fortress.

And if it was impossible to get in, I found myself wondering exactly how difficult it would be to break out.

If the need arose.

Of course, it would never come to that.

Of course.

We arrived at the corridor's entry hatch, Rainer keying in a password on the keypad to the right of the door.

"Current password accepted. Please identify yourself."

"Howard Rainer. And guests."

"Scanning retina. Stand by."

A soft blue beam of light flashed quickly across Rainer's face, he blinked afterwards, rubbing his eyes. "I hate those things."

"Identification verified. Access granted. Welcome to Phoenix, Howard Rainer and Guests."

The PlastiGlass entry hatch slid aside, allowing us access to the corridor. It was warm inside, insulated from the icy hangar by the three-inch thick sheet of glass that had slid tightly closed behind us. The corridor gave way to a glass tube, connecting the hangar to a building, the tallest of all the buildings I'd seen on the compound. Snow smashed against the tube wall as we made our way across it, coming eventually to the entrance of the opposite building, a large circular door that reminded me of the escape pod Dex and I had used when we escaped the burning *EAV PlanetOre Discoverer,* seconds before it blew apart in a flash of fire and light. That had been the only operation Apex had given us as a team.

Dex, Cole and I.

Youngsters.

Before we all became what we would later become.

"Open," Rainer said.

The circular steel door rolled open, and we entered a warm, softly lit lounge area. Couches and coffee tables were arranged at various places in the room, and on one of those couches, surveying the stormy twilight outside, sat Trevor Mason.

Rainer approached him first, moving ahead of us.

"Hello, Trevor," he said, as the other rose and shook his hand.

Trevor Mason was a powerfully built man, towering above even Felony, who was taller than me. He had long white hair, tied back in a ponytail, and a trimmed white beard. His skin was tanned, weathered, leathery.

"Welcome back, Howard," He said, his voice deep, strong. He turned to the three of us, smiled, "Welcome to Phoenix, everyone."

He walked over to us.

"Sarah. A pleasure," he said, gently taking her hand in his own, "a pleasure to finally meet you."

He turned to Felony and I, and we made our introductions.

"Good job finding my lady, Mister Corben."

"Yeah." I said, not quite comfortable with the situation.

He smiled, "And who is your friend?"

"This is Felony. He's Sarah's bodyguard," I said.

Mason raised an eyebrow, "I assure you, Mister Corben –"

"Call me Ash."

" – Ash. I assure you, there will be no need for personal protection here at Phoenix. This outpost is completely secure."

"Yeah. You never know," I replied.

Mason nodded, "Indeed..." A moment's silence. "Anyway, Mister Rainer will show you all to your suites; dinner has been prepared and will be delivered to your respective quarters. Perhaps we can meet for breakfast at, say, nine thirty a.m.?"

227

We agreed, and Rainer led us from the lounge, down another corridor and eventually to a pair of elevators.

Floor?

He told the elevator to take us to level twenty-three, what would turn out to be the third storey from the top, and about thirty seconds later the doors opened into a warm, ambiently lit hallway.

"These suites are the best on the outpost. Reserved for NeuroLOG executives and important visitors," Rainer said, handing out keycards and silver comdisks like the ones we'd used on the hovship, "I'm sure you'll find them much more comfortable than your quarters onboard the *Crusader*. Make yourselves comfortable."

I, for one, had found absolutely nothing wrong with the level of comfort onboard the hovship, actually being surprised that they'd gone to so much trouble. But Rainer was right, I realised, as I stepped into my room.

The place was big, soft lights at floor level giving a warm glow to the plush carpets. Directly ahead of me there was a large bed in the centre of the room, a bathroom to the right, and floor to ceiling windows stretched from the bathroom cubicle in the corner, past the head of the bed and curving around to make up the whole of the wall to my left.

I threw the bags on the floor, took a really great bath, shaved, and lit a smoke. Then I went and stood at the window, watching the hazy, shifting twilight outside.

Well, I thought to myself. Here we are, like it or not.

Antarctica.

Ciegan's End.

What happened now remained to be seen.

"Computer, TV," I said.

"Preferred channel?"

This from an attractive, female voice.

"Er, news. Global."

The wallscreen across from the bed came alive. I hesitated to turn. TV kept giving me bad news these days.

"Volume to four," I said, turning to see the screen.

I was greeted with the sight of the Chairman of the Earth Alliance High Council, Dan Smith, a tall, handsome man in his early fifties, with piercing blue eyes and a chiselled jaw. The guy looked like a good old-fashioned movie star and I had for some time harboured the suspicion that he was, in fact, computer generated.

My case was strengthened by the fact that I had never heard of one occasion when the guy had ever been seen live. Only ever onscreen.

On the other hand, anyone in his position of seniority would do well to stay as well protected as possible.

"...is somewhat larger and very much closer than scientists at the Earth Alliance Space Centre originally thought. Some members of the EA High Council find this quite disturbing and wholly unacceptable, considering its close proximity to the Earth, and we will launch an official enquiry as soon as this is over. Assuming there is anything left of civilization. The size of the meteor, which has been named Mrs. Nesbit, is now said to be roughly half the length of Nu Caynan, more than large enough to wipe out the human race. EA Space Centre scientists are collaborating with the EA Military and certain concerned corporations in an attempt to reach a reasonable solution before Mrs. Nesbit wipes out the human race, which is in the not-too-distant future, I have to say!" A big smile now from Chairman Smith, whose image was then replaced with John Jacob's intense expression, "Another person is back from the grave, putting the total count at thirty-five! This latest sufferer of DMW Syndrome is a woman, who was found wondering through Nu Caynan, lost and confused. Records state her death to have been nearly twelve years ago. It is

229

unfortunate that burials are no longer performed, because I for one would like to see what would be dug up! Cremations are all very well and good, but I can tell you one thing, the EA Records Department has a lot to answer for!"

"Mute."

An alternative arrangement, Dan Smith had said. There is only so much one can do in the event of a giant asteroid, and there isn't enough space underground for a tenth of the population of a MegaCity.

Like I said.

Always bad news.

I turned away, wondering how secure Phoenix was against a meteor half the size of Nu Caynan. Well, unless those clever bastards at the Space Centre came up with something fast, I guessed I was going to find out.

Morning looked exactly the same as night, so when the alarm went off at eight-thirty, I nearly threw something at the flashing wallscreen. Then I remembered where I was. Got up. Lit up. Wondered briefly if it was time to quit.

No, I thought. I'm not a quitter. Besides, the meteor would probably kill me a lot sooner then the cigarettes.

I showered and shaved, and a short while later there came a soft chime from the door.

"Open."

Sarah and Felony stepped in.

"Ready?" Felony asked.

"Yeah." I replied.

Rainer met us at the elevators.

"Good morning, Ash. We will be dining in Mister Mason's personal quarters this morning. Not a regular thing, I can assure you," he said, hitting a button on the wall beside the steel doors.

"Yee ha," I replied, as we stepped into a cool, mirrored lift.

I noticed another security camera, tiny, staring down at us from a corner.

We went up one level, the doors opening onto a large foyer. Two guards stood beside the doors, and they swung them open as Rainer approached.

We entered a huge room, open plan, stretching off to our left and right. The entire floor was surrounded with glass, and I realised that this room covered the entire floor space of the twenty-fourth floor. Another elevator stood in the far corner, no doubt leading up to the top floor and Mason's private living area.

Off to our left, beside a window, was a long dining table. Trevor Mason was seated at its head, speaking quietly with a man sitting to his immediate left. They both looked up as the three of us entered with Rainer, coming up to the table. They stood, the guy introduced as Simmons. He was a reedy little man with darting, beady eyes.

Had to be a scientist, I thought.

"Excellent, glad to have you all here," Mason said expansively as we all took a seat, "Breakfast is served."

Two waiters approached, removing the silver covers from the trays already on the table

"Please, enjoy the meal," he added, picking up his cutlery.

The rest of us followed suit.

We ate in silence for a while, Mason and his friend quietly finishing the conversation they'd been having when we arrived. A few minutes later Simmons stood, made some excuse, and left. He hadn't touched the food.

I realised he didn't even have a plate.

As he left, Mason turned to us, "Please excuse me, there. My job here is never done. No rest for the wicked, heh?"

I nodded, "*So, what the fuck do you want with Sarah?*"

Actually, I didn't say that.

Well, not then and there, anyway.

"After breakfast, I have arranged for a member of staff to give a guided tour of Phoenix," Rainer said, taking a sip from a cup of coffee.

"After that, we can meet here for lunch, and perhaps I could ask you a few questions, young lady?" Mason said.

Sarah nodded slowly, "Yeah. But I don't remember anything from when I was three, let alone when I was a baby."

"All in good time, my dear," Mason said with a reassuring smile, "I'm sure we'll get to the bottom of this."

"So, how safe are we from the meteor, Mister Mason? The EASC has said it will probably hit tomorrow night." I said, enjoying the bacon immensely.

Mason nodded, "I am a member of the High Council. I am fully aware of the situation. Mister Corben, in the construction of this place, certain requirements needed to be met. One was the need for protection in the case of all-out corporate war. World War Four, if you will."

I nodded, "Yeah?"

"Needless to say, all the requirements were met," he finished.

I said nothing, continued with breakfast, which, I have to say, really was very nice.

Afterwards, Mason called for the guy who was going to give us the tour.

Then he turned to Sarah, "I will see you later, young lady."

"Okay. But you have to understand, Mister Mason –"

"Trevor –"

" – that I don't go anywhere without my bodyguard." She finished, placing a hand on Felony's shoulder.

Clever girl.

"Of course, that's quite fine, but I assure you there is nothing to fear. You are in our care, and you have my word as a gentleman that you are perfectly safe. Please don't worry yourself –" Mason said.

"The lady never goes anywhere without me," Felony interrupted.

A beat.

Mason nodded, "Very well then, if that's the way you wish it. Please, enjoy the tour of our facilities." He smiled, "I'll see you all for lunch."

We left. I had to admit that we hadn't been the friendliest of guests, and the guy had been nothing short of polite and charming throughout. I was beginning to think I should re-evaluate my opinion of him.

And possibly myself.

A tall, bald man with a funny moustache met us on the ground floor. His name was Tim.

"Hi, everyone, I'm Tim."

We all greeted Tim.

Tim's job this morning was to give us a guided tour of the Phoenix, and I got the feeling he was far less pleased about it than he was letting on. If I was right, then the guy hid it well, and I respected him for that.

Even if I did find his moustache laughable.

Which it was.

Anyway, the tour was interesting in a dull kind of way. We were shown the different domes, the smaller ones. There were three, two large ones and one smaller than the others. One of the large ones contained a giant greenhouse, which Tim dutifully informed us was where they grew food. Of course, food and beverages and other things were all imported onboard hovships once a month, but, as Mason had said earlier, the outpost had to cover certain eventualities. So it made sense for the place to not only be fully stocked but also be fully self-supporting. The second dome housed scientific laboratories dealing mainly with hardware and software research and development, and the third and smallest was a garden, with a little lake and everything, for execs to relax and have a swim or catch a tan.

DigiSun is a truly wonderful thing.

In order to get from one dome to another, it was necessary to access the main dome, and move along a corridor running along its circumference. The dome was massive. Ridiculously big, and as we passed the fourth door marked

NX CONTAINMENT AREA

NO UNAUTHORISED Personnel

I found myself wondering exactly what type of research required that much space. And what NX meant.

I asked Tim.

Tim wouldn't tell me.

"I'm sorry, Mister –?"

"Ash."

"Mister Ash, but that information is classified. No one goes into the Big One."

"No one?" I asked.

"No one without Mister Mason's personal authorisation."

"Oh... Not even a peek?"

"Sorry Mister Ash, no can do."

"Okay, can you answer one question then, Tim?" I asked, beginning to enjoy myself.

Tim amused me, mainly because he didn't appear to possess a personality.

"That would depend on the question, Mister Ash."

"Well, I suppose it would, Tim... Okay, what is that big old tower sticking out of the Big One for? The array of smaller antennae are obvious. Communications devices for the upload and download of software to satellites and remote stations, right?"

Tim said nothing.

"Right. That's obvious. But the *impossibly* tall one? You guys running galactic TV from here?"

"I'm sorry, sir. That's classified," Tim wasn't looking very comfortable, "Please, Mister Ash –"

"Okay," I said, hands up in a placating gesture, "you're off the hook."

For now.

I made a mental note to find out what the hell was going on inside the Big One whatever the cost. Because I had a pretty strong feeling all of this had killed my best friend, not too mention my ex-wife, and that wouldn't do at all.

Twenty-two

Ash, you're close to losing the only two people in the world who give a shit about you

who give a shit about you

about you

Those words circled around and around in my head as I walked along a connecting tube towards yet another circular entrance, surrounded on all sides by the ice and snow of Ciegan's End.

He'd been right, eventually.

It had just taken a bit longer than expected.

But that was okay, because for now it kept me focussed. For now I had a battle to fight and an opponent to obliterate. Nothing like a personal war to keep your shit together.

After lunch, Sarah and Felony had joined Mason for a drink and a talk, and I'd gone for a walk.

"Don't get lost, now, Mister Corben," Mason had said as I'd left.

Tim had probably told him about my interest in the main dome, and the tower, and that was his way of asking me not to attempt to gain entry into the NX, whatever the hell that was. All of which was funny, because that's exactly what I was going to do, and his polite request made me want to even more.

"I'll do my best. Thought I'd take a walk around on my own. Maybe end up at the garden, or the greenhouse," I replied, grinning, "Not used to all this snow and darkness."

Mason nodded, "Takes a while to adjust. Enjoy it."

"Thanks."

And I left, making my way along one tube after the next, towards the looming bulk of the main dome.

The Big One.

The garden was situated near to the executive apartments; that's why I'd mentioned the greenhouse, which had a tube that ran off the circumference of the main dome, giving me an excuse to be there. I needed one, because as far as I could see every square inch of this place was covered with security cameras. Tim hadn't taken us to the security command centre, for obvious reasons, but I guessed every inch of the outpost was under constant and careful surveillance. Which meant my ugly mug would be smiling for the camera as I attempted to enter the main dome.

I arrived at a circular hatchway with the words

Main Research Dome

above the entrance.

I waved my keycard over a silver panel.

The door rolled open, and I walked through into the wide corridor running along the circumference of the main dome, taking a left and strolling in the direction of the greenhouse. As I passed another NX door, my curiosity hit danger levels.

I had to get in there.

I glanced around casually, taking in the curved ceiling where it joined seamlessly with the wall, which in turn joined with the floor. The cameras in this area of the outpost seemed to be focussed mainly on the entrances to the corridor and the NX area. That meant that if I were to –

"Mister Corben!"

I turned, spotting Tim coming up from behind.

"Hello, Tim," I said with a smile, wondering what the hell he wanted.

"Mister Mason sent me to give you this, " he held out a small silver disk to me, identical to the one given to us by Rainer and which was at this very minute lying on my bed.

"I already have one," I said, not taking it, "But thanks anyway."

Did they think I was stupid? If I had one of those on me, they could track me. If I didn't, and I managed to avoid the eyes of the cameras, I was invisible. It wasn't a difficult choice to make.

"Mister Mason told me to inform you of the dangers of being on a remote outpost like this. Accidents happen frequently. If we get hit with a surprise storm, there's no telling what might happen —"

They *did* think I was stupid.

I nodded, took the disk from him.

"Please keep it on you at all times, Mister Corben," Tim finished solemnly.

"Sure," I said, putting it in my pocket.

"Thank you," Tim said, beginning to walk past me.

I happened to glance at the tag on his laboratory coat as he passed, and I was pretty sure I'd spotted an 'NX' there.

Interesting.

I walked behind him, careful not to make a sound as I followed him. I was giving him a bit of time to forget about me, watching where he was going. He stopped at the entrance to the greenhouse, turned, and I pulled back to the wall, hidden from his line of sight by the wall's gentle curve. I heard the greenhouse tube's hatchway roll open. Roll closed again.

Perfect.

Only, I couldn't follow him through straight away because he'd hear the damn door.

I waited for a minute, then I entered the tube, crossing through into the greenhouse a few minutes later.

I was surrounded by greenery, plants of every shape and size. A metallic walkway stretched around the dome, running along its edge. I looked down, only to see the plants falling away below me as well. The place was bigger than it looked, and humid as hell.

I took a stroll along the walkway, unsure of whether I was being watched or not. There was no way to tell in this place.

I put my hands in my pockets, feeling the cool disk between my fingers.

This, I thought, had to go. Now.

I pulled my hands out of my pockets, surreptitiously flicked the disk over the edge of the walkway and down into the greenness, hoping the cameras hadn't picked that up, and went looking for Tim.

I found him hard at work, seated at a bank of computer monitors surrounded by plants on a steel platform off the main circular walkway. I stopped short when I saw him, realising if there were a bunch of screens, then there were probably cameras too. So I did the only thing a normal mugger would do: I stood behind a big plant and waited for my moment to strike.

My moment came after about fifteen minutes. Tim got up, walked past me.

I moved behind him, said a little prayer that no-one was watching, and hit him over the head with the butt of my gun. I leaned down and felt the pulse on his neck. Beating steady.

"Sorry, Tim."

I slid the blue and silver plastic tag out of its sheath on his coat, examined it. It was a keycard, just like the one Rainer had given us to gain access to our rooms. Only, presumably, of a higher security level.

Possibly the highest.

And I'd been right, the words 'NX Clearance' were clearly there.

I pulled off Tim's pants, and used them to tie him to the steel rail of the walkway. Then I put on his coat, patted him on the cheek and went to see what the hell was going down in the Big One.

Keeping my head down, I came to an NX access door a few minutes later. I waved the card in front of a black panel, the door slid open soundlessly and I stepped inside.

A man stood with his back to me, surveying what I can only describe as a shifting, turning, flickering mass of light and substance.

He turned to face me, his eyes showing surprise when he saw my face.

"Who the hell are you. What's –" I decked him so hard I'm surprised I didn't break my hand. He flew into the computer banks behind him, crashing to the floor in a silent heap.

I walked forward, trying to understand what I saw through the observation windows before me, staring out into the giant, constantly shifting mass of light and images. At one moment I thought I was looking at a peaceful meadow, clumps of trees here and there, the next a metallic structure standing in the middle of a snowfield, part of some type of complex, and then I saw a crowd of excited people at it's base, the sun's rays shining down on them on the vast snowfield, speaking amongst themselves in hushed tones. The scene seemed to shift into place, and I saw the structure abandoned, blood smeared across the walls, a flag at its entrance blowing in a wind that couldn't possibly be in there.

An insignia on the flag.

I knew that emblem, I'd seen it somewhere before.

Recently.

"Help me!"

A child's voice, coming from somewhere inside. A scream. And then I saw her, running from behind one of the structures, running across the snow, pursued by what appeared to be a man, but loping along like a monkey, arms hanging loosely by his sides, knuckles dragging on the ground, uttering a screeching animal noise I knew I'd heard before.

I used the keycard to open the door to my left, ran out across the snow towards the running child, scrambling towards her.

"Come to me!" I yelled, pulling my guns, "I won't hurt you!"

The child swerved, making a beeline for me, the man creature on her heels.

I brought my guns up

"Stop or I shoot!" I yelled, taking aim.

The man brought his arms up, reaching for the little girl, the pair no more than twenty feet away.

"I said stop!"

Reaching for her little shoulders...

I shot.

The man dropped, blood from his leg oozing out onto the white snow, as the child ran into my arms.

"Shhhh. It's okay," I said softly, as the little girl shuddered in my arms, "It's okay."

I watched the man trying to stand up, falling to the ground, trying again.

The child pulled away from me, her giant eyes looking up into mine, tears falling softly down her soft cheeks.

"You're okay now, angel," I said, stroking her golden hair back, "Everything's okay."

She smiled.

And then her hands came up and she clawed at my cheeks, jerking away violently as if pulled by some unseen force, and she lurched off toward the metallic compound, her high-pitched screaming filling the air.

I ran after her, trying to stop her.

"It started with the children."

I stopped short, turned to face the man on the ground, who was again trying to stand, only to fall back down again.

"What?" I said.

He was silent.

I looked at the gashes on his face, "What the hell happened to you?"

He laughed. A short, harsh sound, with not a trace of humour in it. "This place. Terrance fucking Manning. Take your pick."

"Terrance Manning. That was thirty –"

Oh Christ.

The insignia I had seen on the flag was also on this man's jacket. A vertically elongated black 'G'. Two words beneath it:

Project Gateway.

PROJECT GATEWAY

The man looked up at me, eyes cold.

"It started with the children," he said quietly, feeling the gashes on his face, the wetness of his own blood on his cheeks.

"What happened here?" I said slowly, a sinking feeling begin to form in the pit of my stomach.

The man smiled another humourless smile.

242

"They started acting... strange," he said, "Started doing things they wouldn't do normally."

I looked away, across the snow, towards the compound. For some reason I couldn't stand to look at his eyes anymore. It wasn't his wounds, it was his eyes. There was something very wrong with them.

"Like what?" I asked.

"Like cutting themselves, ripping out their hair. A nine-year-old girl started masturbating at her family's dinner table. Right there while they were eating, just brought up her legs, hiked up her skirt and started doing it."

I was quiet.

"That was just the beginning. My best friends' baby boy was killed by three of the evil little bastards. The oldest no older than ten. They broke into his quarters on a dare while the family was sleeping, went over to the kid's crib, reached down, and tore out the baby's eyes. There must have been something slightly wrong with the baby I think, because it didn't even cry. Just lay there, giggling, blood running down its face onto the crib's sheets."

He went silent

"Who was the girl you were chasing?"

The guy said nothing for a while, just running his hands across his ruined face, eyes cast down to the red snow.

Then he looked up at me with those strange eyes.

"That girl," the man said quietly, "was my daughter. She died six months ago, only she won't go away."

Everything shifted around me, as if an intangible blizzard had suddenly sprung up and distorted my vision, and then the scene around me changed again, almost like water colours, mixing into something totally new, and I was standing in the middle of a desert in the twilight. Off towards the distant horizon a lightning storm was approaching. Could've been an EM storm, I couldn't be sure.

To my right was an ancient motorcar, almost totally buried in the sand. The manufacturer's emblem was still on the hood:

A three-pointed star.

Happy birthday baby.

"What the fuck is going on?" I said, looking around.

All I could see was the desert stretching off in every direction, a warm glow on the sand coming from behind the motorcar. A warm glow that could only be coming from a candle's flame.

I took a step toward it.

Another step.

A soft giggle.

Something mumbled.

A laugh in response.

I knew that sound.

I moved forward, "Mel —"

A laugh again. A fluttering sound in my head. The desert was gone, replaced by a room.

A white room.

But I wasn't in it. I was watching from somewhere else. Watching a woman sitting in a steel chair at a steel table in a room with white walls illuminated by intense fluorescent light. The woman was shaking slightly, I don't know why, holding a cigarette in her left hand.

She'd been crying, her eyes red and her cheeks flushed and wet from the tears. I don't know if there was anybody else at the table, or in the room for that matter, but I don't think so.

She turned her head sharply, something I couldn't see catching her attention. Her dark hair fell down her shoulders. She was scared, confused, and totally unaware of my existence, sitting all alone in the cold light of a clinical white room.

I knew her.

A long time ago.

A child's laughter, from somewhere behind me.

I swung around.

I was standing in the snow by the Gateway Habitat again.

The white room was gone.

The main dome was empty, except for me. And then, as I watched, bloody hand prints started forming on the steel walls in front of me, starting at the habitat entrance and moving outwards in both directions, the blood smearing and hardening and going black and flaking before my eyes. The prints were quite low, only a few feet off the ground. I walked forward, came to stand beside the steel wall of the habitat, bent down to examine the prints more clearly.

Small, not the marks made by a man.

It started with the children.

My eyes followed the trail of blood, black against the steel, until they came to rest on a small boy, about ten years old, sitting propped up against the wall in the cold and mumbling something softly to himself. I moved quickly up to him, not wondering where he had been five seconds before. I came up to him, pulled off Tim's lab coat, pocketing the keycard.

"It's okay," I said, wondering if he was a part of this place or the outpost, "I'm on your side... This is for you. It's freezing in here."

He looked up at me, not with fear but with sadness, "My dad's mad at me."

I wrapped the coat around his shoulders, noticing he had something in his hands. I ignored the blood smeared across the wall and had a seat against the wall beside him. It just felt like the right thing to do.

"I'm Ash," I said, looking at him out of the corner of my eye, "What's your name?"

He looked at me, "Jeremy."

"Nice to meet you, Jeremy," I said with a grin, "Hey, you wanna get out of here. Get some hot chocolate?"

The kid shook his head, looking down at the snow, his hands still playing with whatever it was.

"Dad's mad at me," he repeated softly.

"Yeah? I'm sure he'll get over it."

The kid shook his head, staring intently at his hands, "Nope."

"Well, why don't –" I stopped short, catching a glimpse at what little Jeremy was playing with.

I got up, backed slowly away from the kid. He looked up at me, stared at me with those sad eyes, "What's wrong, Mister?"

I didn't reply.

"Mister?"

The boy got to his feet, coming towards me.

"Nothing, nothing at all. Put down the eyes and stay away from me."

"It was jus' a joke... jus' a joke," he keened, the eyes still in his hands, "Little kid didn't need 'em anyway. Not here, not anymore"

"Yeah, I said keep the fuck away from me."

I continued to move slowly back, the kid continued to move unhurriedly toward me. He was smiling now, holding the eyes out, "You afraid of me, Mister? You afraid of this place?"

"Go to hell."

And then he darted forward.

I jerked back involuntarily, cringing, my arms coming up to cover my face. To cover my eyes. A warm gust of wind hit me, rocking me slightly, and suddenly I felt the sun on me. I brought my arms down and found myself standing in the middle of a meadow, a stream bubbling softly over some rocks to my left. I looked out at the horizon, where the deep green land met with startlingly blue skies, the sun shining down gently on my shoulders, and I realised then what the 'NX' had meant on the keycard:

Nexus Area.

This place was a colliding point, a nexus of time and space. And I had an idea I knew who and what had made it that way.

I turned, ready to get to the observation room, to call our friend and host Mister Mason and maybe ask him a few questions. I was stopped by a hand on my arm.

I jumped, spun around.

It was a young woman, maybe seventeen, dressed in the Gateway jumpsuit and jacket, her hair long and golden in the sunlight. She smiled at me. She was really quite beautiful. And I realised I was back at the habitat, but still standing in the meadow. There was no snow, just the light grass swaying gently in a soft breeze and above me a puffy cloud making its lazy way across a deep blue sky.

"Where are you going?" She asked, her voice calm.

"Er, back to...where I came from," I replied.

"No, I need your help," she said, shaking her head, "Please, there's some really crazy stuff happening here. I need your help."

I looked at her, watching her face, her eyes. She seemed worried, a bit apprehensive, but not crazy. Not like those damn kids.

"Are you a member of Project Gateway?" I said, carefully.

She nodded, "*Please, you have to help me.*"

"Sorry, there's nothing I can do. I'm thirty years too late," I turned to go, felt her hand on my arm again.

"It's *not* too late."

I looked at her, at the pleading in her eyes.

"You've got the wrong guy. I'm not one of you," I said quietly, trying not to look at her, "I have to go."

And then I felt her nails dig deeply into my arm, and I turned to see her head moving in towards my neck, her mouth open and her eyes wide and insane.

I grabbed her shirt with my other hand, pulled her away from me, breaking her grip on my arm, and flung her onto the grass.

She looked up at me, eyes hateful. And then she smiled, her eyes all sweetness and light.

"Why won't you come inside?" she keened, "We won't hurt you. We just want more company."

I stepped back, "Thanks, but I prefer my own."

And then two hands grabbed my arms, and I realised I was being held in place. I struggled to break away but it was useless. I looked to my left, to my right. They were Gateway members, the word 'SECURITY' on their grey Gateway jackets. Big guys, both of them taller than me, both of them staring straight ahead. I got the feeling by the way they moved and by the way they held me that they'd had some form of military training. I wondered what organization it had been, what I was dealing with.

The girl laughed, as they began to drag me along with them, "You'll see. It'll be fun."

The blonde girl ran ahead of us, giggling and picking flowers in the sunlight, as the two big men dragged me towards the entrance to the habitat.

"Where the hell are we going?" I asked.

"It's a secret," the girl replied, smiling.

"Rather tell me, I hate surprises —" I was shoved roughly by the guy on my right.

"Do that again, "I said, "and I'll crack your fucking skull."

He didn't reply, just continued to move me across the grass towards the large, wide entrance to the habitat, the large doors which were already staring to slide slowly open, showing nothing but a gaping hole into darkness, into a darkness that I didn't understand and didn't want to. I wished I hadn't given that little bastard the lab coat. It contained the comdisk something that, I had a feeling, would have made a big difference right about now.

Almost there...

The blonde seemed to notice the expression on my face.

"Don't worry," she said, "soon you'll see everything much better."

The guy to my left grunted.

A few feet from the entrance, now, and I could see nothing beyond the threshold. It was like sunlight couldn't penetrate into that place. I felt the darkness reaching for me, welcoming me home, crooning to me.

"No!" I started to struggle violently, trying to reach for the guns that I had, up until then, kept out of sight in their holsters beneath my jacket.

I struggled, but I couldn't reach them, I had no ability to move within the Gateway men's iron grasp.

And then the lights went out, and things got bad.

Twenty-three

The *EAV Gatekeeper* glided in across the white snow in the twilight, slowing as it approached the open doors of a giant, domed hangar. Its cargo was precious.

A cargo of humans.

A new colony, full of hope and excitement and perfect dreams.

The hovship docked in the giant steel hangar, and one by one the people disembarked, stepping out into the Antarctic habitat that was their new home. They walked out into the twilight, a distant sun shining on the very horizon giving them its welcome. One by one they emerged from the massive hangar, and then in groups, until at last all were gathered at the entrance to the Gateway Habitat, talking excitedly and quietly amongst themselves. Every once in a while one of them would glance expectantly up at the podium erected beside the main entrance.

And then I was there with them, standing in the crowd, looking out at the twilight sky and the atmosphere was electrifying. I didn't know how or why I was suddenly a part of things, it just seemed right.

There came the sound of a horn, and all eyes turned to the entrance to the main building. A man stood on the podium, staring down at the masses, arms open wide.

A man I'd seen before.

A man I'd had lunch with that afternoon.

Trevor Mason.

I stared up at him. Thirty years younger, but there was no doubt about it.

He held up his hands, and a hush fell over the crowd.

He smiled, surveyed the people below him.

His people.

For he was their leader, and they his faithful followers.

250

"Some of you are here because you needed something to believe in, and my theory came at the right time."

Silence. You could have heard a feather drop.

"And some of you are here because you felt something in the world was... missing. Something wasn't quite right."

There was a rumbling in the crowd, a sort of hushed agreement.

"But whatever your reasons for joining me here at the Gateway Outpost at Ciegan's End, one thing is certain."

A beat.

"You are all here because you have dreamed. You have dreamed of another place."

A few heads nodded, some words of affirmation.

"And this place in your dreams felt real to you, more so even than the world in which you awoke. You're here because you know something, my friends. You are here because you know *there is more*."

The crowd cheered.

Mason raised his hands again, commanding silence with a gesture.

"And some of us," he said, softly, "are here because we have lost something."

He seemed to be staring directly at me.

Directly *into* me.

"Something very dear to us... "

He *was* looking at me.

"Maybe the most important thing in our lives," speaking so quietly now, almost a whisper over the speakers, "And maybe... maybe I've found a way to get it back."

The crowd was silent as their leader stood on the podium, head held high as he watched his people, his colony.

"My friends!"

251

A pause now, the crowd expectant.

"Welcome to the Gateway! Welcome to your dreams!"

The crowd went wild, hats and paraphernalia flew into the air, and then everything shifted, and I sat in a damp dark metal room, surrounded by blood and blackness. Water dripping. Occasionally I heard a scream, coming from somewhere in the darkness.

And footsteps, a kind of shuffling, coming closer.

And closer.

"Hello?" my voice echoed, a hollow fragile sound.

I realised I was shaking. It was freezing here, I got the feeling my breath was crystallizing in the air a foot away. Not that I could see that far in the pitch-blackness surrounding me.

The shuffling stopped. There was silence for a while, and then the grating sound of steel on steel, a bolt drawing back. The shuffling continued, in the room now, somewhere to my left, stopping again.

I was silent.

Whatever it was hadn't responded to my voice, and I took that to be Yet Another Bad Thing. I sat dead still, the sound of the slow dripping still in my ears, and began moving my right hand very, very slowly toward my shoulder holster.

And then the lights came on, dirty yellow light bleeding down from tubes running across the ceiling. I was sitting in a metal chair in a stark metal room containing no windows, with long tables running down its length. It must've been a dining area for the Gateway inhabitants, but now it was filthy, disused. Dark blood stains streaked across the steel walls, the tables, and the floor.

Before me stood a girl with one arm, holding a doll and smiling at me.

Unsure of how to handle this, I smiled back.

She held out the doll for me, and I took it, my eyes not leaving hers.

252

"Hello —" I began, stopped, feeling a sudden wetness on my fingers. I looked down slowly.

The doll was covered in blood.

I dropped it, repulsed, and the child began to scream. But not sadly, or even angrily, but with a kind of insane ferocity that can't have been human. She reached towards me with her good arm, and I realised with horror that I couldn't move. It wasn't that I was strapped down or otherwise secured, I wasn't.

I just *couldn't move*.

At all.

I couldn't even struggle, just sat there on that steel chair as the little girl screamed her inhuman scream, her good right hand coming closer and closer to my face. Her nails, I saw as they got closer still, were jagged and had tiny pieces of flesh stuck to them. I found myself wondering whose flesh it was, hers or the last person to drop her doll.

The lights went out, and her screaming stopped and again I sat in pitch blackness with no sound but the dripping, the constant dripping. I found myself waiting tensely for the feel of that hand, those fingers, brushing over my face. Those nails, ripping into my skin, tearing, gashing, slashing.

Any second now...

A flutter of air against my face, a bird? Whatever it was nearly put me into cardiac arrest, but I realised I could move again. I reached for my guns, was greatly relieved to find them both present and correct. I pulled them from their holsters, just in case I was confronted with another little girl, and I don't care how that sounds.

"Get it!" another child's voice, a boy this time.

"I'm trying! He's too fast for me!" another boy, maybe a bit younger.

"No, he's not. Come on, Jed, you can get him!" this from the first boy.

And then I was surrounded by light again, found myself sitting on a grassy slope, my back against what turned out to be the PlastiGlass wall of the habitat's recreational dome. Artificial sunlight shone down from the holographic array on the ceiling.

Two little boys, one of them about six, the other around ten, were in a grassy field, the younger of the two attempting to catch a large brown bird, like the one that crashed our jet, only smaller, the older boy sitting on another hillock, watching with amusement. The little guy was running after it, arms in the air, whooping, while the poor bird seemed to be trying with great difficulty to get itself into the air, but was for some reason failing at this. Both were headed for the glass dome's wall.

"Quickly, he'll get through the hatch! Then we've lost him! Jed, Dad'll kill us!"

I looked towards where the older boy was pointing, and sure enough, a hatchway was open in the PlastiGlass wall of the dome, and the little boy and the ridiculous bird were headed straight for it.

Something was wrong.

This wasn't two little boys playing on the fields. Something was very wrong here. I glanced at the older boy, trying to see what was happening, but nothing appeared to be out of the ordinary.

And then I saw it:

A remote controller, hidden in the palm of the elder boy's hand, a glint of something very bad in his eyes. I turned, the bird and the little boy were almost at the hatchway.

"No!" I yelled, getting to my feet, starting to run after the little guy, stopping.

Then I turned and ran for the elder boy, the other guy being, by now, way to far away to try to stop. Besides, having a big old adult running towards him and screaming would only have made him run faster. Well, I would, anyway.

"No, don't do it! Don't −"

There was a sickening 'thunk' and I stopped running.

Turned slowly.

The bird was fine, happily picking at the blood and splinters of brain that had escaped the dome as the hatchway entrance had smashed down on little Jed's head, crushing his young skull in an instant. Blood started to spread onto the grass and the soft, white snow that lay outside the dome, the red liquid dark and shining.

I turned to the elder boy, stared at him.

He shrugged, pushing the button to lift the gateway once more, blood and gore all around it.

I just watched it rise.

"You killed your brother," I said softly.

"I killed my brother," he whispered to himself.

I looked at him, and he started to smile.

The scene swung wildly and again I sat in darkness with the sound of dripping in my ears. Slow dripping. Slow and regular.

I tried to move. Found I couldn't, some drug was rendering my muscles useless to me. After God-only-knew how long, I could take it not a second longer.

"What the hell is that noise?" I yelled at no-one in particular, "What the hell is going on?"

Only silence greeted my ears.

I tied to move again but, of course, I couldn't. My body was totally useless. And then the lights came on again, but this time I wasn't sitting anymore, I was lying on a hospital bed surrounded by doctors and nurses wearing bloodied, dark grey coveralls featuring the Project Gateway logo on the right arm.

I attempted to sit up, but I realised straight away that I still had no control over my muscles.

I swivelled my eyes down, realised I was totally naked except for a wafer-thin hospital gown with the same colours and logo as the others. The doctor and nurses were talking quietly amongst themselves and when I tried to speak I discovered I couldn't do that either. I started to worry about things, and the heart-monitor picked up on it.

The doctor turned to face me. A few of them held medical tools that were covered in blood, and I guessed they must have finished with someone mere minutes before my arrival.

What the hell was I doing here?

"Good afternoon," the doctor smiled.

I guessed he was the one who was going to cut me open, because he had a medical scalpel in his right hand.

"My name is Doctor Kales, and these are my subordinates. We are about to... do some work on you."

I was pretty sure I didn't need any work done.

In fact, I was bloody certain.

The heart monitor started to go crazy.

One of the nurses mumbled something and the others laughed. The surgeon moved towards me with the bloody scalpel, and it was then that I knew for sure that these people were not only going to 'operate' on me using instruments covered in blood, but they fully intended on performing the 'operation' while I was wide awake and the only medication they'd administered or probably even *considered* administering was to paralyse my muscles.

Oh shit.

The nurses drew the gown away, revealing my naked body.

No.

The surgeon brought the blood-covered blade slowly down to my chest, moved it down to my stomach, the tip gently gliding across the surface of my skin.

He was *enjoying* this!

One of the nurses looked down at me, moved her face in close. She was in her early sixties, by the look of her. She had a very homely appearance to her, like she was the mother of someone I knew, and her presence was almost... soothing. Except for the fact that she had no eyes,

Neither, come to that, did the rest of them.

Suddenly, they all stood there with gaping sockets, blood smeared all along the skin around the eyes and down the cheeks.

"Don't worry love, the last guy we did feels much better now," she smiled.

I realised I was going to die.

Either that or be held within this black nexus forever, to be 'operated' on for eternity.

Or both.

I made a mental note to shoot pretty much everyone inside this habitat if I ever got out alive, although right now it didn't look very likely.

For some reason, I though about Melanie.

About the way she looked at me when I said something that I thought was funny.

And then he cut.

It was a sharp, shooting pain as the surgeon made an incision through the skin on my stomach. I would have screamed if I could, but I just lay there, paralysed, staring at the new wound and the shaking hand grasping the scalpel and the blood with a kind of detached horror.

Was he even a doctor?

Was he even fucking human?

He called for a nurse, probably pretty if it wasn't for the total lack of eyes, and together they put into place a steel clamp around my now gaping and bloody stomach cavity.

The homely nurse said something else, and the 'surgeon' agreed.

"Don't worry, Mister. The stomach clamp was just to see if we could do it. You see," she actually looked embarrassed, "we've never used one of those before."

"But don't worry," remarked the surgeon, "It's dead easy."

"Isn't it, Doctor?" The pretty one said, smiling, "We have to use those more often."

He nodded, and both approached my head. This, I felt, classified as an Extremely Bad Thing.

The homely bitch used her fingers to pry open my right eye, while the 'pretty' one brought another, smaller, clamp.

Christ, no.

Together, they clamped my right eye completely open, and the surgeon came towards me once more with his bloody, infected, scalpel.

Please don't.

Closer...

A white room.

And closer...

She was so scared.

The guy flicked his wrist, and in that one swift movement my right eye was severed and removed from its socket, and dropped in a jar to my right.

I started to pass out, but was revived by the homely nurse.

"Don't worry, dear. One more, and this will all be over," she said with a smile, wiping the sweat off my forehead.

No, I don't want to see your world.

I don't want to see.

Help me, Mel.

Please help me.

They clamped my left eye open, and once again the scalpel came towards my face, stopped inches before my open left eye. Something had caught the 'surgeon's' attention, him and the two nurses were staring at something past the small field of my vision.

I could feel the scalpel shaking slightly against my eyelashes, felt the warmth of the blood oozing down the right side of my face, the coldness of the steel clamp holding my stomach open.

I did what any normal person would do.

I passed out.

The last thing I saw as my horrified mind melted away into the darkness was a huge black and orange suit and mask, obviously some type of biohazard suit, moving into my field of vision, towards the doctor. His arm was outstretched, holding something, three words printed clearly down his arm:

NX CONTAINMENT TEAM

And then everything went black, and I fell away into merciful unconsciousness.

Twenty-four

I came awake with a start, realised immediately that I wasn't alone.

"He's awake."

I was lying on a couch in what appeared to be a small lounge, a warm blanket covering me. I had no idea how long I'd been out for. My vision came into focus, I looked around me, found Mason sitting on a chair opposite me, Rainer standing beside him looking anxious, and two bulky security guards standing on either side of the door looking extremely unfriendly.

Mason leaned forward, "Are you insane?"

I felt my face.

I had both my eyes!

Wait . . .

And my stomach was fine!

I put a hand to my aching head.

"Getting there, gimme a few more hours."

Rainer grinned at this.

"Mister Corben, do you know how serious this is? You –"

"Yeah, Rainer," I said, bringing myself to a sitting position, "I know how serious this is. They fucking operated on me! They took out my fucking eye!"

Silence.

Mason nodded, "What they do to you in there is only real *in there*, Mister Corben. As long as you keep your head out here, you're okay."

"You're a fucking lunatic," I replied.

"Ash . . ." Rainer said gently.

Silence.

"You saw me," Mason said, softly, after a while.

I nodded.

"It showed you everyth –"

"Everything, yeah, before trying to turn me into a circus freak."

Mason looked down at this clasped hands, "I see."

I looked up, stared directly at Mason. "Your name is Terrence Manning. You were the founder of Project Gateway, thirty years ago. Because of you everybody on the colony died violent and insane deaths. Everyone except you, a man, and a little girl. You employed me to find and deliver that little girl to you. Why?"

"Who do you think you –" Mason began.

"What the fuck do you want with Sarah, Manning?"

He went silent, watching me with a sullen look.

The guys by the door moved uncomfortably.

"You guys stay where you are. I'm not in the mood for this," I barked.

They looked at Rainer, who said, "Why don't you boys wait outside. Mister Corben poses no threat to us, he has my complete trust."

"Yes, sir," they left the room, went to stand guard outside the door, eyeing me warily as the left.

"What is happening to the Planet, Manning? It has to do with the Nexus, any idiot can see that –"

"And one indeed has –" Manning grunted.

"Yeah. So what have you done? What is happening?"

Manning clasped his hands together, seemed to be very interested in them for about a minute or so. Then he spoke.

Softly, he said, "Well, it has shown you, so . . . Mister Corben, have you ever lost something you loved so much that you would do anything to get it back?"

"Yes."

"A woman?"

I nodded.

"I lost my son. I was a young man, in my late twenties. Married, with an incredibly promising career as a scientist at Astral Mechanics, working on the nature of dreams and alternate universes, close to a breakthrough, in fact," he took a deep breath, exhaled slowly, "I received a call one day. It was from my wife. She was hysterical. She was . . . She said something had happened to Daniel . . . Something terrible. Mister Corben, he had been hit by a hovcar... My boy was in surgery when I arrived at the hospital. The doctor informed me he had suffered massive head injuries, his skull had been crushed . . . between . . ."

The guy wasn't having an easy time with this. Rainer put a hand on his shoulder.

"I'm okay, Howard, I'm okay . . . Anyway, the surgery saved his life. He came home a month later, but he was . . . different. He was brain-damaged, Mister Corben, my boy was brain-damaged at five years old. I can't even imagine what the next three years must have been like for him. All I know is three years later he found my gun, put it in his mouth . . . and . . . he . . ."

"That's enough, Trevor," Rainer said gently.

There was silence in the room.

"I'm sorry," I said awkwardly.

"He was nearly eight. My wife, Jess, found him in his room . . . She left me a few months after that, we got a divorce and I haven't seen or heard from her since. So I buried my son in the ground and I buried myself in the work and that's the way it stayed for two years. I knew something, Mister Corben. Only a theory at first, but I *believed* in it. And those two years were spent creating something. Something great."

"Project Gateway."

Manning nodded, "The Gateway was my obsession, my dream, and it became a reality. I gathered my followers and together, we boarded the *Gatekeeper* and journeyed to Ciegan's End where our newly-completed habitat awaited us, and our minds were opened over the course of the next twenty-odd months using the power of neurotechnology, and the joining of our wills to rip open the border between worlds."

He looked down at his clasped hands.

"But it all went wrong . . . Mister Corben, it was a case of too much too soon. About a year and a half into it, my people lost it. They became insane. And violent, terribly violent. They hurt each other, and themselves... The situation escalated rapidly out of control and descended into pure chaos, and the few of us that for some reason were not affected like the rest went into hiding, barricading ourselves in one of the store rooms. Unable to communicate with the outside world, to call for help, we scraped out an existence within the bunker while outside the world went to hell. About three months later, our salvation came in the form of the Earth Alliance Navy, off the newly landed *Cirrus*. They swooped in and cleaned out, getting almost completely wiped out themselves in the terrible, shifting nexus they found themselves in. It was a bloodbath, the original inhabitants of the Gateway habitat had become like wild animals. Only a few of us made it out.

"But one thing remained in my mind: it had worked. My theory had been correct. All I had to do was release the nexus, the collision of the dreamworld and the ordinary world, *subliminally and very slowly*, over the course of a decade or more using the power of neurotechnology, and it could be a reality. I launched NeuroLOG four years later and opened this outpost a decade after that, building a massive dome over the original habitat to secure the nexus and tap it's power, and when the time was right and NeuroLOG's hardware and software domination of the marketplace was almost absolute, I began the slow business of sending neurological suggestions on the reality of the worlds as two sides to the same coin and the impulses gained from the nexus across the globe through NeuroLOG's widely-established network, to anyone who uses a Neurolink. That's most of the Planet, Mister Corben. I knew that it was then only a matter of time before the fruits of my labour would be seen . . . Mister Corben, that day is nearly upon us. The more people believe, even subconsciously, the more this thing grows. What is happening to this world is this: You dream of your woman, Mister Corben?"

"Yes."

He nodded, "That is because she still exists, in another place, a place you go to when you dream. The ordinary world and the dreamworld are colliding, the borders between the two are being torn apart, and pieces of the two worlds are slipping through the cracks."

"Dead Man Walking Syndrome," I said softly.

"There is no death, Mister Corben. Only another place. Those people were here, and now they are there. The same with geographical locations. You have visited Sandy Island in another place. I'm sure we all have. It is the Planet's changing, evolving, subconscious which is bringing it all together. It is a miracle."

"A miracle? Manning, people are losing it. People are dying. I have seen a man pull out his own eyes –"

"Sarah was born in the Nexus, Mister Corben."

I went silent.

"She knows how to exist in harmony with both worlds. Both worlds existing simultaneously. As one."

"But you –" I began.

"The child escaped unscathed. Did it not occur to you that that little girl was born in the nexus and existed surrounded by complete madness and complete, horrific violence for *months* as things became worse and steadily worse without being hurt, physically or psychologically, before I finally gave up trying to save them and we holed ourselves up in the storeroom to wait it out?

"And when help finally arrived, and most of the rescue team were butchered by the inhabitants, my people, still she wasn't touched on the way out. At one point her father was viciously attacked while en route to the *Cirrus*, he dropped the girl, she can't have been older than a year and a half then, and tried to defend her. The man was savaged, his body ripped and torn, and he fell to the ground in a heap. The child just stood there over the wounded, lacerated body of her father showing no fear, staring calmly at the lunatic. He just stared back at her, as if hypnotised. Then he backed away, very slowly, turned, and ran!

"We boarded the *Cirrus* shortly after and got the hell out of there. We were twelve in the storeroom. Only three of us made it to the hovship, along with two marines. There was only one crewman onboard, the other members of crew having gone insane or been killed and dragged into the nexus. Everyone onboard was injured badly, Mister Corben. Everyone, except Sarah. I believe she has the ability not only to see both worlds as one, but also to save the minds of the ones afflicted with what I have termed The Madness."

"You think she can save the world," I said.

"Mister Corben, in the three months that we were holed up in that store room, nine of the twelve people were affected in some way, until Sarah came to them. She would approach the person, put a tiny hand on their cheek, look into their eyes, and their condition would all but disappear over the course of the next few hours… Yes, I believe that young lady is the salvation of this world."

"You want your son back, Mister Mason, I understand that –" I started.

"And you want your woman back –"

My thoughts strayed to Melanie, the desert, the storm, and the white room.

I could have her back!

And my old friend Dex.

And things would be like they were before.

And...

And neither of them would ever forgive me.

"I miss her more than words can say." I said softly.

Mason nodded.

"But I can't let this happen," I continued, "not at the expense of mass murder. You are using NeuroLOG and the unsuspecting minds of billions of innocent people to make two worlds collide, two worlds that *belong apart*, and hoping your son will come through a breach. I understand your motives. Believe me, I do . . . but the price is too high."

Trevor Mason tried to speak but I interrupted, "My best friend is dead because of a Fragment."

"What's a fragment?" Mason asked.

"Feelings of ill will, bundled up in a warm and cuddly package."

"From the other place?"

"Yes, and I'm sure you'd find many other surprises if you came back to Nu Caynan with me," I said.

Mason shook his head, "Not now. For the moment, my place is here."

"You've heard of the giant asteroid on a collision course for the Earth."

Mason nodded, "What of it? As I have already said, we are quite safe in the event of impact."

"It didn't rock up until after things started getting weird."

Mason watched me carefully.

"Do you know what I think? I think it's part of the collision between worlds," I continued, "And I think there's only one thing to do about it. I think we have to blow this place to hell."

Mason shook his head, "I'm afraid I can't allow that, Mister Corben."

"It must be done," I replied, I looked at Rainer, "Did you know about this?"

"This is the first he's heard of this. Only myself and the two top scientists on Phoenix know the truth about this place, one of whom you knocked out this afternoon. Everyone else on the outpost sees it simply as research into an unstable nexus of space and time, and know nothing of its true purpose."

I nodded, "Well, either way, this place has to go."

"As I already told you, Mister Corben, that is not going to happen."

I pulled my guns, aimed them at his face, "Call for an evacuation and activate the self-destruct sequence."

Mason shook his head, "This place doesn't have –"

"Yes it does. EA law. All biological, molecular or quantum-related research facilities must have a destruction sequence as a safety device," I said tensely, "so I say again: Call for an immediate evacuation and activate the self-destruct sequence."

Mason scoffed, "Or what, you'll shoot me?"

"Don't tempt me."

His eyes met mine, and I could see that threatening him would do no good, wasn't sure what options that left me with.

"Computer, activate the intercom."

"Intercom online"

"To all members of staff, this is Howard Rainer. Please evacuate Phoenix Outpost immediately and make your way to the EAV Crusader at once. Take only what is absolutely necessary. The outpost self-destruct countdown will commence shortly. You must be onboard the hovship within the next thirty minutes, thank you."

Mason was shocked, "What the hell are you doing? How do you know the activation code –"

"It's my job to know, Trevor. And, judging from what I have seen and heard, this operation has gone too far."

"I am a member of the High Council!" Mason roared, "You —"

"Shut up!" Rainer replied, "Trevor, you're playing with the lives of the entire population of this planet. It has to stop. What do you think the Council will have to say about it when I compile a full report on this outpost?"

"You have nothing."

"I have a disk, with details and figures on subliminal broadcasting over the NeuroLOG network. Also, it includes video archive footage of the nexus, and what has gone on in there for the past three years. On top of that, it has full technical schematics of the outpost, and more importantly of the Main Research Dome housing the habitat and the transmitting towers built onto it. Trevor, I have all the information necessary to put you in a padded room for the rest of your days," Rainer said.

"Where the hell did you get this disk?" Mason said, tensely.

"It has been systematically compiled over the period of the last few years, ever since I started to have... suspicions."

"Why?"

"A failsafe, against the day I might need it. It seems that day has come."

"And who, may I ask, was the compiler? As I already mentioned, many of my employees have seen the nexus, a number of them having even ventured within, but only two know the true nature, the true *purpose,* of the Phoenix. And only they have access to that kind of information... "

Rainer said nothing.

"Howard?" Mason said quietly.

"It doesn't matter. He was simply following my orders. Trevor, NeuroLOG has been home to me for a long time.

It has been my life, and I have run this company with my entire being, keeping totally focussed to her needs and turning a blind eye to your outpost. But, in light of this information, I can't allow you to continue with this. The choice is yours. Either way, the outpost goes. The question is, do you want to lose you position in the High Council, possibly end up in an asylum?"

"You wouldn't."

Rainer looked tired, "I would, Trevor... But I'd rather not. Let's just get the hell out of here. Let this thing go."

"No! I will not lose my son!" Mason pulled a gun of his own, raised it at Rainer's head.

"Drop the gun!" I said.

Mason looked at me, "You should have been taken out when we had the opportunity," he spat, "Looks like my people are going soft."

He looked at Rainer, who said nothing.

"Serves me right for involving someone from the outside. Only after hiring you did I stop to consider the error of that decision. Hiring someone who wasn't loyal to me was a bad idea, something I realised too late," his gun was still trained on Rainer, daring him to activate the self-destruct sequence.

"The guys in suits, the people after me, it was on your orders?" I said, wanting to shoot the guy more than anything now.

"Computer, activate self-destruct sequence," Rainer called.

"No!" Mason yelled.

"Please give activation password and authorisation for self-destruct sequence."

"I'm sorry, old friend. I know how much you miss your boy, and I can't imagine how it must feel, but this has to end," Rainer said, sadness in his voice. Then, "Computer, self-destruct authorisation: Howard Rai –"

And Mason fired, taking him twice, three times, in the chest. I returned the fire with pleasure, taking him in his. The two men crumpled to the floor, and I ran over to where Rainer lay. The two security guys burst into the room, guns trained on me, taking in the scene around them. Mason lay on the other end of the room in a pool of blood, unmoving. I think he was dead before he hit the ground. Rainer was still conscious, but losing blood fast. I tried to put some pressure on his wounds, but I knew it was futile. He wouldn't live long.

"Put your hands up!" yelled one of the guards, as the other went to check on Mason.

"If I do he'll bleed to death!" I replied.

"He was protecting me," Rainer said softly, "Mister Mason became violent, pulled a gun on me, started firing. Mister Corben was simply defending me."

"Mister Mason is dead," the other guy said.

The guard looked unsure of what to do, but didn't press the point. Rainer was the ranking member of staff, was in fact the highest-ranking member in the company now.

I looked down at him, his blood spreading everywhere.

"Get some help!" I barked, "We need medical staff here now!"

The one guy nodded, called for emergency medical staff through his headset.

It was too late, and I think Rainer knew that, because he looked up at me, smiled, "I was hoping to retire at Empire Beach."

"Please give activation password and authorisation for self-destruct sequence"

"Computer, authorisation: Howard Rainer, ID five-nine-five-two-three-seven-four. Password: Megan."

"Password and authorisation accepted..."

There was a brief pause, then,

"Warning, Outpost Phoenix will self-destruct in sixty minutes...

Repeat: Outpost Phoenix will self-destruct in sixty minutes..."

boomed from every speaker in the outpost.

I looked at Rainer, "I'm sorry about being a bastard," I said softly.

"I know," he replied with a faint smile, eyes closing, "You can't help it... it's in your nature."

"No! Open your eyes, you have to keep your eyes open!" I slapped him in the face, and his eyes came open.

"What the hell was that for?" he said.

"That thing about my nature," I replied.

He grinned, and the emergency medical staff burst into the room, and one of the security guys pulled me away from Rainer as they settled down to work. I went and sat on the couch, hands clasped tightly together.

Waited . . .

And waited . . .

A few minutes later they stopped what they were doing and put down their instruments, covered in blood and completely and utterly silent. And I knew the truth, didn't even have to ask.

Rainer was dead.

"Warning, Outpost Phoenix will self-destruct in fifty minutes...

Repeat: Outpost Phoenix will self-destruct in fifty minutes..."

"Sir, it's time to go," said the guy who had pulled me off Rainer, "We have to go, now."

I nodded and got up, feeling extremely tired for some reason, wanting only to crawl into a deep dark hole and sleep for a week.

Or maybe a month.

"I need to find my companions," I muttered.

"Sir, you must make for the *Crusader* immediately," and then his voice dropped to little more than a whisper, "I saw you with Mister Rainer. He said you had his trust, therefore you have mine. I will personally guarantee your companions' safety."

Call me crazy, but I believed him.

I got up and left, trying not to step in the blood of a man whom I had come to realise, too late, was my friend.

Twenty-five

I wasn't there to see the final and absolute destruction of the Phoenix outpost and the Gateway habitat it had housed, but I can only imagine it must have been quite a sight. Orange flames lighting up the twilight, the snowstorm we had left in burning away in the blast radius and the heavens above it glowing bright and alive in the darkness.

Afterwards, there was nothing for it but to watch as the snow beneath us turned to water and the sky above us turned from twilight to day.

The journey was, once again, long. Four weeks is not to be scoffed at, but have you ever noticed how much *longer* it seems on the way *back*? Felony, Sarah and I discussed the outcome of NeuroLOG and Mason and Manning and the whole damn mess, and Sarah pointed out some very interesting things:

For a start, she said the world was not ready to experience both worlds at once, hence the insanity that had gripped so many. She said that the return of things to some semblance of normality would probably be a slow process, as it would take time for the damage to people's subconscious to be reversed by nothing more than the mediocre pressures of modern life.

She appeared to be right, as we soon discovered that everything was pretty much the way we'd left it, Shillian was still a weird dreamscape and her airport still a meadow, as a number of mind fuoked airline pilots had discovered just in time. The asteroid was still headed for us when we left Ciegan's End, but everyone in a position of 'authority' seemed to have a different idea of its size and distance from the Earth. Some said it would hit us thirty years from now, others said it was more like thirty minutes. And still others remarked that it had, in fact, already hit us, but was so tiny that we hadn't noticed. This didn't stop the EA Defence Force from shooting the hell out of it a few weeks later with the first show of nuclear weapons since the International Weapons Treaty. No one said where they had come from, but then, no one really thought to ask, what with an Extinction-Level Event being anywhere between thirty years and thirty minutes away.

So we fired everything we had at it.

The meteor broke apart, shattered, and a million tiny meteorites scorched through the atmosphere and disappeared without a trace, a rain of fire raging bright against the black abyss of the night. Not one piece of rock hit the ground, the whole meteor storm vanishing from sight before even one fragment could hit the ground.

Sandy Island also totally disappeared, leaving a number of sets and quite a few people clinging to them in the high seas.

Tommy Slid had been quoted as saying he felt that that was exactly the kind of thing his ex-wife would have done, and that this was in fact the perfect way to end his picture. His ex-wife was, for once, in full agreement and felt the whole thing was yet further grounds for a lawsuit. Tommy again told her where she could insert the idea. Mercury Red was said to be very pleased with the new ending to the picture.

Rescue attempts were made for the people (mostly extras and crew) and sets at sea, and a number of those attempts were successful, but eventually the studio said enough was enough and they could bloody-well swim to shore. Their response was to bind the sets together and use the thing as a makeshift raft. It is generally acknowledged as being the single most bizarre floating device in recorded history.

The Fragment didn't come back.

Between you and me, I think it was getting tired of getting shot. I would be. I didn't know how or why it had come for me so savagely, and I guessed I never would, but I wasn't really bothered.

It didn't return in the next four weeks, and Rainer's trust had ensured me protection from Mason's people, so it didn't appear that I would have to endure any further attempts on my life. I was just glad that it was over.

I thought about what I would do on my return to the world of the living, whatever that meant.

Would I go back to Tanis?

Reopen the offices?

No, it wouldn't be the same without Dex.

Dex, that was one thing I needed to deal with. Over the course of the journey, I found myself with a lot of time on my hands, and a lot on my mind. Three people in particular: Dex, my ex-wife Sharyn (as much as she had irritated the shit out of me) and Howard Rainer, a man I had suspected of some very bad things initially but who had eventually become my strongest ally.

Eventually, the cold gave way to warmth and sunshine, and my thoughts strayed to lighter subjects, helped along by the complete healing of Mitchell's mental state, after someone had had a little talk with him. Sarah never told me what she had said to him when I asked her, she just smiled enigmatically and said, "You wouldn't understand."

I, like everyone else on the Planet, hate it when someone says that to me, but in that particular case I figured she was probably right. Also, I regarded the very fact that I wouldn't understand as a Good Thing. I decided it wasn't worth dwelling on. What was more important was where I was going to spend my impending holiday.

Perhaps, I thought, I should spend some time on the beaches of Tora Sera, getting some sun after all the snow. Maybe I'd give Tommy a call, see how he was doing.

A few days before we arrived at Steiner Harbour, I made the call.

"Ash, waddup man?" Tommy was one of the few people who always seemed genuinely happy to hear from me.

"Finished up, looking to catch some R and R," I replied, glad to see him too, "I'll be in Tora Sera in a few days. What say we meet up?"

Tom shook his head, "I'm in Nu Caynan, man. Editing *The Pros and Cons*, you know how it is."

I said *No, not really.*

"You wanna meet me this side? We can hit a few night spots, make some friends. Where's Dex?"

I told him.

"Shit."

"Yeah," I replied.

"I'm sorry, man."

"Yeah."

There was a short, and very awkward silence, where neither of us really knew what to say.

Tommy broke the spell.

"I'll have a jet waiting for you at Tora Sera when you get there," he said, "You and I are gonna get trashed."

I laughed, and looking back I think that was the first time I'd done that in a while.

"I'll see you there," I replied.

I hung up, and settled back in the couch by the observation window in my cabin, deciding to enjoy these last few days on the sea even if it killed me. Over the last three weeks I'd gotten used to being exclusively in my own company. I would see Mitchell occasionally, but not often. He was the ranking member of staff in NeuroLOG now, having been named by Rainer as his successor, and therefore had his hands pretty-much full.

And Felony and Sarah, well, that's another story. They had become increasingly interested in each other lately, making me wonder exactly how long *that* had been going on for. Knowing me, probably quite some time. What can I say, when it's work, I'm as sharp as they come. But sometimes I'm really a bit slow. At times I will not notice something unless it's right on top of me or coming towards me very fast with a funny look in its eyes.

That's just me I guess. So, when Tommy offered me a few nights of fun and games in the clubs of Nu Caynan, I realised that just maybe that was exactly what I needed.

A few days had never felt so long to me.

PART THREE
Salvation

Twenty-six

Nu Caynan at night, in the pouring rain.

My kind of place.

There were two reasons why Tommy and I ended up at SkyN that night:

One: I needed a new name. A fresh start, if you will.

And two: because I wanted to know how Neth was holding up against the competition, how the war for the Nu Caynan underground was faring.

We arrived at the club in the early hours of the morning, Tommy in a black hat and sunglasses, his 'incognito look', which I pointed out made him look even more like Tommy Slid than he did without them, and me in the usual casual black suit.

We walked past the queue and up to the entrance.

"Hello, is –" I began.

"Shit, you're Tommy Slid!" bellowed one of the bouncers, "You're great, man! Come in!"

And we went in.

It was as easy as that.

We headed straight up the stairs to the entrance to the VIP room, where we were stopped by the guards at the door.

I wasn't certain, but they appeared to be different from the guys on my previous visit. The door was also different. It was quite a lot bigger, for one thing. And it was made of what appeared to be solid steel.

"Hi –" I began again.

"Tommy Slid! Fuck! It's an honour, man!" Tom's hand was excessively shaken, "You want in?"

Tommy nodded, looking bored.

"One moment, Mister Slid," the guard said, swiping a card through a slot in the door, which slid open with amazing speed. I saw that it *was* solid steel, about two feet thick. The guard disappeared through the door, and it slammed back into place, only to slide open again when he appeared back about thirty seconds later.

I was asked to disarm, which surprised me considering the guns had been *given* to me by Neth, and we entered the VIP room. I looked around for Neth, didn't see him.

"Ash!" I turned at the sound of my name.

It was Rachel. She was running up to me.

"Rach," I said. "How've you been?"

She gave me a big hug, completely ignoring Tommy, who was eyeing out the same lesbians from before, who were still at it on the couch. I think they may have been going for a record.

"Not great," she replied, voice hushed. "SkyN has a new owner."

I raised an eyebrow, "What? Who —"

"Not now," she said, "Come with me. We'll get a room and talk."

I nodded, pulling Tom's attention away from the ladies on the couch, and we started to follow Rachel out of the VIP room.

"Ash, my old friend! What a surprise this is."

I stopped dead.

I knew that voice.

It had been a while, a hell of a while, but I knew that voice well.

I turned around, and stood face to face with someone who, more than anyone else on the Planet, should have been dead.

"Hello, Cole."

Cole smiled, "Like my place?"

He gestured around him. The place was exactly the same as the last time I was here.

"Where is Neth?" I asked quietly.

Cole laughed softly, "Would you care to speak in private, Ash?"

I nodded, told Tom to wait with Rachel, and followed as he led the way into a private lounge area off the VIP room. Cole had a seat on a couch at a low coffee table, put his feet on the table, and gestured for me to have a seat.

I ignored the offer, just stood staring at him.

Cole was unfazed, "Fine, have it your way. Neth is dead. I killed him myself. I understand you were friends."

"We had an understanding. You should be dead."

"Yet here I am," he smiled. "still murdering your friends."

"You're going to pay, Cole."

"No doubt," he replied, pensively. Then he smiled brightly. "But not today. You know, I have been trying to kill you for quite a while, Ash. Since I slipped through from the other place. Cigar?"

I declined.

"Suit yourself," he said, snipping it and lighting up. Something occurred to him, "If you had just opened the fucking door of your apartment all those months ago, you would have saved me a lot of time and effort... And men."

The vBomb.

"It was all you," I muttered.

Cole nodded, "Pretty much, yeah. You're a slippery bastard, Ash, I have to hand it to you. Always on the move. Your lovely ex-wife Sharyn was very helpful, her diary contained all the information we needed to trace you and Dex. Lost you after the plane crash, though."

"Sorry about that."

282

"No matter. After you left your only traceable items in Serenity, and Dex's signal died out in the middle of fucking nowhere, we needed to call in some help." He looked irritated. "I really thought the Fragment would sort you out."

"The Fragment?" I said under my breath.

"Unpleasant, isn't it? Courtesy of a friend on the other side. He's getting upset that you keep sending it back empty-handed."

"I try."

I was going to kill this guy.

There was nothing more in the world I wanted as badly.

Something occurred to me.

"The old lady, Sally. Why did you kill her?"

"Our trace on your mobile led us there. She wouldn't tell us your destination, the bitch. So we killed her for fun."

"You're a real gem." I muttered. "You were never after Sarah, then."

"Sarah? Sarah who? I told you already, I've wanted nothing better than to kill you since I slipped through. Tit for tat, and all that."

I looked around the room, trying to find something to attack him with. As it turned out, Mason hadn't put the hit on me after all. He'd had nothing to do with it. I suddenly felt bad for nailing the guy, even if it had been in Rainer's defence.

"There's something I have to know, Cole." I said, trying to remain calm. "How the hell did you get the vBomb into my apartment? That security setup cost me a fortune."

Cole smiled, "I was Apex too, Ash. You're not the only one who can hack a security system." He shook his head then, "You know, I was sure I had you in the flight from Shillian," Cole continued, "It was perfect. I tell you, Davis could not *believe* the evacuation pods! I mean, you disappear for a decade and they come up with all kinds of new-fangled shit."

"Davis?"

"Yeah, he was the guy with the 'chute, my right-hand man back in the day. Maybe you remember him from NeuroLOG, ten years ago. A certain cocktail bar?"

"Not really. You guys all look the same."

"Dex will," Cole said. "He took him out. From a hovcar in the rain right outside the window –"

"Dex is dead."

Cole raised an eyebrow, "Really?"

"Yeah."

He nodded, "Fragments have that effect on people."

I said nothing.

"In order for one to come in, another has to go out. Your friend was in the right place at the right time. No hard feelings, eh?"

I tried not to show my anger, my *fury*, with what I saw sitting casually before me. Cole, back from the grave, sitting there smoking a cigar without a care in the world. After everything that had happened in the past few months, all the strangeness and the violence and the death, to see the man who'd killed Melanie sitting in front of me and gloating about the part he'd played in all that had happened was more than I could bear.

I dived at him, my hands closing around his neck.

I squeezed, putting all the anger and helplessness and loss I had endured in the past ten years into ripping the life from his body.

I heard a gunshot.

Pain, shooting suddenly through my side.

And then I heard a sound behind me, felt hands on my arms and shoulders, and I was pulled off him and thrown roughly to the floor.

Cole got up, walked over to me and kicked me in the stomach.

"Did you really think you could kill me?" he snarled, walking around me.

"I did once already, you fuck –"

He kicked me in the face.

I looked up through the mists of pain to see what I was facing. Cole stood with two guys in suits, one I recognised as the guy from the motel room on the road to Serenity.

I looked at him, "Didn't I shoot you?"

The guy said nothing, just looked down at me.

"So much for re-thinking your life," I said.

He looked at Cole, who nodded, and then he kicked me in the face and it felt like my brain had been jarred loose and I could have sworn I saw her smile.

"Mel."

It just came out.

Cole seemed amused by this.

"You miss her, Ash? You want her back?"

I started to get to my feet but was kicked in the face again, fell back down.

"You're quite sprightly for a man with a bullet in your gut," Cole remarked.

I didn't reply, was starting to feel dizzy.

"She's gone, you know. You killed her."

I looked up at him, couldn't speak.

"You should have left Apex alone, Ash. Yep, she'd still be alive if it wasn't for you."

Cole smiled, putting his gun to my head.

"It's quite something. The amount of resources I devoted to having you capped, all the guys I sent out on their various Ash-based missions, only to end up doing it myself in my *own fucking nightclub*."

285

He pushed the gun hard into my skull as he said those last words, and I didn't move a muscle, just looked up at him.

"You killed me, Carter. You put a bullet in my head," he said then, his eyes glazing over, "Do you know what it feels like to die like that?"

"I'm sure she experienced what it felt like to die like that," I spat.

Cole's voice was harsh, "Those were my fucking orders! It was me or her. If I'd said no, Apex would have made me pay with my life. The people I was answering to weren't like Felony. They weren't out to protect my interests, they were out to protect their own. They would have put a bullet in my head."

"So you slit her throat instead."

Cole lowered the gun, his eyes appeared to be far away.

"I almost didn't," he said. "I roughed her up a bit, psyching myself up to do the job. Tied her up, stripped her, just as I was ordered to... And then I stopped, thought maybe I could get away with leaving it at that, started to walk away. But I knew the truth and frankly, I couldn't afford to take the chance. So I turned around and..."

"Slit her throat," I finished for him.

"Yeah. And then you came along just as I was building a name for myself in the underground, and you shot me in the face and put me through a hell I can't even put into words. I'm a changed man now, Ash. There's no limit to what I'm capable of now."

My mind flashed back to the two girls, what where their names?

"Natalie. And Jennifer," I said out loud.

"Ah yes, the little girls. That was Davis. He booby trapped your office, then he saw the girls and thought they'd make a good conversation piece, thought maybe it would attract you when you heard about it. He buggered that up a bit, really. All it did was attract the cops, who got blown to shit as soon as they opened your door. So much for the routine scan."

286

The pain was agonizing now, and I clutched my side, trying not to let it show.

"You people are monsters, Cole." I spat. "And no matter how much worse you are now, you were a fucking monster back then too. You got off light."

He raised the gun to my head again, pointed at my broken and bleeding face.

"Do it," I said then, "I'm tired of running and I'm tired of fighting and I'm tired as hell of having guns pointed at me. Pull the fucking trigger."

He didn't reply, just pushed the gun into my cheek.

"The transition phase from this place to the next is very bad when you die violently," he said, obviously savouring this. "I don't know why that is. Maybe it's just because we're bad people, who knows?"

I looked into his eyes, realising for the first time that he was, in fact, completely mad. And then things got *really* interesting.

Suddenly, the door was kicked in and shots were fired. Both of Cole's guys jerking back and flying through the air in a hail of bullets, smashing into the furniture and lying there, unmoving. Cole ducked behind me, using me as a shield, gun still pressed against my cheek.

Tommy stepped into the room, one of my guns in each hand, followed by the two security guys from the entrance to the VIP room.

"Computer, call the front desk!" Cole yelled at the wallscreen.

Calling...

The screen shattered as a bullet hit it dead centre.

"What took you?" I asked.

Tommy grinned, "Gimme a break, man, it wasn't that bad. I heard the gunshot, heard your voice after that, and decided to do something about it. But I couldn't exactly come in empty handed, not to mention being one against three. So I had to get these guys on our side."

"How did you get that right?"

287

"Money... And parts in my next picture."

"And we get to meet Mercury Red," one of the guards said, grinning.

"You two are dead men," Cole said.

"Neth made it known throughout the Nu Caynan underground that he would employ everyone under you at twice the salary," the guard replied. "Without you to argue the point, this could work out quite well... So you, I think, are the dead man."

Cole sighed behind me, "Mercenaries, you just can't trust them. Well, you killed Davis and he was the only man I could really trust. So you're going to have to pay for that."

"I thought you said you killed Neth," I said.

"No, 'fraid not," Cole replied, "I tried to, but he got away. He's been hiding out with what people he has left, waiting for his moment to strike at me. I was just trying to piss you off."

"Looks like that moment has come," I said. "News travels fast around here."

"Very fast," Tommy said, "I've called him. He's on his way. As soon as your people downstairs see you with a bullet in your head, I think they'll accept Neth's offer."

"You have Neth's mobile number?" I said, surprised as hell.

Tommy grinned, "I'm Tommy *Slid*, man. Also, where do you think I get my stars their narcotics from?"

"Good point."

"I'm not dead yet, Carter. We're going for a walk," Cole said, pulling me painfully to my feet and wrapping one arm around my neck, "And as soon as we get downstairs, I'll have security take each of you outside and *fucking skin you*."

"Shoot him," I said sharply.

All three of the men had their guns trained at my head, trying to get a shot at Cole. He was right. If he was dead, all we had to do was wait for Neth and present the body. But if he left the room alive there'd be trouble, and Neth would be hopelessly outnumbered, and we'd all get it in the head.

"I can't get a shot, Ash," Tommy said.

"*Then shoot me*!" I half yelled, a full yell being out of the question due to reasons of intense pain.

"*I can't!*"

Cole started to move us slowly towards the door. I had by that stage lost quite an impressive amount of blood, and wasn't really feeling up to struggling. The only reason I can think of why Tommy hadn't taken a shot at my leg, thereby incapacitating me and screwing Cole completely, is because he'd seen how much blood I'd lost already. Also, Cole was a big guy, and the chances were he'd probably just drag me along to the door, incapacitated or not.

So we had a problem.

"Get away from the door," Cole said.

"Don't move," I said.

They moved, and Cole moved us slowly past them, through the doorway, and out into the deserted VIP room.

"Where is everybody?" I said, feeling queasy now, the world seemed to be moving around me. Spinning and dipping. Moving closer, then suddenly further away.

I shook my head, trying to clear it.

"We cleared the room and locked the door before going in to get you. Safer that way. No prying eyes," Tommy replied from the doorway, still keeping the gun at head level.

"And no unexpected guests," one of our new friends said.

Cole reached into a pocket, pulling out a keycard, as we slowly approached the steel door.

He grinned, "Time to go, boys."

We got closer to the door and I knew exactly what would happen when we got there:

Cole would reach behind him, swipe the card. We would move quickly backwards through the doorway together. The door would slam shut in front of us, leaving Tommy and the other two in the VIP room. Then he would shoot me in the head, call for security to take out the others, and prepare for Neth's arrival.

I know this because that's exactly what I would have done, and we'd received the same training.

It was inevitable.

And time was running out fast.

"Tommy, shoot me," I said calmly.

"I'm feeling a bit jumpy, gentlemen," Cole said, "If something startles me I might just pull this trigger."

"Then we'll pull ours." Tommy said evenly.

"Either way, I'm fucked," I declared, "Just shoot me, Tom."

Tommy took aim.

We arrived at the door and Cole reached back with the keycard. The door slid open and Cole pulled us through, the door slammed shut in front of me and then bang.

And that was it.

Twenty-seven

The gun left my cheek, the arm fell away from my neck and, behind me, Cole hit the ground with a dull thud, blood flowing from a wound to the head, and he wouldn't be rising again.

I turned to see Neth climbing the stairs opposite the lift, training a gun on Cole's still body

I grinned weakly at him.

"You okay?" Neth asked, noticing the blood on my clothes and covering the hand that was clutching my side.

"Yeah. Great. How are you?"

Then I collapsed.

I'm told Neth's personal doctor is pretty good, and I guess he must be, because when I finally awoke I felt okay, really, in the best room SkyN has to offer, with Rachel beside my bed wiping my forehead with a soft damp cloth. The lighting was dim, ambient, soft and warm. I couldn't help but feel the same way. Rachel has that effect on people.

"Hey," I said, barely more than a whisper.

She smiled her beautiful smile, "Hey."

"I'm still alive," I said.

She laughed, "Yeah, it's a shame."

"Yeah... How long have I been out for?"

"Quite a while. It's just after sunset," she replied, wiping my cheeks softly with the cloth, "You slept through the night and just went on going."

"Where's Tommy?"

She pointed.

I looked across the room, where Tommy was asleep on a couch against the wall, a thin blanket over him.

"He sat beside the bed throughout the night and held out as long as he could today," she replied. "Eventually fell asleep a few hours ago. I woke him up and forced him to lie on the couch."

Tommy stirred. Rubbed his eyes.

He looked at me, saw I was awake, grinned.

"Ash, how ya feeling, man?" he said, getting up and coming over to the bed.

"Not too bad," I replied. I tried to sit up, felt a hot stab of pain, and lay back down again.

"Don't move, Ash." Rachel said evenly. "You were shot. Take it easy or so help me I'll tie you down."

"Sorry."

"No sweat, baby. Just looking out for you."

Rachel placed the cloth in a bowl of water, "I'm going to get Neth. He said I should call him as soon as you're awake."

She left the room, and I looked at Tommy.

"Thanks."

"Not another word about it, man. You'da done the same."

We discussed briefly what a lucky bastard I was, and I remarked that if he hadn't made a certain phone call I wouldn't be lying there, I'd be lying in a morgue. It was then that Neth came in, accompanied by Rachel. He was in a black silk robe, a silk cord tied around his ample stomach. He looked fresh, like he'd just stepped out of the shower.

"Ash, you okay? Doc patch you up good?"

"Yeah, I'll be okay. Tell him thanks, and send me the bill."

"I'll tell him thanks. But as for the bill, don't be a dick," he replied.

I grinned, made a remark about his incredible sense of timing the night before and he laughed at that.

"Well, when you hear an old friend needs your help, *and* you get to take your territory back, you kinda skip to it," he said, lighting a smoke. "Sometimes it pays to be timely."

Rachel took the cigarette from him and killed it in an ashtray, "Are you insane?"

"What?" Neth said, shocked.

"The guy's recovering from some serious physical trauma," Rachel said briskly. "You can damn well smoke outside."

I grinned, "No Rach, it's fine. Matter of fact, I think the psychological trauma is of a higher priority right now, so light me one too."

She wasn't happy with this, but she let it go, mentioning something about if the doc heard about this.

We lit up, and I asked Neth about the takeover.

"Well, the guys at the front door didn't accept my offer initially, and all the others were either in the process of considering it or shooting at us. Then I shot what's-his-name-"

"Cole."

" – whatever, in the head, and everyone started to consider it. And now, well, I'm back in action."

"Good for you," I said, trying to get up again, wincing.

Rachel pushed me gently back down, "You're not going anywhere until you're good and ready."

"Yeah, you tell him," Tommy said.

"Yes ma'am," I said, sinking into the soft cushions, realising there really wasn't much reason to get up right now anyway.

293

"Yeah," Neth grinned. "Rachel will take good care of you."

She punched him on the arm.

I spent a week at SkyN, being cared for by Rachel. Nothing happened between us, nothing like *that* anyway, but if I hadn't been so hung up on Melanie and so burned out on Sharyn, something would have. Rachel was sweet, caring and incredibly sexy. Sort of like Sharyn had been, only with a personality that I didn't want to nail to the wall and use as a dartboard.

My stay gave me time to think about what I wanted to do next, and I'd started to feel more and more that I wanted to return to Tanis.

Tora Sera is great, but it's a holiday place. You can't live there. Not unless your life is a permanent holiday, and that would drive me insane.

Besides, I missed my hov, which I may have mentioned to you is a really great piece of machinery, and I wanted to get that damn vBomb out of my apartment.

So I said my goodbyes to the people at SkyN a week later, told Rachel to take care of herself and Neth that if anything should happen to her in her chosen profession I would personally kill the ones responsible. He'd said he would first, and I'd left. I think our understanding became a friendship that day.

I went up to SlidCo Studios, in the higher parts of the city of Nu Caynan, to give Tommy my regards and wish him luck in the cutting room.

"I hate this part of the job," he'd grumbled, shaking my hand.

"Why don't you give it to an editor to cut?"

"What? Are you mad?"

I grinned, "It'll work out great."

"It always does, I'm Tommy S –"

"Slid, yeah, I know."

"Take care of yourself, Ash, man. And I'll be expecting you at the premiere of *Pros and Cons*."

"I'll be there," I said, turning to go.

"Yeah, so will my ex-wife." Something seemed to occur to him, "How are you getting back to Tanis?"

"Plane."

"Really? You want to take mine?" he said.

"No, I couldn't."

"Yeah, sure. Take it, man."

"No, really."

"Yeah."

"N –"

"Take it!"

And then I left Nu Caynan, courtesy of Tommy's personal jet, and made the return journey to Tanis, for once not being blown out of the sky or hit by a giant bird. I thought it pleasant to travel by air without having a near-death experience; there was definitely something to be said for it.

I sat back in my seat, staring out at the clouds below me, and wondered what it would be like to live a normal life.

Wondered if I even knew what that meant.

Nope, probably not.

I arrived back at Tanis, disembarking and being greeted with a beautiful, sunny morning. The ocean was shimmering, the way it does, the sun glinting on the water, and I felt something that I hadn't felt in quite some time: I was home.

The next few days were more eventful than I would have liked them to be. The cops had been electronically notified as soon as I'd gained access to my apartment, something I'd known would happen as soon as the computer gave me the visitor list. They'd wanted to know about the decapitated heads outside my offices, had popped around to my apartment, ran a routine scan, and found the vBomb. I had just poured some coffee and had a seat in my study one stormy night when Officer Dick had arrived, dripping water all over my foyer floor and asking about the kids and the bomb.

"Call NeuroLOG, ask for Mitchell."

He'd called right there and then, and Mitchell had confirmed that I'd had been in Nu Caynan at the time, in the services of NeuroLOG. Officer Dick had said fine, but what about my partner, Dexter Kellerman?

"Him too."

And that had been that.

As I've said, this is a corporate civilisation, and if a company like NeuroLOG backs you, consider yourself sorted. I could have walked into a restaurant, pulled out a gun, shot fifteen people, and ran away. If NeuroLOG said I had been on Mars at the time, the cops would drop it, even if they had ten eye witnesses who gave evidence to the contrary.

That's just the way it is.

So Officer Dick left, and I had a seat in my study, kicking off my shoes, putting my feet on the coffee table, and lighting up a smoke.

Blew a smoke ring.

And another.

"Computer, TV."

"Channel?"

"KKP News," I said, eyes going to the wallscreen.

"... in Oaken City Psychiatric Hospital, where the various sufferers of DMWS, or Dead Man Walking Syndrome, have been relocated and are now being treated. There are currently twenty-four patients who are still under their supervision, the others having been discharged to their respective families –"

"Mute."

I blew another smoke ring, staring at the screen. Psychiatric Hospitals are very depressing places, and the last thing I felt like doing was having a guided tour of one. In truth, I was hoping for the latest on Shillian. Also, I was wondering how everyone was dealing with it.

On screen, the camera zoomed through one dismal, sanitary white corridor after the next, overhead lights casting a clinical bright light on everything. I recognised the place, but I had no idea why. Doctors walked by in gleaming white coats, holding DigiPads and looking official at each other as they passed in the halls, nurses pulling some ranting loon towards an unknown destination, the whole place giving the air of depression, misery, and utter cleanliness.

I had visited Oaken City on a number of occasions, but I didn't recall ever having visited a mental asylum there. Still, I had to admit the tranquillity of Oaken Lake had to be conducive to good mental health. It was a quiet place, peaceful, built on an island in the middle of the lake, where the rest of the world couldn't touch it. My family used to holiday there, my father and I doing the whole 'fishing at dawn' thing, but that had been many years ago, when I was a child.

Yeah, if ever there was a place to put people, out of the way and peaceful. Away from the hustle and bustle of MegaCity life, then Oaken Lake was the place.

Incoming call...

"Answer."

It was Tommy.

"Ash, man. How was the flight?"

"Very nice." I replied. "I thought maybe the topless stewardesses were a bit over the top, though."

"There's just no pleasing some people."

I grinned at that.

"How's the final edit coming along?" I asked.

Tommy groaned. "Don't ask. Tell me again why I don't just use a damn computer?"

"Because you feel that nothing can compare with the lush and sublime visuals that only celluloid can provide."

"Oh yeah... Right. Damn."

"Keep the faith, Tom. You're nearly there," I said, "Have you heard from Sarah and Felony?"

Tommy nodded. "Yup. They've holed themselves up at the Palace. Can't imagine what they must be doing with their time."

I laughed. Felony wasn't a young man, but he still had some mileage left in him. My guess is, he can still give any young buck a run for his money.

"I guess I'll see them at the premiere of *Pros and Cons*," I said.

"They'll be at there," Tommy agreed. "Will you?"

I nodded, "At the very least, you're gonna need protection from your ex-wife."

He grunted, "Don't even joke."

"I wasn't."

Something beeped off-screen. Tommy turned to have a look.

"Ah, crap. Speak of the devil."

"Or closest ranking equivalent."

"Ha ha. Gotta run, Ash. See you at the premiere. I'll send the jet."

"No need for the –"

He was gone.

" – topless stewardesses."

I drained the mug of now cold coffee, got up, suddenly feeling very, very tired.

I pulled off my shirt as I entered the bedroom, walked over to the window without turning on the lights, looked out at the night. The rain was beating at the glass, drumming almost rhythmically, and from far off across the sea I could just make out the approaching storm. Vague flickers of light flashed across the distant horizon, distorted through the haze and the darkness. I lit a smoke. Had a drag. Killed it, and threw myself onto the bed.

I was out like a light.

Drifting off to some far-off place.

At first all is quiet. The night sky filled with stars and a spattering of clouds, silver grey in the Moon's light. The breeze this evening is warm, blowing gently against my face. I stand there, staring up at the night.

Something is happening. I don't know what it is, and I don't know how I know. But something is wrong. I look around, not sure where I am, and suddenly I realise she's gone. I feel a surge of panic.

Fight it down.

This is why I am here. I'm searching for her, and the search has led me here, to this strange otherworldly city. I have to find her, have to find her before it's too late. Can't forget, the way the others have.

I look out towards the horizon, the city skyline a myriad of glowing lights against a pitch black sky.

There is a moment of intense silence. The wind stops, a leaf coming to rest on the pavement beside me. All is completely, utterly still. There is no sound, not the chirp of a bird nor the barking of a dog. I realise suddenly that the world is holding its breath.

And then the heavens explode and rocks fall from the sky, screeching through the atmosphere, burning across the night sky like the tears of a long-forgotten god. And the clouds are changing, becoming jagged lines, streaking across the pitch-black heavens, painting the darkness above with the colours of wild flame. And the Moon, staring down like a demon, is like blood in the eye of chaos, laughing as at last the cancer of this planet is removed. The screams of a mother, child cradled in her arms, body limp, lifeless. She looks up at me, her eyes hollow, her pain easing even as I watch, her body empty now, vacant of the soul that once burned inside.

Where is she? Where the fuck is she? I have to find her. I start running, making my way towards the city looming ahead, burning and crumbling even as I watch. Massive chunks of rock crash into the world around me, smashing into parked cars and sleeping households, the ground trembling, the air thick with smoke and flame and the screams of the frightened, the helpless, and the dying.

I have to find her. I have to find her.

She isn't here.

I know that voice.

I turn towards the sound, seeking out its source. He stands in a pool of darkness, a shadow cast by some unseen thing, his face hidden from me.

Where is she? I say, my voice barely more than a whisper

You know where she is, old friend

Where is she? Stronger now. Harsher.

She's in a clean place. A cold place.

Above us the sky is raining fire, and all I want is to see her again.

It's all I've ever wanted.

Since before we ever met.

Before I was even born.

I don't know what you mean!

You will, old friend.

A piece of rock flies across the night, coming closer by the second.

You must go, Ash.

But –

GO NOW!

I awoke screaming her name, clutching at the sheets, chest heaving as I gasped in lungfuls of air, the rain lashing at the window pane and the storm, now at its full power, raging above and around the city of Tanis.

I looked up at the dark ceiling, my mind still in the other place, trying to control my breathing. Trying to relax. In the dream I was looking for someone. Finding her was all that mattered.

The stranger's words echoed in my ears.

Cold.

Clean.

"Mel."

I was out the front door before my shirt was on.

T w e n t y - e i g h t

I drove through the night, the rain lashing at the windscreen, painting images of a life I'd thought forever lost to me beneath the sands of time. I drove through the darkness, no light but for the twin beams emitted from my hovcar and perhaps something more, illuminating not the night outside but the darkness that had for so long clouded my sight.

A candle.

Lit far across the night.

Calling to me.

Its soft flame a beacon, lighting my way.

And even as the storm around me danced with the memories of another life, my mind danced with them.

And as I drove I dreamed.

And dreamed.

Scenes and images of another life coming back to me as if I never left.

As if I never would.

Her head on a pillow as she watches me awaken, coming once more into the world after being somewhere else for a while. She smiles, leans toward me, kisses my forehead.

So softly.

My eyes open slowly.

Outside, the sun is just beginning to rise. A cool breeze comes through the window, rustling the curtains

"Mel, I –".

She kisses me, and the words go right out of my head.

Storm lights blinked in the darkness as I passed the city walls of Nu Damascus, radiant red halos hazy in the downpour. Ahead of me, a hov pulled out onto the highway. I glanced at the driver as I moved slowly past it.

A man.

Maybe my age.

Maybe not.

His face was vaguely illuminated in the blue glow emitted by his dashboard dials. He didn't look at me, not so much as a glance, and I found myself wondering what kind of crazy bastard would leave the safety of the city walls on a night like this.

Maybe he was suicidal.

Or insane.

Or maybe he was chasing a dream.

A meadow.

The grass is immaculately mowed, the trees tall and perfect and proud. In the centre of the meadow is a blanket, and upon the blanket lie two people.

A young couple. Lying together. Holding each other close.

The man whispers something.

Silence.

He begins to wonder if his words were heard.

And then she squeals, grabbing his face in her hands and kissing him all over as the sounds of her delight are carried off on the breeze. Carried off with two words, barely heard across the distance of time.

Two words.

"Marry me."

I braked hard, swerved to avoid a tree that had fallen in the road, pulling a hard right and then a harder left about a split second before leaving the road and flying off into a ditch.

The storm was getting worse, the wind lashing at my hov like some ancient, primeval force. I gripped the wheel tighter, focused on the road ahead, seen only vaguely through the beams of my headlights, and made hazy and indistinct by the downpour that thundered down upon the surrounding land.

"Computer, search for proximity to EM storms."

Radius?

I thought about it. Distance from my current position to-

"One hundred kilometres."

Scanning...

It was pointless, I knew. An EM storm could gather up at a moments notice, but hell, I had to try. The least I could do was see if there already was one flying around, hopefully before I drove into it.

No detected EM storms within specified parameters.

Good.

I accelerated.

The sun is low on the horizon, a dark orange orb hovering above the darkening water, continuing its slow descent into the sea even as they watch.

She sits beside him on the sand, but her eyes are not on the sunset, or the gently rolling waves, or the myriad colours above them, but on the small object glittering on her finger. He watches her caressing the diamond with delight and with love.

She looks up at him, smiles her beautiful smile, leans over and kisses him softly on the cheek.

He knows this is all he wants in the world.

This is all he ever wanted.

But there is one thing that must be done before it can be perfect.

Apex

The time is coming. It's so close now. .

He takes her face in his hands and kisses her.

Soon, and everything will be alright.

I entered the foothills of the Tre Borez mountain range, speeding up into the trees. I'd left the highway a while back, taking the turnoff that would lead me to Oaken City, nestled deep in the mountain range that was the Tre Borez.

The range was made up of three major peaks, in a circle, lesser ones between them, and Oaken Lake nestled in the heart of the deep valley the mountains created.

The place was as close to picture perfect as you could hope to find.

I'd even taken Melanie there, once, for a weekend. We'd stayed in a little inn run by a nice old couple. Mel had loved it.

We were going to have our honeymoon there.

It had all been arranged.

Lights twinkling, reflecting on the shifting surface of the dark water. A young man stands beside a young woman, staring out at the night, his arm around her, her head resting on his shoulder.

Across the river the city glows, its many billions of lights seeming to beckon to them, but it is here in the darkness that they feel safe.

She lifts her head from his shoulder, turns to look at him.

"Run away with me, Ash," she says softly. "Let's leave this place."

"Not now," he replies. "Not yet."

He pulls her closer, kisses her. "But once this is over, we will. I promise, baby."

I promise.

I rounded a bend in the road and Oaken City lay beneath me, a bed of thousands of lights flickering away in the haze of darkness and rain, becoming brighter and brighter as I accelerated down out of the mountains.

There is sand outside. It blows in the darkness, lashing this way and that as the storm hits the desert. And electricity fills the sky even as the rain thunders down upon the earth.

It is cold outside, so very cold.

But inside, it's warm.

Candle light surrounds them, protecting them from the darkness and the terrible beauty of the storm outside.

They are safe here, safe, as they lay together, her head resting gently on his chest, she watches him. His eyes closed. His breathing steady.

"Ash." A whisper, nothing more.

His eyes open, he turns his head slightly, smiles at her.

"I'm awake."

"I know. I always know."

He nods, "True. It's frightening."

"Ash?"

"Yeah?"

She says nothing now, only watches him.

He raises an eyebrow, "Yeah, babes?"

"I had a dream."

He says nothing, letting her speak in her own time, softly brushing her dark hair away from her face.

"I dreamed you left me. All alone. I don't think you did it on purpose, but it happened that way."

"I would never leave you, Mel."

"I know." She smiles then. "Just a dream."

He smiles back. "Just a dream."

Just a dream.

I drove through the gates of Oaken City Psychiatric Hospital, coming to a stop at the main entrance, and was banging on the door a few seconds later.

I checked the time.

5:45am.

I banged again.

A wallscreen to my right lit up, an elderly lady in a white coat staring intently at me.

"Yes? What do you want?" she demanded.

"I've come to get someone. A patient of yours. A DMWS sufferer." I hunched my shoulders, trying to shield myself from the driving rain.

She looked me up and down. "And you are –?"

"Cold and wet. So please open the fucking door."

The screen went black, a few seconds later the door slid aside, and I entered the lobby of the hospital.

It was softly lit now, a lot less harsh than it had been on TV. The old lady I'd seen on the vidscreen approached me, flanked by two large and somewhat unfriendly-looking orderlies.

She regarded me sternly. "Who is it you are looking for, Mister –?"

"My name is Ash Corben. I've just travelled here from Tanis. I believe my fiancé may be a sufferer of DMWS."

"Identification, please." She said, hand outstretched.

I gave her my ID card. She checked it carefully, then nodded and handed it back.

"Her name, Mister Corben?" she asked, moving around a counter to a nurses' workstation and settling down in front of a computer.

"Melanie," I swallowed. "Melanie Portman."

She got to work on the computer, and I went to stand at the window, watching the rain come down, wondering what the hell I'd been thinking of and mentally preparing myself for disappointment.

"Room 37, Mister Corben. Third floor."

I hadn't even noticed that I'd been holding my breath until it exploded out of my throat.

"What?" I said, turning to look at the old lady.

"Room 37," she repeated. "Third floor. The elevator is to your left. James will escort you."

We went up to the third floor and James pointed the way to room 37. "I won't go any further, Mister Corben. Just call Michelle if you need anything. She's posted a bit further down the hall."

I nodded, walked down the hallway like I was in a trance.

"Mister Corben?"

I stopped, turned to James. "Yeah?"

"Prepare yourself. She is in a state of catatonia. She probably won't recognise you. It is a symptom of this ailment. Some experience it, others don't. Just thought you should know."

I nodded again. "Thanks."

I continued down the hall, coming at last to room 37. The words **Melanie Portman - DMWS** were scrolling across a small screen embedded in the door.

I knocked.

No reply.

Tried again.

Nothing.

I took a deep breath, let it out slowly, and hit the **OPEN** tab.

The door slid back silently, the ambient light from the hall outside casting the softest glow into the dark room. I stepped inside, the door sliding closed behind me.

It was dark, the only light coming from the glOlamps hovering outside in the rainy night, illuminating a hunched figure, covered in a blanket, sitting in a chair by the windows.

I stood dead still.

"Mel?" It came out a croak, barely audible against the sounds of the wind and rain.

Silence.

I moved forward then, my legs seeming to move of their own volition, coming to stand beside her. Melanie sat in the chair, bundled up against the cold, hands crossed in her lap, staring out into the night, and looking like she hadn't aged a day.

I swallowed hard.

"Mel."

She said nothing, made no move, giving no sign whatsoever that she had heard me. Just sat there, staring out into the storm.

I kneeled beside her, reached forward and took her hands in my own. They were cold, so very cold. My hand came up to her face and I turned her head, bringing her eyes into contact with my own.

She looked at me, blinked once, but said nothing.

"Baby, what has happened to you?"

She blinked again, showing no emotion, no recognition registered on her beautiful face. It was like she wasn't there anymore.

A tear slid down my cheek.

"It wasn't a dream, Mel." I brushed her hair back from her face, the way I used to. "We stood together by the water, watching the sea. The wind blew ocean spray onto our faces."

Silence.

No response but for the rain as it hit the window panes, carried on a strong gust of wind.

"I promised we would leave together. We would go away. I promised, Mel." Another tear slid down my cheek, I tried to fight the horror and loneliness and pain that was welling up inside of me. "It wasn't a dream, Mel. You never left me, baby. You never left me."

I broke down.

I don't know if it was the vacant look in her eyes or the shock of seeing her again or her icy hands or the promise that I had never kept, but I cried and cried and cried, my head coming down and resting on her legs, my arms falling down to my sides, my chest heaving and my shoulders shaking like a little child.

I had faced all of the darkness in the world, and fought to keep something and lost it, fought to lose something that would never leave my mind. I had forgotten how many people I had killed and remembered every lie I'd ever told her, every bad thing I ever did didn't matter as long as she loved me. I had lost her, walked away when she'd really needed me, and only returned to her hours after she'd died.

And now she sat in a chair before me.

Come back from the dead to bring me back to life.

And I couldn't get through to her.

So I cried.

And cried.

And I didn't stop until someone put a hand through my hair, stroking it softly, bringing my head up to look into my eyes.

"Ash?"

I looked into her big beautiful eyes, not breathing.

Then my hands came up and grabbed her, pulling her to me.

"Ash? Where am I?" What –?"

I gripped her tightly. "Mel."

"Where am I, Ash?"

"Mel."

I clutched at her, my heart feeling like it would explode at any second.

"It's okay, Mel. It's okay. Everything is okay now."

"I dreamed about you, baby I –"

"It wasn't a dream, Mel. It never was."

It never was.

She started to cry, I cried with her, and we held each other as if we were the last two people in the world.

And for all we cared, we could have been.

E p i l o g u e

We meet once more, on the edge of the water at the dawn.

I have left the highway far behind me. Abandoned the search, having found, at last, what I was looking for in the most unlikely of places.

Mist swirls around us, rising up from the ground, dancing like ghosts on the night. I stare out at the ocean, at the rising of the distant sun, the water the deepest blue, waves breaking onto the sand, a deep roar in my ears.

He stands beside me, while behind us the fragments of a city that had come to us so strangely seems, at last, to be leaving. Returning silently back to its own place and time, taking with it the masses of bewildered people who were its inhabitants.

I know who you are now *I say*

Really?

You are an old friend, from another place. The place where the city has come from.

Yes

Your name was Dex

A smile **Yes**

You disappeared. You were... you were killed... In the other place.

Dex nods **I was pulled from the other place, yes. But dead? Do you not believe your own eyes?**

I can't reply.

You have found the one you have searched for? *Dex says.*

I nod

In the other place *he says*

Yes, old friend

He smiles **Ash, enjoy what time you have with her. But remember, sooner or later she will return to this place. She slipped through, but she cannot stay on the other side. The breach between worlds is healing even as we speak.**

He sees my expression

He knows me well

I'm sorry, old friend

I nod

But *he continues* **as she must return to the place where she belongs, perhaps so must I**

I turn to look at him

He smiles **See you on the other side, old friend**

See you on the side.

I awaken with her beside me.

Outside, it's just getting light, the night receding, gently giving way to the cool light just before the dawn. Soon, the sun will rise, a golden orb will rise into the sky and the clouds above will burn with the colours of wildfire.

Once, I spoke to you of that one perfect moment.

Well, for me there is another.

It is her hair on the pillow, before the sun has begun its slow ascent across the heavens. Her eyes closed, she sleeps, unaware that I am watching her every move, the gentle rise and fall of her chest. It is the warmth of her breath against my cheek. It is every single moment I spend with her and every word she whispers to me as we lie together on top of the bed sheets we bought together.

She didn't drag me there this time. I went with her willingly. Because I love her, and time has changed nothing.

It is true that nothing lasts forever, and one morning I'll awaken and she won't be there anymore. And it is true that my life has been a testimony to that. But no more than yours or anyone else's. And as much as things will change, as much as you lose and as hard as it hits you, there is one thing that endures. One thing that remains through it all.

The thing you love.

You hold it inside of you and you cradle it in your heart and you keep it a secret and you never let it go.

It defines your world.

Nobody can touch it, and no one can take it away from you.

It's yours forever.

313

www.ingramcontent.com/pod-product-compliance
Lightning Source LLC
Chambersburg PA
CBHW070807180626
46818CB00001B/151